MINDER RISING

CENTRAL GALACTIC CONCORDANCE BOOK 2

BY CAROL VAN NATTA

WWW.CHAVANCH.COM

MINDER RISING
Copyright © 2015 Carol Van Natta
First Ebook Published May 2015
Published by Chavanch Press, LLC
ISBN:978-0-9831741-5-8

Cover design by Gene Mollica Studio
Edited by Shelley Holloway
Author website: Author.CarolVanNatta.com

DESCRIPTION

* * * * *

A millennium into the future, all children are tested for minder talents, and the best are recruited for the Citizen Protection Service.

Agent Lièrén Sòng is recovering from a near-fatal crash. He should want nothing more than to get back to interrogating criminals for his covert CPS field unit, but being sidelined gains new appeal when he makes friends with a woman and her son. Imara Sesay, road-crew chief and part-time bartender, breaks her ironclad rule never to get close to customers when she asks Lièrén to teach her son how to control his burgeoning minder talents.

Unexpected deaths in his field unit make Lièrén suspect he isn't a lucky survivor, he's a loose end. He should pull away from Imara and Derrit to keep them safe, but when the local CPS Testing Center is entirely too interested in Derrit's talents, Lièrén must make an impossible choice. Can he stay alive long enough to save Imara and her prodigy son?

* * * * *

2015 SFR Galaxy Award Winner

PROLOGUE

* Planet: Concordance Prime * GDAT 3238.203 *

TIMING WAS EVERYTHING. Fortunately, the target's habits were known and his clothing distinctive, so it was easy for her to track his progress along the pedestrian walkway. The city of Spires was famous for its transparent roadways and walkways, making it possible to watch him from below, where only the most paranoid would think to look. They'd given her a tracker synced to a tracer the target unknowingly carried, but it was subject to ghosting, probably because everyone in crowded Spires carried tech, even farkin' babies and pets, and it swamped the signal. The target headed to the metro platform, as she'd been assured was his habit. She'd timed it earlier, watching random pedestrians, so she knew it would take about ten minutes to get through the crowds, past the kiosks, and up onto the platform where she wanted him.

The stolen ground hauler's cab was the bubble style, offering a panorama view of traffic, but it made her more visible than she liked. Carefully, slowly, she used her telekinetic talent on the heavy ground hauler's controls to creep forward, a few centimeters at a time, while keeping her body relaxed and bored, as if she was still parked. It didn't help her concentration that the cab smelled like a colony of sewer rats had died in it, though it explained why the cab had been left wide open. She had to make it look like the ground hauler was being directed by the traffic-control system, because the occupants of other vehicles would complain to the controllers if they noticed her vehicle wasn't. People should just mind their own business.

Two more minutes to wait. Once she was on the ramp, she wouldn't be able to stop, and only had four minutes before the ground hauler arrived at the platform, where her target would be waiting. The ground hauler was just the right height to cause a tragic accident. She felt a momentary pang of regret for the other passengers who would be on the platform, but shrugged it off. There were too many damned people in Spires. Really, she'd be doing the city a favor by reducing the surplus.

One minute more. She was tempted to turn the entertainment back on, but she was tired of hearing the politicians posturing about some local march by the Talent Support and Advocacy Committee. Sure, supporting minder veterans was a good cause, but the TSAC, or tea-sackers, as she liked to think of them, seemed more interested in media coverage than in helping minders. Not that the politicians weren't equally guilty of that. She was glad she'd never had to catch-and-release one of *those* wastes of carbon. That was the problem with Spires. As the prime city of the Central Galactic Concordance government, its primary business was political power, which drew money and influence peddlers like flies to a compost pile. Maybe she'd luck out and the "accident" would take out some politicians and lobbyists, too. If so, she'd deserve a commendation.

She leaned forward, watching the road-surface lights glistening in the soft rain as she prepared to merge into the traffic flow and take the ramp. Suddenly, all traffic slowed to a stop. From her higher vantage point, she could see into some of the vehicles, where countdown clocks were lighting up. She only had about a five-minute cushion and couldn't afford the delay. Maybe it would be short. She casually reached under the dash and reconnected the traffic-control system by touch. The news wasn't good. The system announced there'd be a six-minute wait to clear a path to get fire rescue to a building fire. She'd just lost her cushion.

She swore as she disconnected the controller again. Returning tomorrow was impossible, since she was supposed to be hours into interstellar transit by then. She couldn't keep the stinking ground hauler long enough to find her target again, since the theft had undoubtedly been reported by now, making the vehicle glow plasma hot on the stop-and-detain list. And she didn't have time to locate and steal another vehicle, override its access, and spoof its traffic-control unit.

She glared at the now out-of-reach platform. Like everything else in Spires, the gleaming showcase of the galactic government, the platform was transparent, with a soft pink tint to denote the gathering area, where the target would soon be standing, self-satisfied and oblivious. Even the farkin' support pillars were clear, to add to the illusion that the lofty citizens of Spires were walking on farkin' clouds.

She eyed the pillars again, an idea forming. If she couldn't get up there to take out the waiting passengers, maybe she could take out the whole platform. The ground hauler was heavy enough, and with enough speed, the closer pillar wouldn't stand a chance. With luck, the momentum would take the hauler to the farther pillar, guaranteeing the platform would fall.

It would take careful timing, but she could do it. She reconnected the traffic-control unit and programmed address coordinates that would put her in the correct lane to take her right by the pillars, then watched the clock like a hawk, willing the countdown to continue uninterrupted. When it was down to seconds, she carefully centered her teke talent on the spliced connection. She was more of a heavy teke, so doing the fine work with the splice was like trying to pick up a toothpick wearing exosuit gloves. She watched the other vehicles start to move and had an anxious moment when she thought the traffic system wasn't going to allow her hauler into the flow, but it finally slid into an open slot. The system obligingly gave her priority for the lane, and that was all she needed. She let the splice go, dropping her vehicle from the system, and punched in maximum acceleration, overriding the safeties. The sweet creators of chaos were with her and miraculously opened an almost clear path to her new target. She kept the vehicle straight, gaining satisfying velocity. The millisecond she had a clear view of the support pillars, she angled the vehicle toward them, froze the steering control with her talent, and scrambled into the rear seat to strap herself in.

The safety equipment did its job in cushioning her from the impact, but she hadn't expected it to take so long or be so farkin' loud, though it was probably just adrenalin heightening her senses.

She grabbed her bag and used her teke to help her get out of the ruined cab. Her first look at the destruction was rewarding. The first pillar was completely sheared, and the second shattered and twisted. The platform above it was now at a ninety-degree angle, and satisfyingly empty. Torn fiber cables and handrails flapped in the breeze. On the street in front of her, a few bodies were strewn about, but none of them were the man in the gradient-blue vest and matching kilt. It was too much to expect that her target would have splatted at her feet.

Fortunately, she'd planned a contingency for this scenario. She opened her bag and removed her rigged device. She flipped its switch, then tossed it into the cab, where an acrid smoke began spewing out and soon filled the cab and billowed out. Hidden by the smoke, and holding her breath, she pulled on a white tunic with red armbands and buckled on a red utility belt, the universal gear for emergency responders. She pulled on a dark red rain hat over her hair, giving witnesses and security cameras one less thing to identify her by. Lucky for her, the rainy season had come early this year.

She slung her bag over her shoulder, then stepped away from the cab, as if she'd been looking for the driver, and was nearly knocked flat by a dazed pedestrian.

"Oh god, oh god, oh god," sobbed the man. "All those people!"

She grabbed him by the shoulders. "Where are the rest of them?"

"What?" He coughed from the smoke.

"Where is everyone else?" She pointed to her red armband.

The look on his face said he'd remember the carnage forever. He pointed to the intersection and the ramp. "Up there."

She let him go and started to lope toward the intersection, but changed her mind and ran up the parallel walkway instead. It was smarter not to be seen coming from the direction of the ground hauler. Besides, it was starting to rain harder, and the road was slicker than the walkway.

She made a show of stopping at bodies when she found them, glad they were obviously already dead, because she didn't know the first thing about how to treat the living. None of them were the target, which meant she'd have to get closer to where the majority of victims had landed. The klaxons and whumping sounds of emergency air vehicles began to multiply, and she knew she had to hurry.

Why couldn't the target have been in High Spires, where a simple push with her mind would have him plummeting a few thousand feet? It would have been a more fitting death for a high-and-mighty telepath who stuck his talent where it didn't belong. That way, innocent passengers wouldn't have been killed because of him. True, she would've had to have been fairly close, because the man was a full-grown adult, not some snot-nosed kid or a frail great-great-grandmother. It would have been harder to do it undetected, since the city was too farkin' crowded, but she was good at what she did.

When she rounded the corner, she knew she was farked. Too many people had already converged on the scene, and too many of them were in white with red armbands. She might be able to pull off a claim of "just lucky to be in the area" to civilians, but she couldn't fool the professionals once they asked about her organization and specialty.

She ducked into a recessed doorway and pulled the last item from her bag. The ugly brown raincoat would cover the tunic long enough for her to snag the nearest unoccupied autocab. She left the empty bag crumpled on the street, trusting it'd be mistaken for just one of dozens that had fallen with the waiting passengers.

She'd have to tell the others she wasn't sure of the kill, and it was an understatement to say she wasn't looking forward to that. Some of the blame fell on their shoulders, giving her all those strictures and limitations about how and where it had to be done, and disagreeing with each other about the timing, but the crux of the matter was that she couldn't say with certainty whether or not the target had been eliminated. And she couldn't lie, either, since most of the others were telepaths, and wouldn't hesitate to pluck it out of her mind. Farkin' untrusting assholes.

She'll be happy to fly that evening and never look back.

Chapter 1

* Planet: Concordance Prime * GDAT 3238.203 *

MINDER CORPS FIELD Agent Lièrén Sòng stared at his no-kick fizzy drink but didn't see it. He had shrunk his world to as small as he could make it, but even from six meters away, he could feel the big bald man sitting at the bar broadcasting a prickly synaptic haze of barely contained violence as he stared at the dark-skinned woman behind the bar, as if trying to hypnotize her. Lièrén might have let it go, might have followed protocol to stay out of it, but he couldn't. He counted the bartender as a friend, even if she didn't know it.

The bar had cleared out early that night. Only a half-dozen patrons occupied the booths and nursed their drinks, chems, and solitude. The piped-in music, a lilting jig in ancient British folk tradition, now jangled in his head like a wind chime warning of an approaching storm. It made him want to put his hands over his ears, but that wouldn't shut off his sifter talent.

It was yet another problem piled onto a truly lousy day. He'd awakened from his prescribed afternoon nap with a jolt, another dream of falling. Unsurprising, since only six weeks ago, he'd actually fallen several thousand meters out of a high-low flitter that was breaking apart and on its way to a fiery crash and burn.

After three weeks of trauma care and reconstructive surgery, he checked into the long-term residence hotel for the duration of his continued rehabilitation, which included being treated by another sifter for his post-traumatic experience therapy. His recovery had been slowed due to withdrawal symptoms from his Citizen Protection Service-mandated program of enhancement drugs, which he couldn't take while his new cloned liver integrated with his body. Beyond the headache, dry mouth, and sweat flashes, his primary minder talent felt thick and muddy. It didn't help that he'd run out of the temporary replacement enhancement drugs the CPS's medics had prescribed for him. He hadn't noticed until he'd gotten back to his hotel room that day, which wasn't like him. He was forgetful, but usually well organized.

He wanted his ordinary, balanced life back, where he mostly stayed in ships and space stations, and where the weather was controlled and it didn't rain whenever it felt like it. There were too many empty drawers to fill in the hotel room, a silent reminder that his few personal possessions had been destroyed along with the flitter. His replacement clothes, even though autotailored to his exact measurements and range of motion, felt too new.

He shouldn't be feeling sorry for himself, because at least he'd lived through it. His senior field unit partner and friend, Fiyon Machimata, hadn't been so lucky.

If Fiyon had been with him now, he'd have insisted on going someplace more upscale. The Quark and Quasar, which was a part of the residence hotel, was designed as a family-style pub and was much more congenial than the hotel's restaurant, which had marginal food and surly service. The pub had two- and four-person booths and an eclectic mix of round tables of varying heights, suitable for adults and children alike. The decorator had lined the walls with mysterious metal pieces purporting to come from preflight Earth sailing ships and farm equipment, but Lièrén suspected they were copies of random machine parts that caught the designer's eye. Behind the bar's simulated wooden façade, the prep area and the dispensary were modern, if not exotic or extensive.

When he'd first visited the bar after moving into his hotel suite, he wasn't sure he liked the music, which was billed as "preflight British traditional," even though whoever selected it had a rather elastic definition of the style. It had grown on him in subsequent visits, to the point that he looked forward to the live musician scheduled to perform the next week. It was… odd to be able to plan things like that. Usually his job kept him constantly traveling.

The lowlight of his already *zhào chū* day had been being stuck in the metro station while the city figured out how to reroute the skytrams because of an accident. A ground hauler had crashed into the pillars of the passenger platform, killing at least thirty people outright and flooding the area trauma centers with the injured. If he hadn't stopped to help an older couple with toppled packages and wayward grandchildren, he might have been back in the trauma center again himself, and back to waking hallucinations of falling. He was glad he didn't have to go anywhere near the gruesome ground levels where the victims had landed.

After another nightmare had terminated his too-short nap, Lièrén had been too irritable, thirsty, and unsettled to stay in his hotel room another minute, so he'd gone to the bar. It had been surprisingly crowded for an early weeknight, and he'd retreated to a back corner booth to get away from the pressure of the unknowingly broadcasting patrons. He was only a low-level telepath, so their current, running thoughts didn't bother him from a distance, but his high-level sifter talent meant he couldn't avoid feeling the ebb and flow of them. Without the CPS enhancement drugs helping him control his talent, the active minds around him felt like constant raindrops on a sunburn.

The usually boisterous server, Rayle Leviso, who chatted with and teased everyone, had thankfully left him alone that evening. Once the bar emptied, Rayle had slid out early, too, leaving only Bartender Sesay… Imara, she'd invited him to call her, to deal with the few remaining customers. She was cheerfully competent and wasn't given to idle chatter, and it didn't hurt that she was easy on the eyes. Even her outgoing son, Derrit, was thankfully quiet tonight.

In the earlier crush, Imara had asked if Derrit could sit with him to do his homework. Lièrén had nodded and said less than was polite, but his pounding headache made it difficult to do anything more. The medics and healers had done admirable jobs in repairing his ribs, diaphragm, lung, and liver, but they couldn't do anything about the withdrawal symptoms, owing to his sifter talent that made most chemical painkillers useless. His choices had been to stay in the rehab unit for another three weeks with the constant company of a healer, or deal with the pain and discomfort on his own. He valued his privacy more than his comfort, although it was hard to remember why on nights like this one. At least he wasn't having to regrow teeth—he'd heard from other rehab patients that it took months for the new ones to feel like they belonged in their mouths.

Tonight was the first time Lièrén had spent much time with Derrit, and he'd been relieved that the boy's mind was blessedly quiet. Once Lièren had considered it, he realized Derrit was a natural shielder. Talent detection hadn't ever been one of Lièrén's strong suits, so the boy was probably at least mid-level, if not better. When the crowd had thinned and more booths opened up, Lièrén could have asked Derrit to move, but he'd left the kid alone. He looked busy and productive, and that kind of concentration was hard to achieve for eleven-year-old boys.

Hell, it was hard to achieve for thirty-two-year-old men. He'd been given part-time CPS desk duty in a local field office while his flitter accident was being investigated. In an odd quirk of fate, though his field unit was officially based out of the main office in High Spires, this was the first time he'd ever been on Capet Dedrum itself, more commonly known as Concordance Prime, or visited its galaxy-renowned showcase capitol city.

Repeated interviews with the staff from the CPS Office of Internal Inquiry suggested they thought there was something questionable about the accident. Since his assignment for the last twelve years had been conducting covert field interrogations, it was easy for him to identify the agenda behind their questions. He'd already requested an advocate to look out for his interests, as was his right as a de facto member of the military. He knew he was innocent of any wrongdoing, but the OII investigators might take some convincing.

So far, his desk duty had been to catch the field office up on its neglected data cubes—cross-referencing, prioritizing, tagging, and threading—which wasn't helping his headaches. He liked administrative work, and took pride in creating and keeping order, but it was mind-numbingly boring after a while.

Because of his "trade office" experience and training, he was supposed to be available to the field office for occasional tasks suited to his talents, but they hadn't asked, probably preferring to use sifters they knew and trusted. It was just as well, since he still had little stamina, and his talent continued to feel different and unreliable while on the latest temporary drug protocol. The local field-office supervisor, Tom Yamazaki, was new to Con Prime. Despite his Japanese last name, he didn't speak the language, and precious little Mandarin, which he'd need if he planned to make a career in Spires. Lièrén had only met Yamazaki once in person and hadn't been introduced to the other agents in the new office, who all must have gone to the same conservative autotailor to get the group rate. They acknowledged his presence from time to time, but mostly, they ignored him.

It had been disheartening to realize that with the death of his partner, his only friends now were Rayle and Imara. They'd shown more concern and care than people he'd known for years. Only his supervisor had sent a generic "get well soon" ping. To the overworked medical and therapy personnel, he was a CPS auth code and a barely remembered name. To everyone else, he was just another tourist on the metro.

And now, it looked like the capstone to this particularly lousy day was the bald man at the bar who'd been heavy-handedly hitting on Imara and getting nowhere. He was probably drawn by her pretty face and wide smile that invited laughter, and her crazy, coiled hair that always looked like it was on the verge of breaking free from its restraint. To Lièrén's chagrin, he'd only noticed the situation because young Derrit had seen the trouble and was watching them like a hawk. Lièrén had a sinking feeling it would be more trouble than Derrit could handle.

Rule number one in covert field units like his was not to draw attention to himself or the unit, and rule number two was to follow rule number one. Lièrén had led anyone who asked to believe that his title of "field agent" was CPS-speak for "office twonk," and that his unit's mission had to do with trade support. Procedure said he should leave now, or conveniently fall asleep and see nothing, but the bald man's haze of violent discord was slicing through Lièrén's talent like a fistful of forceblades.

Derrit abruptly stood and began sidling toward the bar, focusing on his mother with the intensity of a laser beam. Lièrén's headache flared, and second later, the bald man grabbed Imara's hand. Lièrén sat, frozen in indecision.

In the blink of an eye, the bald man muttered something in what sounded like German, then stood and tried to drag Imara from behind the bar.

"Leave her alone!" shouted Derrit, closing in fast and latching onto the man's arm.

The bald man snarled and backhanded the boy, sending him flying a meter or more into some chairs.

* * * * *

Imara Sesay was sorry she'd let Rayle leave early for rehearsal, now that the hairless *chitsiru* seated at the end of the bar had taken to staring at her like he was a cobra and she was his next mousy meal. The bald man and his buddy, another asshole, had arrived an hour before, obviously pre-chemmed, so she'd refused to serve them anything with a kick. The second asshole had gone back to his room to sleep it off, but asshole number one stayed and tried to interest her in a hot-connect in his room, or even the bar's storeroom. He'd spent the last thirty minutes refusing to believe her "not interested" replies to any of his increasingly crude invitations, and disdaining the joyhouse discount token she'd offered.

She straightened and evened the edges of her trays and glasses as she casually looked around to see if there was any help to be found in the customers, but the bar was practically empty. Under the counter, she activated the security alert system and, after a moment's hesitation, keyed a Priority Two ping, meaning they should come as soon as possible, but it wasn't an emergency. In the four years she'd been a tender, she'd never had to call a Priority One. She was relieved to see that Derrit was safely out of the way with the nice CPS man, Field Agent Lièrén Sòng, who was still recovering from a horrific accident.

She'd planned to make Derrit move to another booth, but as long as Lièrén wasn't complaining, she left her son where he was. Not that Lièrén ever complained. He was unfailingly gracious and soft-spoken. Even in pain, as he clearly was tonight, he'd never been rude. She liked Derrit to get exposure to other people, more specifically males, since Torin had died five years ago, leaving her without a husband and Derrit without a father. She'd been known to convince the occasional patron to give Derrit impromptu lessons in exchange for free drinks or chems. As a result, Derrit knew how to use a phase blade as an impromptu spot-welder, how to position softlights to make people look good on holo camera interviews, and how to calculate the lift-weight ratio for a hexquadium antigrav flitter.

When she'd first met Lièrén three weeks ago, he'd seemed surprisingly frail for a handsome man in his prime, but nearly dying in a high-low flitter crash would do that to anyone. He'd only survived because his fall had been broken by some trees, or so the newstrends said. He no longer held his upper torso as carefully, and he hadn't lately dozed off while waiting for the hotel restaurant to deliver his food, but he was far from fully recovered. He was nice to look at, with his well-defined shoulders and narrow, tight hips. Too damn bad he was a transient.

She probably shouldn't have allowed herself to privately call him by his first name, but she liked him. Maybe he'd at least stay long enough to teach Derrit something. Even on nights like tonight, Lièrén was still polite and patient, traits that would be useful when teaching a gregarious eleven-year-old with energy to burn and a nanosecond attention span.

The overbuilt bald man at the bar waved to get her attention and grabbed his mostly empty glass.

"Hey, *Törtchen*, how about sharing some of that sweetness with me?" He waggled his glass and sloshed the dregs of spiced fruit juice around, but he was staring pointedly at her breasts and licking his lips. He'd opened his tunic earlier, as if the bar was too hot, making sure she noticed. His muscled, hairless chest had the perfectly even golden tan only found in a body parlor. Since he was following the latest fashion trends for hairlessness and skin tone, he should have had them do a little subcutaneous fat removal while he was at it. Starting with between his ears.

She forced a chuckle and pasted a professional smile on her face. "Did you just call me a pastry?"

"No, that's *Torten*. You're too dark and juicy for that. Why don't you come up to my room, and I'll teach you some more German, like *saugen meine Schwanz*." His leer was so overdone that she almost laughed for real, but she didn't think he'd appreciate it. He'd already taken her lack of interest as a combined insult and challenge. She wondered what exotic chem he'd taken before he arrived, because it sure as hell made him delusional if he thought she was putting her mouth on *any* of his anatomy.

"No thanks," she said. "Refill?"

"How about I fill you instead?" He made a rocking motion with his hips.

The guy just wasn't giving up. She turned away so he wouldn't see the look on her face, which would probably piss him off. Irritating customers was against hotel policy. She wasn't shocked—the newest noob youngster on the road crew where she worked days came up with better sexual innuendo—but his one-track mind had gotten old, fast.

"Fine," he said sourly. "Give me a refill." He pushed his glass toward her.

She saw movement out of the corner of her eye and turned to see Derrit sidling up to the bar, like he wanted to ask her something. She tilted her head and gave him a look that told him to go sit down, but he ignored it. She gave him a harder look, not wanting him anywhere near the asshole, as she reached for the glass.

She was startled when the bald man's hand closed over hers. All of a sudden, her head felt like someone was squeezing her temples from the inside.

"Let go," she said between clenched teeth, trying to pull her hand free.

Instead of releasing her, he snarled, "*Gottverdammte Schützennen*," and started to pull her around the corner of the bar. What the hell did he mean "goddamn shielders"?

Derrit grabbed the man's arm and pulled hard. "Let her go!"

With hardly a glance, the man backhanded Derrit, sending him flying back into some chairs. Imara began kicking at his shins and swearing loudly, hoping someone from security would hear her. Damn her pride for not calling a Priority One.

He slapped her, hard, apparently thinking that would shut her up. She spat blood. "Farking *trottel*! That all you got?" Even as she called him a moron, she started to crouch down low enough to throw an uppercut punch into his crotch, but suddenly the pressure in her head turned off like a switch and the man slowly collapsed to the floor.

She watched him slump against the bar, then looked up to see Lièrén Sòng leaning over the man, his hand on the man's neck. Derrit, bloody nose streaming, was crawling toward the bald man, a truly angry look on his face. Before she could process what was happening, Lièrén gave Derrit a hard look.

"Don't do it," he commanded forcefully. Quiet, gracious Lièrén was nowhere in that tone, and it was enough to stop Derrit in mid-reach.

"Don't do what?" she asked, looking back and forth from Derrit to Lièrén, who looked paler than she'd ever imagined an ethnic Chinese man could.

She saw Lièrén glance at the four remaining patrons, most of whom were carefully looking anywhere but toward them. He met her gaze.

"This *húndàn* is a straight telepath." His voice was low as he indicated the bald man. "Derrit was going to clean him, but with anger driving his talent, the man would probably end up blank-slated."

Imara only barely stopped her jaw from dropping in shock. She looked to Derrit, then to the man on the floor, then back to Lièrén. "What did you do to him? The bastard, I mean?"

Lièrén sighed, and a hint of reluctance crossed his usually serene expression. "I'm a sifter."

"A what?" Imara was having trouble kicking her brain into forward motion. She grabbed a bar napkin to wipe the corner of her mouth where she felt blood seeping. Her jaw was going to be sore for a while. Adrenalin made her hands shake.

"A different kind of telepath. You have to decide now what to do—call the police, call hotel security, or let Derrit and me fix the man's memory."

"Fix it how?" Her filer's memory finally started working, and she remembered what she'd heard about the types of telepaths. Sifters mostly worked with brain chemicals.

Lièrén's reluctance became more pronounced, but she thought it had a tinge of resignation. "I'll twist him, and show Derrit where to clean."

"You're a twister, too?" Imara felt herself go pale. Twisters could undetectably change people's memories. It was a frightening talent.

Lièrén nodded. He was proposing to invade the telepath's mind to alter or erase the inconvenient memories, with Derrit's help. She told herself she'd have time to be astonished later.

She looked at Derrit as he used his sleeve to blot the blood from his nose, which had slowed to a drip. While she'd really like to leave the bald man a lasting, painful legacy for daring to hurt her son, the hotel management's unwritten policy was "no trouble with customers meant no penalties for employees." She went with her gut feeling that she could trust Lièrén.

"Twist and clean him." She hoped it was the right choice. The last two patrons in the bar were too chemmed or drunk to move. The smarter ones had already cleared out. "But do it fast," she said quietly. "Security will be here soon, because I sent them a Priority Two ping earlier. Whatever you do has to match the flat video from the security cameras, in case they look."

Lièren nodded. He looked pale, but steady, as he motioned Derrit closer. He crouched down in front of the man and gently took Derrit's hand and put it on top of his own, the one touching the man's neck.

She watched them both for a minute. Derrit's open and expressive face showed a variety of emotions, chief among them wonder and delight. Lièrén's face was serene, almost like he was meditating. He was probably killer in bluff games like hype or poker.

Imara felt like her mind was trying to fly apart at the seams, so she gave herself the task of arranging the bottles and boxes on the bar's display shelves into perfect symmetry. She wasn't a very good liar because her filer's memory never let her forget the truth. To save her job and keep Derrit safe, though, she'd lie like a rug, as her granny liked to say. It was dawning on her that her son was going to be a powerful minder, stronger than his shielder father. She'd already suspected Derrit was developing a shielder talent, but the cleaning was a surprise. She wondered how Lièrén had known.

She kept glancing at the entryway, expecting the evening shift security team, Poltorak and Okonjo, to walk in any second. She needed to clean the blood from Derrit's face, but she didn't want to disturb him. She managed to unearth a knit shirt left over from a live band appearance. The shirt would be too big on Derrit's skinny frame, but better that than the bloody one he was wearing. It wasn't Derrit's first fight, but it was the first one with a grown man. She could tell his nose was already swelling up, and he might have the start of a black eye. All she could do was apply a flexible cold pack until she could get him to the medical clinic for a quick treatment. Since she was the only licensed tender available until the night shift arrived, it'd have to wait a few hours.

She wanted to pace, demand answers, and try out the bar's flame torch on the bald man's bushy eyebrows, in no particular order. Instead, she scrubbed and polished the bar top until it gleamed, sliced fruit rind twists by hand with exacting precision for the next shift, and refilled the napkin dispenser. It felt like it was taking hours, but a glance at the clock told her it had been less than ten minutes when Lièrén and Derrit finally stood up.

Imara triggered the cold pack she'd pulled from the bar's supply and handed it to her son. "You know the drill. Fifteen minutes on, ten minutes off. Lie down in the booth." Derrit did as she asked without hesitation, meaning his nose was hurting a lot.

"Sit, before you fall," she told Lièrén in the same no-arguments-I'm-your-mother tone, pointing to the barstool next to the one the bald telepath had monopolized. Lièrén smiled faintly. He looked exhausted and pale, but she'd seen him look worse, those first few days after he'd moved to the hotel.

Just as she opened her mouth to pepper him with questions, Poltorak and Okonjo finally arrived.

"What happened here?" asked Poltorak. She was a short but wide woman with a thick Russian accent and a ready smile. Okonjo was a tall, thin black man who looked like the wind would blow him over, but he was a ramper, a minder talent that made him stronger than he looked and wickedly fast. On him, bald was a good look.

Imara pointed to the telepath, still slumped on the floor, but now stirring. "Pre-chemmed guest. Wanted me for sex, and got unhappy when I turned him down, which is when I sent the Priority Two. He tried to get physical, then passed out. I didn't serve him anything with a kick—you can check the dispense logs." It was the truth as far as it went, and skipped over Lièrén's and Derrit's involvement. Fortunately, Poltorak was just as familiar with the hotel's unwritten policy about no trouble and didn't ask any more questions.

"Is good, then. We take him back to room, let him sleep." She and Okonjo helped the woozy telepath sit, then get to his feet.

Okonjo looked to Imara. "English?" She nodded. "Mister... sir..." asked Okonjo solicitously of the man he was supporting. "What room are you in?"

Imara surreptitiously watched the telepath's face for some sign of cognition, but he was really looped.

Okonjo sighed and thumbed his percomp to ping the front desk. "Iggy? Got a guest, can't remember his room. Use security QB-2 and take a look." Okonjo and Poltorak turned around with the man so he faced the discreet camera eye above the bar. Okonjo tilted the man's head back so his face was clearly visible.

"He came in with an associate who called him 'Karl,' and he speaks German," said Imara helpfully, loud enough for Iggy to hear. "The other guy mentioned the fourth floor."

After a moment, Iggy came back with a fourth-floor room number. Okonjo and Poltorak half-carried, half-walked the man out of the bar.

Imara waited a few long seconds more to make sure they were really gone, then turned to Lièrén. "What will he remember?" She kept her voice low and quiet.

"That he had fantasies about you, but the last chem he took was chaotic, making him feel dizzy and fluxed, and then—fade out. The next thing he'll remember is whatever the security team does with him. Even if they show him the video, he won't remember assaulting you and will probably blame it on a bad chem reaction. Since you didn't serve him any, you're clear."

Imara was impressed by how well the story fit together, and disturbed. She hadn't realized how… chillingly effective high-level minders could be. "What did you do to him to make him drop like he was in 3G gravity?"

"Sifters can modulate synapses, neurotransmitters, and hormones. I flooded his receptors with a monoamine…" He trailed off, looking almost embarrassed. "I apologize for the tech speak. Think of it as doping, like applying a happy-drug slap patch."

She wanted to ask a hundred more questions, but she needed to prioritize them. "Let me get you something to drink, on the house."

"Thank you. Water would be welcome." His shoulders were drooping, and one of his eyes was half-blinking with each heart beat. Damn, but the man was polite, even when he was in agony.

"Would you like a painkiller to go with the water?" She dropped three ice cubes in a glass and started filling it. "I have several in the dispensary…"

He shook his head. "You're kind to offer, but most chemical painkillers don't work on sifters. I'd need a healer to follow me around for a few hours."

"Really?" No wonder it was taking him such a long time to recover. She couldn't imagine not being able to slap on a pain patch after a hard day on the road crew. "Well, *that* flatlines."

"Yes," said Lièrén, the corner of his mouth twitching with amusement.

She handed him the glass. He nodded his thanks and took several swallows before setting it down on the coaster in front of him. "I have a new liver, among other things. While I'm recovering, I can't be on my normal enhancement drug program, and the withdrawal makes me dry-mouthed."

It was the first time he'd confided so much in her. She knew firsthand about withdrawal symptoms. "The headaches, too?"

"Yes, and sweat flashes." His smile was sardonic. "Still, I'm getting better every day."

Despite his humor, she could tell he was all but done in for the night. "One more question, and then I hope you'll go back to your room and rest."

He ducked his head once. "As you wish, Bartender Sesay." His overly subservient tone made her laugh.

"Cheeky brat. I told you, call me Imara. How did you know about Derrit's cleaning talent? I guessed he was probably a shielder, because his father was, and I'm a filer, so it stands to reason he'd have some sort of talent. How did you know Derrit wanted to clean the telepath guy?"

He shrugged one shoulder, then winced. His neck muscles were probably as tight as a drum, considering how long he'd been enduring the headache. "Sifters can detect talents, though I'm not all that good at it. Derrit was angry enough to drop his shields, so I felt the… activation of his cleaning talent. It can be difficult to control when you're mad."

"I see. That's how you knew the asshole was a straight telepath? He was activating, too?"

"Yes, though mid-levels like he is are usually better at containment. Whatever he chemmed himself with weakened his control. I could feel it even from back there." He pointed to the far booth where Derrit was still lying with the cold pack across his face.

Imara badly wanted to get all the answers she could from him immediately, but she couldn't justify torturing him any longer. He was only staying with her now out of good manners, and perhaps protectiveness. "You've got to get some rest, Agent Sòng. The security team will monitor the assho…uh, valued patron, so Derrit and I will be fine."

He gave her a tired but genuine smile. "I would be honored if you would call me Lièrén."

"*Shì de, dāngrán, zūnjìng de xiānshēng.*" Yes, of course, honored sir. She gave him an exaggerated bow. "Whatever honored sir desires."

He laughed. "You speak Mandarin very well."

"It was the official language on Capet Dedrum for six hundred years until the CGC moved in and made English the galactic standard. Mandarin is still primary with the long-timers, so it made sense to learn. My tonal control is iffy, though. I've come close to unforgivably insulting people more than once."

"In that case, I'll remember to ask first, rather than assuming I've made you mad." He drank the last of his water and stood. "Goodnight, then."

As he stepped back, she had the absurd impulse to ask when she'd see him again, like she was a fifteen-year-old at the end of a first date. Instead, she gave him a casual salute and a smile.

Once he was gone, she pulled out the knit shirt she'd found earlier and took it to the far booth, where her son was just sitting up.

"Here, trade me shirts. How's the face, *bata*?"

"Mom!" he complained, drawing out the vowel. "I'm not a baby." He stood and pulled off his own bloody shirt and handed it to her, then pulled the other one on. It hung nearly to his knees.

"No, you're not. How's the face, doddering old man?" She tilted his chin left and right, examining his face for bruising. The sooner they got to the all-hours medical clinic to get the bruising and swelling taken care of, the happier she'd be. She might even have them do something about her sore jaw and cut lip.

Derrit rolled his eyes. "It's okay. It hurt worse when I ran into the light pole." He'd been a lopar, recklessly horsing around on a friend's street coaster.

Imara felt supremely lucky that it was a rare dead night at the bar. She looked at the one patron still there, an older-looking woman slumped and gently snoring in the booth closest to the hall to the fresher. Bookkeeper Shola was a bi-weekly regular who claimed to be an insomniac, but somehow managed to sleep several hours in the bar, regardless of the noise level. Imara would wake the woman when her shift ended, as usual.

She turned back to her son. "So, tell me what happened tonight."

"You're not mad at me, are you? For getting in a fight?"

She brushed the unhurt side of his face with her thumb. "No, but you know I worry about you. Mother's prerogative. You have to learn when to pick your battles. He could've really hurt you."

"Tatay would have kicked his ass."

"Your father was an adult man, and you will be, too, someday, but not yet. Tell me about what you and Agent Sòng did together."

Derrit's eyes lit up. "It was absolute zero! He spoke in my mind, like Tatay used to, and showed me the guy's memories and what needed erasing. I could see... well, feel him working, and it was like he was, like, weaving a basket. He showed me how to pick up the right strands. Agent Sòng's mind is... smooth, maybe, like road glass, but the blond guy, his mind is yuck. Like when that waste reclamation line burst and you had to recycle all your work clothes."

"And how do you feel now? Your father used to get heavy sinus congestion if he overused his talent." She smiled and brushed the tip of his swollen nose with her finger. "It's probably hard to tell right now, but think about it, okay? Human bodies provide negative feedback for a reason."

"Mom, what does a cleaner do? I didn't know I was one."

"You have a net account. Why don't you look it up and tell me?" She pointed toward the bar's net terminals along one wall. "And look up sifter and twister, while you're at it." It was a good way to distract Derrit from the pain he wasn't admitting to, and finding out more about Lièrén. Or at least about his talents.

Imara was very tempted to distract herself by mixing something from her dispensary, but she knew from hard-won experience, it didn't solve anything. She'd had enough of making herself numb after Torin's unexpected death, and would never go back there again. Detoxing on her own had been painful. She had to be coherent and present so she could do what was best for her son. Plenty of people wouldn't look past their fearful distrust of minders to see the warm, fun-loving, protective boy, who was so much like his father that it made her heart swell with bittersweet memories.

CHAPTER 2

IMARA PUT THE last drink on the bar and caught Rayle's eye so he'd know the big table's order was ready. He was always gregarious, but tonight, he was practically incandescent, flitting in and out among the tables, dancing and sometimes singing to the music, teasing the kids, and flirting shamelessly with the adults. It was a boisterous crowd, and there was nothing Rayle loved more than an audience. His hair was newly sky blue with winking lights, his eyebrows and eyelashes had a blue neon metallic sheen, and drops had made his irises look shiny silver, all in preparation for the upcoming dance performance he was in. He'd been a part of the publicity session just that morning. He was offering tickets to anyone who seemed remotely interested.

Because she was watching for him, she noticed when Lièrén Sòng arrived, a day later than she'd expected based on the pattern he'd established. All the booths were taken, including his preferred small one in the back, so he chose to sit at the end of the bar. Rayle noticed, too, and after serving the big table and stowing the tray, he made a beeline to Lièrén to take his order, even though it was usually Imara's job to serve the people at the bar. It amused her that Lièrén would always get excellent service as long as Rayle was around. Or if she was around, if she was honest.

Out of habit, she glanced at Derrit, who was playing an online game at one of the kiosks. She allowed him an hour an evening, to make up for being stuck in the hotel. One of the few perks she got as an employee was free use of the net terminals, which made it easier to put off updating the housecomp and percomps for her and Derrit. Spires, even out in the Rim where their apartment was located, was a hideously expensive place to live, which was why she supplemented her day job as a road-crew leader with bartending for the hotel.

Over the last three days, Imara had thought a lot about what to do about Derrit. She'd been careful not to make him feel that she disapproved of his talent, because she'd had enough of that as a child, and she'd only been a farkin' low-level filer, hardly a minder worth registering in the eyes of the CPS Testing Center. Premium talents like Derrit's were a double-edged sword. He'd have more career choices than she ever did, but resentment and prejudice could make a minder's life hell.

He was still a child, no matter how responsible he was for a boy his age. She was concerned that he didn't know what he was doing and could get hurt, or might unintentionally hurt someone else, and that he wouldn't tell her because he wouldn't want to worry her. Her husband Torin had been very protective and had a tendency to keep troubling details from her, and she recognized the same habit developing in her son. Torin had started it because too many details used to overwhelm her, but she was older now and better at staying focused, and she didn't want Derrit to adopt Torin's behavior.

She was kept busy for the next ten minutes with dispensary orders. Rayle could prepare the flats and fizzies, but only she was licensed to dispense the kickers—alcohol, chems, inhalants, or alterants—that made up about half the bar's business on busy nights. She trusted Rayle's judgment, but it was ultimately her decision as to whether or not to serve the kickers, because it was her license. It was legal in Spires for a tender to serve high-test to a ten-year-old, but it was also likely to get the tender personally sued if the kid sustained lasting injury because of it. Her personal policy was to not serve kickers to anyone under seventeen, and the hotel's managers backed her up because *they* didn't want to get sued, either.

Finally, she had a lull, and she drifted down to the end of the bar where Lièrén sat. He looked healthier than he had three nights ago. He smiled when he saw her.

"If I might ask, who selects the music for the bar?" He gestured up toward one of the ceiling speakers. The song playing sounded a lot closer to Japanese *surashu* thrash than a British pub tune. His brown eyes were almost black, and when he looked at her, it felt like she had his undivided attention. It was unexpectedly nice. Most of her customers usually had a dozen other things on their minds, and rarely saw her as a person.

Imara smiled back. "Probably some automated algorithm that chooses based on lyrics or whatever keywords the artists tagged it with. Why?"

"Rayle is having trouble improvising choreography that doesn't look like an insect attack."

She looked to where Lièrén was pointing, then laughed out loud. It drew Rayle's attention, and he wended his way through the tables to join them.

"What's so funny?" he asked.

She gave him a teasing smirk. "You. Where'd you find the termite hill to dance on?"

Rayle rolled his eyes and leaned closer to Lièrén to nudge his shoulder playfully. "Says the woman who says she can't dance at all."

Lièrén smiled but didn't nudge back. "I can't, either, though I respect your difficulty in performing to this particular piece. I think the singer is complaining about glass shards in his Scotch, which would explain the shrieking."

Rayle was about to answer when a customer from across the room shouted for him. Rayle gave a little salute to Lièrén and darted away.

Lièrén gestured toward where Rayle had stood. "He looks very, uhm, blue tonight."

Imara laughed, delighted that Lièrén was feeling well enough to joke with them again. "It's for a show. Don't tell him you noticed, or he'll be delighted to show you that *all* of his hair is now electric blue. The man has no shame." She shook her head. "At least dancers aren't expected to get full-body makeovers for their roles like holovid actors are." She pointed to his empty glass. "Another red fizz, or maybe some water?"

"Yes to both, please." She quickly took care of him, then checked on the other people at the bar and filled several orders for Rayle. As nice as it was to have a busy night, because it made the time go fast and the tips were good, she really wanted a few quiet moments with Lièrén. She wanted to ask him a favor.

The next chance she got, she asked if he'd eaten yet, and offered to order something.

Lièrén gave her a slight smile. "A kind thought, but I'll pass."

She didn't blame him—the hotel restaurant was unpopular for good reason. "I could send Derrit to the kitchen to make a sandwich. He makes a pretty mean flatbread with toasted cheese, and that's not just a mother's pride talking."

"Thank you, no, but perhaps later." He looked regretful. "The new drug regimen affects my appetite."

"Sorry to hear it." She rested her forearms flat on the counter and rounded her back in a stretch. She'd been on her feet for the whole shift. "May I ask, do all CPS minders get enhancement drugs? I've only heard general conversations, but it seems like they do."

"The telepathic and telekinetic minders do. The enhancement drugs also help with focus and maintaining control. I'm not sure about the patterner class. Filers like you, and the forecasters and such, don't seem to need it."

"I don't know about that. I used to get distracted by, well, everything under the sun, but I've worked on it." She shrugged. "Of course, I'm only a mid-level, and a late bloomer at that. I don't envy you being told to take daily drugs because it's 'good for you.'"

"The benefits outweigh the cost. I will admit to not liking being told to exercise for that reason. Being closely monitored while using force exercisers and treadmills is… uninspiring."

"You should come to a dance class with me," said Rayle, who had stepped up behind Lièrén without him noticing and overheard the last few words. "It's impossible to be bored when you're dancing."

Lièrén shook his head. "I am not yet able to participate in such activities." He sounded actually regretful, not just polite, but Imara didn't know him well enough to tell the difference.

Rayle winked at Lièrén. "I'll take that as a 'maybe.'" He turned to Imara. "The long-limbed, sexy man in the clingy green kilt at table six wants another gram of loupomak. They're celebrating because he won a frontier planet homestead lottery." He rolled his eyes. "They'll probably tip me in lottery tickets. Can't pay the rent with lottery tickets."

Imara never forgot a bar order, so she didn't even have to think about it. "Nope, he's already had two. Offer him some intwinden or canab. Or a Red Blossom token, to take the edge off."

"Red Blossom?" asked Lièrén.

"Joyhouse up the north walkway," replied Rayle as he fished in the drawer, then held up a red, oval-shaped smart chip with a red flower on it. "First come, first served!" He twirled away.

Imara snorted. "You'd think that joke would get old with him, but you'd be wrong."

Business picked up again, and she had to abandon Lièrén for a while. She was worried that he'd leave before she got the chance to talk to him. He'd probably stay if she asked, because he was always accommodating, but she didn't want to take advantage of him. Well, she did, because in addition to being nice, he was a handsome, sexy man, but he was also a transient who could be gone tomorrow. She had an ironclad personal policy not to get involved with transients, no matter how plasma hot they were. She'd seen enough of that with her mother's always-outbound parade of lovers. The favor she wanted to ask was for Derrit, not for her.

Derrit was working on an assignment for school that he wasn't ready to show her yet. He got that trait from his father, who had loved building suspense before revealing some secret project. Like the time he'd learned to crochet and made an afghan throw for Derrit as a solstice gift. That the afghan was decidedly polygonal instead of square hadn't mattered to her adoring son in the slightest. On busy nights like tonight, she set up a tiny table near the pantry for Derrit, or he'd never get any work done, especially when other kids came in. Derrit was very social, again like his father. She herself was shy by nature, or at least she had been, until she'd had to learn not to be, so she could put food on the table. Reticent road-crew employees got little respect, and bashful bartenders got few tips.

Miraculously, Lièrén stayed, and took the opportunity to snag his favorite booth once it became free. Remembering his dry-mouth problem, she sent Rayle with another glass of water. It was sometimes still hard to remember that in Spires, or more officially, Novi Nadezhdi, potable water was plentiful and cheap enough to offer for free. She'd grown up in a near-desert, where the nearest oasis was a hundred kilometers away, and water was how wealth was measured.

After refusing to serve brandy to a thirteen-year-old, it got her wondering how old Lièrén was. Certainly over seventeen, because the CPS didn't hire children as field agents, but he looked about twenty-five. Even without the standard rejuve treatments that everyone got, he'd probably look young most of his life. Whereas her people, especially the women, looked like the proverbial old crones by the time they were fifty, without treatments, and she was behind on hers. She didn't skip the regular health maintenance checkups and procedures, because she was all Derrit had, but body work at her age was considered elective. She even skipped the expense of a body parlor for her hair, meaning it had grown longer and shaggier than ever, despite occasional home trims. On the other hand, her great-times-three grandmother was still alive and running her own sheep station at age 168, so at least she had natural longevity going for her.

She knew why she was worrying about her looks, when she usually couldn't be bothered. He was sitting in the back booth. Even though she was only thirty-seven, she was still probably too old for him. Twelve- or fifteen-year age differences didn't matter much these days, what with increasing human life spans, but it was still a consideration for a successful relationship. She rolled her eyes at the direction of her thoughts. She had no business whatsoever thinking about a relationship with a transient. Maybe *she* needed to visit the Red Blossom to take the edge off.

Finally, the big party at table six broke up, which seemed to be the signal for other patrons to leave, too. The crowd thinned out, and Rayle took a break so he could make something to eat in the kitchen. As employees, they were allowed to use it unless the restaurant was busy, which was hardly ever. Derrit had made himself an omelet there earlier. Thank Neptune he thought cooking was an adventure, and was now responsible enough to be trusted in a kitchen.

She loaded the glassware into the quicksan in the corner, rather than send it to the kitchen. The unit was fast, but small, so it would take several loads. It wasn't worth the argument with the resentful restaurant staff to ask them to do it, even though it was their job. She straightened up the supply bottles and boxes, and entered ordering notes for those that were running low.

The second Rayle came back, she asked him to watch the bar for a few minutes. She poured a flat orange for Derrit and took it to him, then took her glass of *kelasa* and slid into the vacant seat in Lièrén's booth. Whatever he was reading on his very elegant, high-powered percomp was making him frown, but when he looked up at her, he smiled.

Suddenly, she was nervous. "I'd like to make you a proposition."

At his raised eyebrows, she realized how it sounded. "Oh, sorry, not like that. I'm trying to propose a trade… I'd like to…." She was sounding like a complete idiot. "I'm not chemmed, I promise. I want to ask you for a favor." She took a deep breath. "I'd like you to teach Derrit to use his talents. I know you're still recovering, so I'll understand if you're not able to, but I'm just a general filer, and I can't do it, and I don't know anyone else. In trade, I'll serve you whatever you want for free, as long as you're here. I know it's not much, but he could really use the help in learning to control his talents."

She looked at his altogether too-handsome face as he considered her words. She hoped for Derrit's sake he'd agree, and at the same time, hoped he'd take her for a babbling fool and turn her down, so she wouldn't be tempted by him anymore.

CHAPTER 3

AFTER THE INCIDENT with the telepath, and after revealing his twister talent, Lièrén had expected uncomfortable questions, accusations, or avoidance, but he certainly hadn't been expecting Imara's request and the trust it implied.

"I'm honored to be asked, but please give me some time to think about it," he temporized. His first instinct was to say yes, because it was Imara asking, and he liked her boy, but it wasn't as simple as that.

"Of course," she said. "I'll be at the bar." She slid out and away fast.

He toyed with his glass of water. He didn't know whether or not working with a child on minder skills would be against CPS protocol for field agents, though he suspected that if asked, his supervisor would forbid it. The whole unit was reeling over a murder-suicide of two of their own.

Lièrén had spent the previous evening with the Office of Internal Inquiry, repeating *ad nauseam* that, although he was in the same field unit, he rarely interacted with others, since their job was retrieval and security, while his and his partner's specialty was interrogation. He hadn't heard from anyone in his unit except his supervisor since his accident, and had no idea what the victims were doing on Con Prime. He didn't volunteer the fact that his now-dead partner Fiyon hadn't trusted any of the other agents in their unit, for reasons he never explained. The OII could develop their own opinions.

From what the OII said, Agent Carlo Baretti had pushed his lover, Agent Traci Apfel, off one of the famous lotus park platforms in Spires, then jumped to his own death. Lièrén felt guilty that, between their separate jobs and his own poor memory, he could barely remember the talents, much less the faces, of his dead coworkers. Considering their obviously dysfunctional relationship, they likely had other things on their minds besides visiting an injured coworker they hardly knew.

It had taken some time to convince the OII that he didn't have any useful information to provide them. He would have told them if he did, because the CPS needed his unit to be functional, and his absence wasn't helping. With Fiyon dead and Lièrén disabled, the unit was down to one part-time interrogator, Talavara, who was a low-level twister, but impatient and careless as a telepath. Lièrén had only met her in person a few times, but Fiyon had often grumbled about having to clean up after her.

Teaching Derrit would distract Lièrén from feeling sorry for himself, a distressing habit of late. He'd once imagined the CPS would keep him on New Kulam at the Academy or the prestigious Minder Institute as an instructor, but his mid-level twister talent had been strong enough to make him more useful in the field. Sifters were often used in interrogation, adjusting brain chemicals to encourage trust and relaxation, and because of their lie-detection capabilities, though his didn't used to be that good. Lately, perhaps because he'd had little else to think about or occupy his time, he'd been noticing the lies more. The OII interrogators had tried lying to him as an investigation tactic, until they remembered his talent. Then they'd brought in their own sifter.

People lied all the time in the bar, usually about how much they'd pre-chemmed themselves before arriving. Fortunately, Imara and Rayle together were good at figuring it out for themselves. Imara was hard to read, but he was fairly sure she only pretended to like sports when customers wanted to talk about them, and Rayle wasn't seriously interested in most of the people he flirted with.

Lièrén was grateful that Imara's questions hadn't yet strayed to *What exactly do you do for the CPS?*, which he couldn't answer without lying and would have to report it. Lièrén already knew he was on thin ice for not reporting what he and Derrit had done to the telepath, but he was reluctant to stir up trouble for another minder, however antisocial. Minders had a poor enough reputation as it was. It was better for minders to take care of other minders quietly, among themselves. Lièrén had found the twisting easier than usual, which he assumed was because of the adrenalin and working with the unexpectedly powerful Derrit. The post-twist headache had been as vicious as always, but at least he'd slept through that night without the usual falling dreams from the accident.

Since lunchtime, his talent had felt like tiny pins and needles in his head. As a high-level sifter, he was accustomed to being stronger than most; he wasn't accustomed to being slow in anything regarding his primary talent. He hoped the new enhancement drugs, which he'd taken an hour ago, would fix the problem. He'd had to wait two extra days to get the replacement enhancement drug order refilled, some problem with a custom compound and a different pharma supplier.

The extracurricular activity of teaching Derrit certainly wouldn't impact Lièrén's current usefulness to the CPS. Owing to the investigation, plus the various follow-up procedures, medical checkups, and therapy sessions that were part of his treatment plan, he could only be in the office part-time, on irregular days and hours. Yamazaki, his supervisor, had assigned him the catch-up filing task for lack of anything better, and had truthfully apologized for it being such a nasty job. Lièrén was grateful that Yamazaki could give him something useful to do, and told him so. It wasn't Yamazaki's fault that he got saddled with a non-local team's injured field agent, especially considering the perceived cloud Lièrén was under with the internal investigation still pending.

He was diverted from his musing by Rayle and Imara at the bar.

"…restaurant staff was in a panic," Rayle was saying gleefully. "One of the station delivery tubes is clogged, and it's backing up the system, making them leak all over the tables. The manager ordered them to shut down until maintenance can get to it, so they have to send all their customers to us."

Rayle's enjoyment was infectious, and was answered by a smile from Imara. "Which tube? Hot water?"

Rayle shook his head. "Kaffa. Someone forgot to replace a filter, and the granules got in the system. They've got housekeeping scrounging around for extra towels. It's an unholy mess." All the hotel room freshers had solardries, quick-dry concentrated-heat blowers, so Lièrén imagined the hotel didn't have very many towels to begin with. A lot of people considered them unsanitary.

Imara, who had been wiping down a carafe, looked thoughtful, then eyed one of her dispenser hoses. "Tell them to try coupling their fizzy line to the main tube and flushing it to the drain. The extra gas pressure ought to get the particles moving along." At Rayle's crestfallen look, she added, "Don't worry. Knowing them, they'll drag out the cleanup for at least a couple of hours. We'll still get all the customers, and you can sell more tickets to your show."

He grabbed her hand and kissed it. "Excellent plan, my precious, practical darling!" He executed a graceful spin as he turned to leave.

Lièrén couldn't help but smile at Rayle's irrepressible personality, while admiring Imara's clever solution. He wished he was that fast a problem solver.

The pressure in his bladder reminded him he'd been downing liquids almost nonstop since he'd arrived, so he went to the fresher, and took the opportunity to try smoothing his hair down with a little water. It had looked stupid ever since his nap, and he hadn't been in the mood to take a shower before coming to the bar. He really needed to find a decent body parlor sometime soon, or he'd look like a frilled cockatoo. He made a mental note to ask Imara for a recommendation. If he trusted Rayle's choice, Lièrén was afraid he'd end up with a cherry red mohawk with glow-in-the-dark skull studs.

When he returned to his booth, he found Derrit seated, waiting for him.

"Nanay says you're still thinking about teaching me," he said without preamble.

"Nanay?" asked Lièrén.

"It's 'mother' in Filipino. It was what my dad called her. He's dead."

The boy's matter-of-fact tone about his father's death was unexpected. As his own recent survival attested, modern medicine had reduced human mortality rates. Parental death wasn't a common experience for children. He himself had been only one of two orphans out of thousands of students at the Academy. He nodded respectfully to Derrit. "I'm sorry for your loss."

Derrit shook his head. "He wouldn't have liked us still being sad."

He glanced toward his mother, who was chatting with a patron, then back to Lièrén. "She told me not to bother you, but I wanted you to know that I really want to learn. It's not like Sula's mother, who made her take classical teslaharp lessons because it looked good on school applications." He was very earnest. The Filipino heritage explained the boy's slanted eyes and lighter brown hair, though he'd clearly gotten the springy, pointed corkscrew curls from his mother.

"If I may ask," said Lièrén, "why are you so interested?"

"Dad told me before he died that I needed to look out for Nanay once he couldn't. I'm not big, yet, like he was, but if I get better at all my talents, maybe I can keep buttwashes like that telepath from hurting her." The fierceness in his tone reminded Lièrén of how angry the boy had been that night.

It dawned on Lièrén why Imara had always been harder for him to read. "How long have you been using your shielder talent to protect her?"

Derrit shrugged. "I don't know. I just kind of think about putting up shields for her, and they happen."

"How do you get them to stick? The few shielders I've known have to be nearby and concentrating."

Derrit shrugged again, more uncomfortably this time. "I don't know. Am I doing it wrong?"

Lièrén shook his head. "I don't believe so." He didn't want the boy feeling ashamed of his talents, but Lièrén didn't know much about shielders.

Derrit's expression morphed into hopefulness. "That's why I need you to teach me."

"How old are you?"

"Eleven, but I'll be twelve in a month," he said with pride. He clasped his hands and shoved them in his lap, as if to keep them from fighting with each other.

Lièrén hid a smile at how eager Derrit was to be older, impressed with how mature and responsible the boy was for his age. He remembered his own days at the CPS Academy, wishing constantly to be treated like the older students he had classes with. He'd probably been a snot-nosed brat compared to Derrit.

He made his decision and nodded. "Yes. Please tell your mother I'd like to speak with her when it's convenient for her."

Derrit smiled widely, then scrambled out of the booth and shot like a meteor toward Imara. In mid-flight, he veered off to Rayle and pointed him to the bar, then pulled his mother's hand to practically drag her to Lièrén.

"You two have a lot to talk about," said Derrit, who nudged her toward the open seat, then scampered back to the bar, where Rayle was watching with open amusement.

Lièrén spoke before Imara could sit. "My apologies for the interruption. I should have anticipated Derrit would be impatient. I can wait until it's convenient."

Imara laughed as she sat. "Now is good." Not for the first time, he was struck by how much her smile lit up her face, turning pretty into extraordinary.

"I will do my best to teach Derrit, but you must understand that there are other, better teachers at the CPS Academy. I'm not recruiting for them, but they have the experience I lack. Also, I am still adjusting to new enhancement drugs, so my own talents may be… unpredictable."

"You seemed to do okay a few nights ago."

"Yes, but I believe that's partly because Derrit has strong talents. Did you know he's been shielding you?"

Her eyes widened. "He has?" She was still a moment, then sighed. "I'll have a talk with him. I shouldn't be surprised, I guess. Torin—Derrit's father—was always hiding things from me so I wouldn't worry. Derrit is very like him. Torin hated medics and didn't trust healers, so when he got sick, he didn't tell anyone until he collapsed one day on the job. By then, it was too late, and he couldn't be saved."

Her tone was even and her expression calm, but he got the impression she still felt... betrayed that Torin hadn't trusted her. Lièrén made a mental note to talk to Derrit about giving Imara the choice of whether or not to be shielded. It had no effect on her filer talent, but unless the shielding was done correctly, it bottled up any other talents she might have, which was why shielders were used in security work. Although she claimed she was only a general filer, with the enviably comprehensive memory of everything, Lièrén wouldn't be surprised if she had another talent, too, maybe more than one. His own sifter talent said she might, though it was equally likely his misbehaving talent was wrong.

He was heartily sick of not being in control of his talents, and of drug withdrawal and side effects, and the near-constant headaches, flatlined sex drive, and still not having stamina even after six weeks of surgery, treatment, and therapy. Other than that, he thought sourly, he was the bloody picture of health.

Once again, he was feeling sorry for himself, when he should have been paying attention to the attractive, friendly woman across from him. "We can begin the day after tomorrow, if that's acceptable. That is your next evening here, isn't it?"

She smiled once again. "Yes, and thank you. I'm sure Derrit probably already told you, but he's really looking forward to whatever you can teach him, for as long as you stay."

"You honor me with your trust, and I will do what I can for him. Have you scheduled his Testing Center appointment yet?"

"Yes, it's in a month, a couple of days before his legal birthday." It was common practice to celebrate birthdays annually based on the local planetary cycle, but as far as the government was concerned, the official, legal birthday was based on the standardized Galactic Date and Time, or GDAT.

Out of the corner of his eye, he noticed Rayle discreetly signaling Imara. He opened his mouth to tell her, but she must have seen it and was already standing.

"I'll send Derrit with more water," she said as she stepped away. She didn't move like a dancer, like Rayle, but her natural athleticism gave the impression of competence. He could well imagine she commanded her road crew with ease, even if he had no idea what a road crew did. While he was a good pilot, both atmospheric and interstellar, he'd never learned to operate ground-based vehicles. And road-crew work in Spires, with its curving silicate roadways and elevated architecture, must be especially challenging.

When Derrit brought the water, he sat across from Lièrén instead of leaving. "So what's the first lesson?"

Social niceties were hard to come by for impatient eleven-year-old boys. Lièrén smiled. "Research. I need to learn more about your talents, as do you."

"Mom already made me read a bunch of stuff on the net. Isn't there anything I can, you know, *do*? To like, you know, practice?" He was fidgeting with eagerness.

"Not yet." Lièrén didn't want to start anything so late in the evening. While it was only a little after eight, he still tired easily. He did want to talk about what happened with the telepath, though, and now was as good a time as any. "You've had an introductory sex class, haven't you?"

Derrit looked puzzled by the subject change, but answered readily. "Yeah, in spring, when I got my implant." Lièrén nodded his approval. A few of his fellow Academy students hadn't even known what the word "contraception" meant, and had needed remedial sex education to explain what was going on with their hormones and bodies when puberty hit.

"Remember what we saw in the telepath's memory? The... images he associated with sex?"

Derrit nodded, his eyes a little darker.

Lièrén didn't like bringing it up, but it had to be dealt with. "What the telepath wanted, what he likes, isn't about sex, it's about control and domination. He gets pleasure from inflicting unwanted pain without consent. He's just this side of being a predator, and whatever chems he took that evening impaired his judgment."

It was an ugly aberration that someone not quite twelve shouldn't have to know about yet, but Derrit's cleaning talent made it inevitable, sooner or later. Cleaners were often used in justice cases.

"Good sex, healthy sex, is consensual. That means each sex partner knows what he or she is getting into. It should be safe, pleasurable, and fun."

Lièrén watched the anger grow in Derrit's face and body as he realized what the telepath had wanted to do to hurt his mother. "You should have let me flatline the slagger."

"It's not that simple. Thinking and fantasizing aren't the same as doing, and the telepath wasn't in control of himself. Yes, he was stupid to get warped on an unknown chem while traveling, which is why we left that part of his memory alone, so he'd learn." Lièrén reached across the table and put his hand on top of Derrit's clenched fist. "You have a powerful talent, Derrit, and it comes with extra responsibility. You must be certain that erasing memories is the right thing to do, because it's not like a game. There is no reset option if you make a mistake. People are scared of cleaners with good reason."

As the implications sank in, Derrit's fist relaxed. Lièrén sat back to let Derrit think about what he'd said.

After several moments, Derrit looked over at his mother, who was laughing at something Rayle had said. "Rayle talks like he wants to have sex with everyone, and I know he likes having fun. Do you think he wants to have sex with my mom?"

Lièrén blinked at the change in subject, then realized he should have expected it. Kids Derrit's age were never more than a thought or two away from the topic of sex. Some never grew out of it.

"Perhaps he does," said Lièrén, though he believed Rayle preferred males, or at least, was more truthful when flirting with them. However, if Rayle did want to hot-connect with Imara, Lièrén couldn't fault the man's good taste. "I don't know Rayle well enough to say."

A wave of exhaustion suddenly washed over Lièrén, like an interstellar drive suddenly running out of flux. It hadn't happened for the last couple of nights, so he'd hoped he was getting better, but apparently and depressingly not. His headache was back, too. He wondered if it was the ordinary price of being a sifter, or if it was just him. The only other high-level sifter he knew was his CPS-ordered therapist, for dealing with the post-accident stress, and Lièrén had to be careful about what ended up in his official records. Confidentiality took a back seat to the CPS's need to be able to trust its covert field agents.

"Are you okay, Agent Sòng?" asked Derrit. "You look sick. Can I get you something?"

Lièrén smiled, absurdly comforted by being fussed over. "Thank you for your concern, Master Derrit. I'm just tired. It's time I went back to my suite." He started to use his percomp to settle his bar tab, when he remembered Imara's offer of a trade. If he insisted on paying now, it would upset her. Life's little negotiations were sometimes a delicate balance.

He slid out of the booth and stood up, and Derrit followed suit. Lièrén blinked against the pain caused by the bright lights. One of the reasons he liked the little back booth was its comparative darkness, which was easier on his persistent headaches.

Imara came out from behind the bar. "Leaving?"

"Yes, and thank you both for another pleasant evening." He made sure to include Derrit in his praise.

"May I escort you to your room, Agent Sòng?" Derrit asked in an unexpectedly dignified tone.

"Derrit, I don't think…" began Imara.

Lièrén interrupted. "I would be most honored, Master Derrit." He liked the thought that Derrit worried about him, and children should be encouraged to take care of older people, even though Lièrén was only thirty-two.

Imara gave him a quick, genuine smile before hiding it from Derrit, and Rayle winked at him from behind the bar as they walked by.

At the door to his room, Lièrén again thanked Derrit.

"You like my mother, don't you?" Derrit asked.

Lièrén slowly unlocked the doorway to give himself time to respond to the loaded question. "I respect your mother a great deal," he said carefully. It was better to speak the truth, when possible, if not exactly the truth the questioner was looking for.

The answer seemed to satisfy Derrit, because he nodded. "See you the day after tomorrow."

As Lièrén sealed his door and dimmed the lights to a more comfortable level, he wondered if Derrit was hoping he'd start something with Imara. If so, Derrit was doomed to disappointment. Lièrén would eventually be healthy enough to return to his regular field-unit job, which had destroyed all his previous relationships. In the last couple of years, he'd given up even trying for long-distance love affairs, or even casual hot-connect-when-convenient arrangements. After a while, even the most tolerant of lovers stopped believing that working on tedious trade disputes took him away for months at a time. His partner, Fiyon, had often groused about what a dumb cover story it was, and Lièrén had to agree.

He stripped off his clothes and left them draped on the chair. He'd take care of them in the morning. He wondered who his new partner would be, or if maybe he'd be assigned a new rookie to train. On second thought, that seemed unlikely, since he only had ten years of experience, far less than anyone else in the field unit. Even when they replaced Baretti and Apfel, it would probably be with experienced CPS minders, not recent graduates.

He smiled ruefully at himself as he slid between the soft sheets of his large bed. He was just like Derrit, wanting to be taken seriously by the adults.

CHAPTER 4

"CATCH HIM!"

A fluffy-tailed red fox puppy made a mad dash around Lièrén's feet, then took off toward the ornamental maple trees at the center of the park, hotly pursued by five laughing, shouting children, the oldest of which was twelve. Lièrén laughed, as did the woman next to him.

Nàiměi Sòng, seated to his left on the bench, turned to look at him. "*Didi*, it's good to see you smile." She was his oldest sister, and this year only, twice his age, a fact he'd teased her about earlier, which was why she called him by the family nickname of "young brother" now. She had intelligent eyes and graceful mannerisms, and thanks to the Sòng family genes and good body-shop work, she looked barely over thirty.

"It's good to be smiling, *lǎo mèi*." He emphasized the "old" part of her nickname that meant "old sister." He gestured toward the rambunctious children. "They have so much energy. How could I not?"

It was a warm, sunny day without being too hot. For once, no rain was in the forecast, but the park wasn't as crowded as it could have been because of the wind. He was glad he hadn't chosen to wear a kilt that day. The greenery was a pleasant change from the hard reflective surfaces of Spires glass. The swarms of adbots that annoyed tourists on the walkways were blessedly few and far between in the park, in part because they were distracted by fluttering plant leaves.

Nàiměi had wanted to visit one of the twelve famous lotus blossom elevated parks, but Lièrén had talked her out of it, vaguely citing safety concerns, and pointing to the recent "death by misadventure" off one of them only last week. That was the CPS's official story for the murder-suicide of his two coworkers. The OII investigators had found a journal that revealed Baretti's unhealthy obsession with Apfel. Lièrén had taken it at face value when the OII mentioned it, but he'd since come to wonder how the periodic telepath counseling sessions they all were required to have had missed it. In any case, he didn't want any of his family near the skyward parks, regardless of how safe the city claimed they were.

"Death by misadventure, hmm?" asked Nàiměi skeptically. "More likely it was idiot daredevils, imagining they were immortal. Like a certain younger brother on a tightrope between school rooftops."

That had been a misadventure, all right, but he and the other students had survived, thanks to the telekinetic in the group, and it had become an Academy legend.

"Don't worry, Nàiměi," he'd told her. "The accident cured me of any such ambitions I might have had. I find I don't care for free-falling."

Lièrén was grateful to be feeling better than he had only a week ago, even though his thighs and back were stiffening up from his morning at the gym. The constant headaches had finally eased up, and the medics had cleared him for moderate exercise of his own choosing. He'd elected to begin a gentle program of blended martial arts, a slow meditative form and a combat style for building strength and flexibility. When he'd been in school, he'd originally chosen martial arts as the least objectionable of the required exercise programs they offered, and had come to enjoy it in time. He'd fallen out of the habit while working for the field unit, since he couldn't predict when he'd be available for classes, but it felt good enough now that he planned to make a better effort once he returned to duty.

Little six-year-old Jing, the youngest and least athletic of Lièrén's grand-nieces, had given up chasing the puppy, and now approached Lièrén, looking at him hopefully. He held out a hand to her, and she took it as an invitation to clamber into his lap and snuggle. She was small, warm, and wiggly.

"*Nǐ xiǎng tīng tīng yīnyuè?*" she asked, holding out one of her earwires to him.

"We're speaking English today, Jing," admonished Nàiměi. She was determined that her grandchildren wouldn't be limited to the Mandarin that prevailed in the family compound, which these days was more the size of a small town. Families with frontier origins often increased their homestead by acquiring additional parcels of land for housing multiple branches as the family grew and prospered. The enterprising Sòng family had long ago expanded and incorporated their real estate holdings, which served as the launch pad for their extensive portfolio diversification.

"Yes, *nǎinai*… Grandmother. Would you like to listen to some music, *lǎo shūshu*?" It amused him to be called "old uncle" at his age, even though he really was her great-uncle. He imagined Nàiměi had felt similarly when he'd been a child and started her "old sister" nickname. He was the only progeny from a later, second marriage for his father, after a divorce from his first wife, the mother of Nàiměi and her five brothers and sisters. The mixed generational blend was common among families that had thrived for centuries.

He couldn't imagine what it must have been like in preflight days, when people were lucky to live long enough to get to know their grandchildren. His great-grandfather, Sòng Tiān Cì, had at least fifteen children that Lièrén knew of, and as widely traveled and unapologetically lusty as the older man was, maybe more. Most of them had children and grandchildren themselves, meaning Lièrén's branch of the Sòngs was well populated and genetically diverse. And that didn't even count the "adoptions," the legal loophole the family trust exploited to bring desirable outside skills into their various enterprises.

"Yes, thank you, it's kind of you to share with me." He took the earwire from her and adhered it to the side of his face. The music was a lively children's song about the seven moons of Zahmanha. The words were silly, but the tune was infectious, and Jing sang artlessly along with the chorus. Lièrén was content to hold her and nod his head to the beat.

Huan, the oldest boy, called to Jing, and she scrambled off Lièrén's lap to run after him. Lièrén removed the earwire and offered it to Nàiměi.

She took it with a smile. "Tell me about your personal life, *didi*," she said as she put the earwire in her pocket. "Do you have someone to make you happy? Someone to celebrate your birthday, or to wait up late for?"

Lièrén had known this conversation was coming from the moment Nàiměi had announced her impromptu visit. While it might well be an educational field trip to Concordance Prime for the grandchildren, she'd undoubtedly been deputized by his great-grandfather and the board of the Sòng Family Trust to check up on him after the accident. Nàiměi's mission in life was to get all her siblings blissfully paired off and raising the next generation in her branch of the Sòngs, and he was the last holdout.

"Not at present," he replied. He thought back to his birthday eight months ago, but couldn't remember if he'd gone out or stayed in his quarters. Whatever he'd done, it must not have made an impression.

She made a disapproving sound. "Well, you should. You need balance. You love children, and you're good with them. You should have some of your own."

"There's still time," he said mildly. With human fertility now extended to age ninety and beyond, most people waited until they were in their forties to have their first child, after they'd established a career and could afford it. Of course, his body first had to recover enough for him to have sex.

"What about that tall blonde woman? The one Uncle Po met when he visited you at that space station, seven or eight years ago."

He wondered who she was talking about. Not that he'd had all that many girlfriends, but his relationships tended not to last because of his job. His sluggish memory finally cooperated. "Birkett Hjolland. She signed a cohab with someone else while I was on a long assignment."

"She didn't deserve you, then. What about that other woman, Rana? Mira? Mika? And the man, whose name I forget."

That he remembered all too clearly, because it was the last relationship he'd failed at. "It didn't work out. There was a sharing problem."

She nodded sagely. "The other man didn't want to share the woman, I take it?"

"No, he didn't want to share me. I'd hoped he'd be there for her when I wasn't. As always, my job kept me away for too many weeks at a time, and the whole thing collapsed."

Nàiměi sighed. "I hate to sound like Great-Grandfather, but have you considered finding another, less difficult career than the CPS? It isn't the only option, even considering your twist talent."

Lièrén tried not to wince. This was the other conversation he'd known was inevitable. Sòng Tiān Cì was of the opinion that the Citizen Protection Service was the root of all that was evil in the Central Galactic Concordance, and that when Lièrén had tested so highly at age twelve, his greedy parents sold him to the CPS Academy in exchange for money and prestige. His great-grandfather also accused Lièrén of being lazy and taking the easy path in accepting the field-unit position after graduating from both the Academy and the CPS Minder Institute with top-tier evaluations. Lièrén had received many pings from him over the years that were all variations on demanding that Lièrén live up to his potential and come to his senses about the CPS.

"I like what I'm doing." Even if he didn't like everything about it, he wasn't about to admit it to his family. He'd never hear the end of it. "Besides, in twelve years, I become eligible for a very generous retirement plan."

"Surely you don't need the funds," said Nàiměi, peering at him with narrowed eyes. "You haven't taken up gambling, have you?" She detested gambling and was probably worried that he'd somehow become corrupted by Spires, where there were betting shops and lottery kiosks on every corner.

"No, but… " He searched for a truth she'd accept. "It's bad business practice to leave earned income on the table." He gave her a small smile. "You must admit that Great-Grandfather is hardly the best judge of my choice of employer. He thinks the CPS has been secretly infiltrated by aliens from the Andromeda galaxy who are intent on destroying civilization as we know it."

Nàiměi laughed, as he'd intended, because it was true, especially since humans had yet to run into any hint of alien civilization in the multiple thousands of planets they'd cataloged and the nearly six hundred Earth-like planets they'd scraped and terraformed. Most of the family agreed that Sòng Tiān Cì's picture should be next to the galactic dictionary's entry for "eccentric."

"I concede your point. Did you hear that to celebrate his hundred-and-eleventh birthday, he entered the Ursa Majoris Thousand Parsec Distance Rally with his race yacht and came in second? I think he mostly did it to get a rise out of Great-Grandmother."

Lièrén snorted. "After he disappeared for the entire second year of their marriage because he was crewing on an exploration spacer, I doubt anything he does surprises her."

"Very true," she said with a laugh, then patted his hand. "Find another lover, Lièrén—or two or three—however many will make you happy."

"One is sufficient, thank you." He'd tried the triad experiment more out of loneliness than adventurousness.

"I'm serious, Lièrén. We almost lost you with the accident. Life is too short and too precious to waste being alone. Any prospects?"

She was more single-minded than the puppy that was now determinedly chewing on his nephew's pant leg. "No," he said, then added teasingly, "unless you count the bartender and the server at the hotel bar."

He should have known better, because she pounced immediately. "Details, *didi*. Is either of them female? How old is she?"

Lièrén laughed and held up his hands in surrender. "Server Leviso is male. Bartender Sesay has an eleven-year-old son, so she's probably at least in her late forties. I'm too young for her."

She gave him a knowing look. "But she's not too old for you, I think.

You like her, or you wouldn't have mentioned her."

Lièrén knew when to be quiet and quit digging the hole he'd gotten himself into. Besides, Nàiměi wasn't wrong. He did like confident, clever Imara, but their respective lives had no possible intersection once he returned to field work.

Nàiměi took pity on him and changed the subject to tease him about his ultra-styled clothing that she claimed made him look like a cross between an air-race pilot and a romantic version of pirate clan. Every bit of clothing he owned had been destroyed in the flitter crash, so he'd shopped on the net via a local autotailor for replacements. At the time, he must have still been befuddled from a recent surgery, because his selections had been… interesting. He certainly stood out compared to the ultra-bland corporate fashion the local CPS agents favored. He hadn't had the patience or time to shop again, and preferred to wait until he could have more appropriately conservative clothing shipped to whatever ship or station he'd be assigned to.

Nàiměi, in between mostly polite interruptions by various children, who were well trained in the family's tradition of respect, and thwarting the puppy's impulse to urinate on her sweater, told him about her various business ventures, and some new lines of business brought in by one of the newer family adoptees, all of which were doing well. She epitomized the family's entrepreneurial spirit far better than he ever would, which was why he worked for others and she'd already been nominated for a seat on the board of the family trust.

By now, his family was used to him not being able to talk about his activities or assignments, although he knew they suspected his unit's mission was more complex than handling trade disputes. He mentioned that the accident had killed his partner, Fiyon Machimata, because she'd met him once, but apparently, it wasn't news to her. It reminded her of the tragic death of one of their myriad cousins, an ex-CPS Minder Corps veteran, who had died of multi-system failure at only age sixty-six.

"Great-Grandfather, of course, has been telling everyone who will listen that it was a new maintenance drug that killed her." Minder veterans sometimes ended up needing a lifetime of drugs, an unfortunate downside to the enhancement drugs that made active-duty minders more effective.

"Of course he has," agreed Lièrén. No one who had anywhere else to be on time got Sòng Tiān Cì started on the pharmaceutical industry, another of his favorite conspiracy hobbyhorses.

"Do you remember that skinny little imp, Chiang? Cousin Liu's youngest?" She continued when he nodded. "He grew big and tall and joined the Jumpers. He's got so much animated body art that it must be like sleeping with an ad wall in the room. Of course, no one says that to his face, except Great-Grandfather. He's conflicted, since the Jumpers are part of the CPS, but he's very proud of Chiang."

It wasn't the first time that Lièrén had experienced a pang of envy that his own career as a CPS minder was less acceptable to his great-grandfather than what other family members did. When Lièrén was sixteen, in the middle of his fourth year at the Academy, his parents had died when their interstellar transport was raided by a jack crew. His great-grandfather had come to New Kulam personally to see him at the CPS Academy to break the news.

The loss had pained him, but in some ways, they'd been long gone. When his parents had delivered him to the Academy, he'd only seen them three times after that via live holo calls on his birthday. They were always traveling for business and never home when he was. He'd spent breaks and holidays with Nàiměi's family or his great-grandparents. Sòng Tiān Cì had spent that visit and the next five years trying to convince Lièrén to leave the Academy, then to leave the Minder Institute, then not to accept the special field-unit position they'd offered, a rare honor for someone as young as he'd been. No matter what Lièrén had achieved, it seemed he'd never win his great-grandfather's approval.

"*Lǎo shūshu*, would you like to hold Hóng Lǐyú?" Jing was standing before him, holding the extremely tolerant puppy like it was a baby. A long-snouted baby who was assiduously licking her face with a long, thin pink tongue.

"Thank you for such a generous gift, Mistress Jing, but he looks happy with you." Lièrén waited until Jing solemnly nodded and walked away, then turned to Nàiměi and whispered. "She named it 'Red Carp'?"

Nàiměi gave him a shrug that said "children will be children" and stood. "Help me collect the monsters. We have tickets to the Central League historical exhibit tour, and it'll take us an hour to get there. Spires is more crowded than ever." She called the children, who obediently converged on her, though their dragging feet revealed their reluctance to leave the park.

"Everyone wants to be near the halls of power, I suppose," said Lièrén as he scooped up Jing and her puppy. She giggled in delight, and the puppy yipped in chorus. Lièrén was pleased he was able to lift her easily. Four weeks ago, he could barely hold himself up without pain. He gave her a kiss and set her on her feet, then pulled the leash from around his neck and attached it to the puppy's harness.

Nàiměi pulled on her sweater as they walked. "Even if I were rich enough to live anywhere in the galaxy, I wouldn't choose Concordance Prime. It's never good to have your face and name known by the authorities. Especially if you're a minder."

He forgot sometimes that Nàiměi was a mid-level finder with an affinity for business opportunities. In some ways, the patterner class of minders had it harder, because their skills caused deep-seated, simmering resentments, instead of immediate fear the way telepaths and telekinetics did.

He gave her a teasing smile. "Maybe Con Prime should be considered a punishment post, like being sent to an extreme weather planet, or on an exploration spacer."

When they parted company, he exchanged hugs with the children and his sister, but drew the line at kissing any puppy named after a fish. Nàiměi extracted a promise to be better at staying in touch, telling him he'd been too long apart from those who loved him.

After they had piled into the large autocab and it had vanished into the swarm of low-altitude air traffic, he took his time making his way back to the hotel, choosing to walk part of the way instead of riding the metro.

He had the disconcerting sensation of being set adrift, as if he'd lost his mooring. Looking back on his existence the past few years, he felt like he'd been an observer instead of a participant in his own life. Maybe the floating sensation was natural after a near-death experience, but it was more likely caused by no longer having his regular enhancement drugs. The worst of the physical withdrawal symptoms had finally faded, but he suspected his persistent, creeping melancholy and yearning for connection were attributable to the nearly weekly changes in drug protocols.

The latest drugs had him feeling itchy, like he was listening to constant white noise, with absurdly emotional responses to silly music, caring children, and a sister's love. Worse, his talent was feeling as jumpy and unruly as a red fox puppy, like it hadn't felt since he was in the Academy. He was more sensitive to people exercising their minder talents, and to the synaptic discord in the minds of liars. He would have liked to ask the opinion of the sifter assigned to him for therapy, but he was too timid and deferential for Lièrén's liking, and he'd have to report every word to his coordinating medic and the CPS, which was a sure way to be stuck on Con Prime even longer. He'd been specifically instructed to report any talent improvements he'd experienced, and so far, he'd reported no changes. His regular enhancement drugs weren't perfect, but the side effects were worth the talent focus and control benefits.

On impulse, he bought a broadcast earwire so he could listen to the newstrends as he walked. He'd hardly even checked galactic headlines in years. He was so out of touch with current cultural references and common slang that Nàiměi had to translate some of what the children said, and explain the terms. He'd become a *hè ăixīng*, a brown dwarf star, someone stuck in the past, longing for the good old days that never were.

Unsurprisingly, since the CGC High Council was currently in plenary session, political stories dominated the spectra. The High Council voted to slash the CPS's budget request for more Testing Centers. A planned TSAC march by veteran minders in High Spires to deliver a petition to the CPS planetary head office was drawing angry objections from some and fulsome support from others. A high officer in the CPS was fighting a public relations firestorm, claiming she'd been taken grossly out of context when a public vid had surfaced of her declaring that minders who participated in the TSAC march were looking to create another Rashad Tarana atrocity. The vid was damning. What was it about politicians that gave them amnesia about modern recording technology?

He stopped for a takeout meal to carry back to his hotel room. Night had fallen, so he darkened the windows and brightened the lighting. He used to turn on holos for company, but now they made his head hurt, so he turned on some music instead. He ate, took his new daily enhancement drugs, and picked up CPS messages.

He was shocked to learn that his field-unit supervisor, Uvay Garbey, a sifter and twister like he was, had collapsed from a heart attack two days ago and hadn't been discovered in time before irreparable brain damage had set in. She'd been young, only ninety-four, and had never mentioned a history of coronary disease. The internal memo mentioned that it had been quite a shock to everyone. The memo included the code to an anonymous cashflow account for everyone to make a contribution to the field unit's remembrance offering for the family, and Lièrén gave generously. The last section of the memo announced that Field Agent Cini Talavara had been appointed as acting supervisor until the CPS appointed a permanent replacement.

That was now five out of nine people in his field unit who were dead or incapacitated. Even his accident-addled brain knew such a high casualty rate was unlikely to be chance. The unit might be covert, but plenty of jackers who preyed on interstellar shipping, blackmarketers, indenturee traffickers, and fugitives knew it to be effective, to their cost. Had the unit become a thorn in someone's side? Or was someone out for revenge?

He knew the OII would be digging harder than ever. It was tempting to let them handle it, but he knew Talavara well enough to know she'd firewall any outsiders meddling in unit business, especially the OII. No one liked the OII, but she was militant in her hatred of them. He couldn't take the chance that the OII would stop whoever was targeting the unit before they got around to fixing what was likely their only failure—him.

He eyed his percomp with the idea of doing a little data diving in the unit's case files to see if he could find a pattern that fit the deaths so far, but he was tired from too much walking, and his throbbing headache was back. For once, he couldn't attribute it to anything but stress.

As Lièrén prepared for bed, he wondered what Talavara's next move would be. Fiyon Machimata had disliked her. Lièrén thought of her as a competent agent with multiple talents, but being a good retriever didn't necessarily make her a good leader. He hoped he'd live long enough to find out.

CHAPTER 5

THE ENORMOUS, CLEAR pillar was rising smoothly, almost as if floating on the light breeze, and then it wasn't. The closer end drifted and suddenly picked up momentum, heading straight for the tall road-crew leader. Knowing he hadn't seen the threat, Imara launched herself into Rackkar's knees and tackled him to the ground. The end swung by where Rackkar's head would have been and over the curved roadway before swinging like a pendulum back the other direction.

Rackkar Horis scrambled to his feet and shook his fist at the operator of the antigrav suspension lifter. "Farkin' A, Faith! Quit playin' lopar, and get the X-axis under control!" He was red-faced and steaming. His grip tightened on the oversized spanner wrench like he was ready to throw it through the lifter cab's windshield. He was the epitome of a road-crew man, big, burly, and mean looking.

Imara beamed him a big smile as she stood up and dusted off her ugly but nearly indestructible uniform shirt and pants. She'd been trying to civilize him since he'd joined the crew, and she was proud of his restraint. A couple of years ago, he'd have dragged the kid out and tried to feed her, head first, through the conduit extruder.

"Sorry, boss," shouted Faith. "You okay?"

"We're fine," shouted Imara. "Try it again. Don't adjust the Z-axis so soon."

Faith, who was barely twenty and full of the oblivious optimism of youth, gave a thumbs-up signal and went back to the controls. The pillar went agonizingly slowly this time but finally slid perfectly into place. It made up the last piece of the clear vertical support for the new metro platform and walkways. Imara insisted that all her road crew cross-train on the commonly used equipment, which was why she had a noob like Faith learning to use the lifter. Imara also insisted on first names with her crew, a trick she'd learned from her dad, to help make them a team instead of a random collection of individuals.

She was glad she checked in on this repair site first. Since the collapsed metro platform affected a visible part of the Spires skyline, it had been moved up in priority, forcing Imara to juggle work teams and schedules. Never mind the plain folks out in the Rim, the flatland neighborhoods that surrounded Spires, who would have to wait another month to get their sinkhole repaired. Imara's family had been as poor as desert rats, so she felt for the Rimmers, but everyone in Spires knew that politics—and optics—drove *everything*.

She rubbed the sore elbow she'd cracked when she'd tackled her crew lead. "Rack, while I'm thinking of it, I'll be out a week from next Tuesday. Derrit's got his twelve-year minder testing."

"Okay," he said. "You worried?"

"No," she said firmly. Rackkar's dislike of the local government colored his opinion of all large organizations, government or otherwise.

He frowned. "Once he's tagged as a minder, there's no going back."

Imara shrugged. "Yeah, but he's already a minder, whether or not the CPS registers him. Better to have it on the record. That's why he's getting private tutoring." She'd let Rackkar assume Lièrén Sòng was a freelancer, rather than a CPS employee.

"He's a good kid. If anyone gives him shit about being a minder, send 'em my way." Rackkar brandished his spanner with an itching-to-fight grin.

"You got it," said Imara, smiling. Rackkar, for all his near-pathological dislike of authority and explosive temper, had a good heart.

"Hey, boss," said Rackkar. "Didja hear? Some H.C. halfwit wants the city to install translucent nets under the lotus parks to stop suicides, like that farkin' pair of jumpers last week."

Imara rolled her eyes. "No, I hadn't." The galactic government's High Council was a continual wellspring of knee-jerk, short-sighted ideas, like their ridiculous resolution to order the city to channel the upcoming TSAC march onto narrower roads, so as not to disturb the "citizens," meaning the High Council and their staffers. Since disturbing the citizens was the whole point, the TSAC was likely to do the opposite of whatever the council wanted. Most of the road crew was of the staunch opinion that the Concordance government was a boil on the ass of the galaxy, and that the elected city government was a pimple wanting to be a boil.

Chioma, an older woman who looked like everyone's sweet aunt but could peel paint with her acerbity, chimed in. "Yah, wait till the tourists see

all the pretty, *dead* birds that get caught in them. *That* will go over well."
Colorful, long-tailed birds of paradise were iconic fauna in Spires, almost
as famous as the skyline itself, and gave rise to one of the city's other
nicknames, "Cuckoo Land." It had taken fifty years just to train the birds
not to slam into the lighted glass walls. Tourism was the city's second-
largest source of revenue, surpassed only by the political lobbying industry.

Wallo, a skinny, very dark-skinned man with a surprisingly deep and
melodic voice, handed out the drinks it had been his turn to fetch. "What
will go over well?" As usual, he'd forgotten to get one for Imara. She waved
him off when he offered to go back again.

"What I wanna know is," said Rackkar, "what farkin' new chems that
ground hauler driver was on that made him fark the controls and commit
mayem on our farkin' roadway?"

"That's 'may*hem*,' moron," sneered Chioma. "So you think the driver
used his dick on the 'tronics? Probably a better use for it than you ever
thought of."

"Wanna borrow the suspension lifter tonight, Chioma?" asked Rackkar,
all too innocently.

"Why?"

"For your husband, since he obviously can't get it up around you."
Rackkar gave her a smirk that dared her to top that. Wallo snickered.

They were worse than hormonal teenagers. Imara cleared her throat
loudly, and they all looked abashed. She allowed them wide latitude in
teasing and joking around, but put her foot down when it got too personal.

She sent Chioma to show Faith and Wallo how to check that the other
pillar base, which they'd formed earlier, had cooled enough to install the
fiber connectors, then asked Rackkar for a quick status update. Her crew
of twenty was the top-performing unit in the city. It got them saddled with
the hard gigs like this one, but it was job security for them all, plus more
variety. Rackkar's team was working below while Maseló's team of six
handled the platform and walkways above. Because the platform was built
with tetrahedron blocks, but the pillars were made of hexes, and the storm-
drain conduits were extruded tubes, the final join would be tricky. She told
Rackkar she'd swing back by later that day to help.

The sprawling Novi Nadezhdi metropolitan area, comprising High
Spires, Half Spires, and the Rim, was a hodge-podge mix of silicate-block
roadways. The lane markings and directions could all be changed with a
few commands from the central traffic computers, which in theory also

controlled all ground-based vehicles. It was illegal to go off grid anywhere in town, but harder to catch and enforce in the Rim. The ground hauler that had wrecked the metro platform had been stolen from there.

As Imara turned to go, Rackkar asked, "Should I be saying congratulations?"

"For what?" she asked. She was only half listening as she considered how and when to move their only working plaz-sealer to reduce delays. Her boss was arguing over the cost of printing the parts needed to fix it, but was fine with it costing twice as much to idle the plaz-sealer crews, because it was a different accounting category. Typical.

"The manager job they offered you."

"Oh, that."

Rackkar was trying to act nonchalant, but Imara wasn't fooled. They'd joined the crew together five years earlier, and he didn't want to see her go, but wanted to be happy for her. Rackkar had come a long way since those first few weeks when he just about bit the head off of anyone who questioned his actions. She'd finally figured out that he was aggressively covering for his abysmal, nearly dyslexic ability with numbers. Using some stickers she lifted from her son's crafts box, she'd created an icon and color-coding system that kept Rackkar from making mistakes. In exchange, he'd taught her brawling skills.

The coding system ended up making the whole crew more efficient and got her promoted to team lead. When they'd invented the crew-shift lead position just for her, Rackkar had been promoted to her old position. She didn't know if he wanted her shift-lead job or not, but it would be hard going. His social skills weren't much better than his math skills.

"I don't know, yet. My lawyer is still looking at the contract." She started to say more, but her percomp signaled an incoming live ping from Derrit. Traffic noise made using her earwire impossible, so the conversation wouldn't be private. Her percomp's holo display had broken years ago.

"Hey, *binata*. I'm on the street with Rackkar's team. What's fluxing?" She was trying to remember to call him "young man" in Filipino, since he'd recently become sensitive about being called "baby." It was a deliberate connection to his father's heritage.

"Arlie Sage is selling her old glideboard, and it's a real good price." Imara didn't approve of air boards for kids, but she felt guilty he couldn't learn how to operate ground vehicles the way she had, in wide-open country roads. She knew he already rode his friends' boards, anyway. If she told him

"no" outright, he'd just do it without telling her.

"It's your money," she said as casually as she could. Arlie was a likable school friend, but the girl was a menace in the airways.

Rackkar, who was fond of Derrit, gave her a look like he thought she was being too hard-nosed. She snorted. "Wait till you have kids," she whispered. She knew he'd be a complete pushover.

"I was, uh, hoping to borrow some from you. I've only got enough for half of what she's asking. I'd pay you back, I promise."

"Does that price include the safety equipment we talked about? That was our deal, remember? Otherwise, the board stays locked in the closet."

"I'll ask her," he said, but his tone said he didn't hold out much hope. Thank Neptune he wasn't much of a drama diva, or he'd have been pleading for another ten minutes. Unlike her younger sister, Piera. When they were growing up together, she could make a simple "no" sound like their dad was refusing to save her from a ravening monster about to chew her leg off.

Derrit was the other reason she hadn't snapped up the manager job. While it was a higher-paying contract, and more predictable work schedule and income, it would also mean she'd have to cut back the number of days she could work at the bar. Derrit loved meeting all the people who passed through the bar, and she thought he at least ought to have a say in her decision. Money was nice, especially in stratospherically expensive Spires, but it wasn't everything.

Telling Rackkar she'd be back in a few hours, she programmed the supply hauler's autodrive for the next construction site, then fired up the in-cab comp connection so she could update the centralized repair records on the way. At the rate they were burning glass on the platform repair, she'd need to order sooner than usual. Her current boss and the bit-counters, none of whom had ever spent a single farkin' day in the field, didn't seem to understand there was always some waste when they made custom fittings. Not every scrap could be recycled.

She barely noticed when the automatic traffic-control system rerouted her vehicle to avoid Neptune-knew-what. While she liked driving, it was nice to let the system do it for routine trips. She thanked her lucky stars she ended up in the repair crew, not traffic control and enforcement, which had been her original goal. She'd take melt burns and smelling like cerium paste any day over dealing with parades, TSAC marches, opening day of a High Council session, and VIP processions, not to mention setting autocab flight paths and metro transit schedules.

When she'd first looked for work after Torin died, the only thing she'd been qualified for was vehicle maintenance, based on her experience in her dad's shop. She could operate anything on the ground or in low air, and fix most of them, but she had none of the official certifications that got applicants in the door on civilized planets. The best money was on the crew, so she'd wormed her way in, one quick repair and one favor at a time.

The bartending job had been another favor, too, from a friend of Torin's who'd put in a good word. She'd known less than zero about dispensing, but with her comprehensive filer's memory, she'd learned fast. Learning to overcome her tendency to be easily distracted and to not depend on others had been the harder lessons. Torin, with his generous, laughing nature, had delighted in treating her like a hothouse flower, and she'd let him. All she'd wanted was a partner who loved her and a passel of children on a farm on some planet where it rained more than twice a year. And the trip down memory lane wasn't getting her work done.

She turned up the music in the cab. Whoever set it last liked *surashu* thrash, with its screaming, thrumming beat and harsh hexanic orchestration. It reminded her of how Rayle had tried to dance to it the other night, and laughing with Lièrén about it. Thinking about *him* wasn't going to get her work done, either, so she found a channel with a nice, swingy matulain fusion.

After tomorrow, she was going to luxuriate for two full days in a row. Two whole days off, from both jobs. It hadn't happened in a couple of years, and she intended to treat it as a mini-vacation, since she'd never be able to afford a real one. Derrit would be in school both days, and she'd already loaded her vid, reading, and music queues in anticipation. She also planned to do something with her hair, though she didn't know what yet, other than deal with the silver threads that made her coils look iron gray in her reflection in the cab's bubble windshield.

Her only regret was that Derrit would have to wait four days before seeing Lièrén again for training. She ignored the little voice in her head that said she'd regret not seeing him until then, too. It was a waste of energy wanting things she couldn't have.

CHAPTER 6

EX-JUMPER LAKSHMI PATWARDAN was prepared to dislike Field Agent Lièrén Sòng based on his personnel file alone, and the stiff, serious look on his face in his official holo pretty much guaranteed he'd either be one of the priggish saints, the arrogant pricks, or the heedless lopars that the CPS Minder Corps seemed to specialize in. At least he'd uncomplainingly accommodated her request to meet on the *Nieji Adoor*, her personal interstellar ship, which was a small point in his favor.

Her official excuse for meeting on her ship was because it was easier to maintain confidentiality, but it was mostly because she needed as low a gravity setting as she could get. Although her mind was still sharp as a shrike's, low-G was the only way to tolerate the Stage-4 waster's disease that was making her a prisoner in her own body, and would eventually kill her faster than low-G syndrome ever would. It was one of the nasty little caveats not mentioned in the CPS Jumper Corps recruitment brochures.

"Thanks for coming," she said. "You're on time, so you must have missed the transfer accident." Space stations, always looking to cut costs, often overbooked their ground-to-space transfer ships. One docking accident could screw up passenger schedules for hours.

"It's a pleasure to meet you in person. I rented a shuttle and flew myself. Your hospitality gave me the excuse to regain some temporary independence."

"How so?" she asked.

He shrugged a shoulder and gave her a slight smile. "I never learned to operate ground vehicles, so I've had to rely on autocabs and public transportation while recovering from the accident."

If he was sneering at her through his politeness, he hid it very well.

He was better-looking in person, and his strategically gaping vest and red shirt, and tight, racer-striped, wide-waisted black pants with an asymmetrical peplum were a far cry from the stodgy corporate suit in his photo. He had a nice physique but was considerably shorter than she was. Then again, everyone was. At well over two meters, she was tall, even for a Jumper. He moved well in the three-quarters gravity setting, suggesting he had experience.

She ushered him into the office area and offered a comfortable chair and refreshments, then trotted out her standard speech to explain how the CPS advocate process worked. She was an independent specialist in CPS procedure and policy, and her job was to represent the CPS employees' best interests in investigation cases. She reminded him that, under Concordance Command regulations, having an advocate was a right, not a privilege, and that he should ignore anyone who tried to tell him otherwise. The CPS sometimes liked to pretend they were exempt from the military code of conduct. She couldn't help but add a non-standard caveat.

"I can't legally be compelled to repeat our conversations or communications, but that doesn't mean a rotted kumquat if I get jacked for a session with a CPS or OII telepath who wants to muck about in my mind." She tried to keep the needles out of her tone, but wasn't sure she succeeded.

He nodded. "Thank you for your honesty. I'm sorry if you have been subjected to that in the past."

Lakshmi eyed him suspiciously, thinking he might be mocking her, but he seemed sincere. So far, he'd been deferential and humble, which was rare for any high-level minder in the CPS, most of whom believed they were the universe's gift to humanity. She let herself relax a little. Stress was bad for her.

Still, she preferred people with more in-your-face emotional transparency. It was too easy to imagine he was hiding a lot, above and beyond what the covert types usually hid. What was his unit's cover story again? She peeked at the records and snorted softly. Trade facilitation, indeed.

It occurred to her that the CPS-mandated enhancement drugs might be flattening his emotional affect, and asked about them. He explained he'd just started yet another protocol because of the recovery treatment plan.

"Do you take them regularly, or just when you're tested?"

He looked confused. "I couldn't pass the random tests if I weren't taking them as prescribed."

She gave him a crooked smile. "Oh, you'd be surprised at the number of ways I've heard to fool them. Implants, neutralizers, flushlines, lookalikes..." She trailed off, inviting him to share his method.

He shook his head, frowning slightly. "I'd think it would be self-defeating to reduce one's effectiveness that way."

Lakshmi tried to keep the incredulous look off her face, seeing as Sòng looked perfectly serious. Maybe she'd been right about him being a saint, even if he wasn't priggish. Had she ever been that blindly trusting of the CPS? She looked at her hand, shaking with the effort of holding onto her coffee cup, and admitted that she had. The difference was, she'd wised up a lot sooner.

"So," she said, "what kinds of questions have our OII friends been asking you?"

"Initially, they were concerned about the accident, but now, they're more interested in why someone might be trying to kill all of us." His impeccable Standard English accent made it sound so casual.

"That's... unexpected," she said slowly. "Care to elaborate?"

He told her how three of his coworkers had died in the past week, including the supervisor, and counting his partner's death in the accident that had nearly killed him, that only left four field-unit members still functional.

He brought out his percomp, an ugly but powerful unit that looked like it went with the corporate suit, not the racy flier outfit he was now wearing. "When I downloaded the unit's historical case files and reviewed them for commonalities, I didn't..."

She cut him off before he could continue. "Did the OII ask you to do that?"

He shook his head. "No, it was my initiative. I haven't spoken to the OII about it yet."

"You might want to find another way to get that data next time, if there is a next time. I don't recommend it. Eventually, the OII will pull access records, and they'll have some pointed questions for you." She hoped he was smart enough to realize he'd need a good explanation ready when they did.

She asked him to relay as accurately as he could the questions the OII investigators had asked him so far, and wrote questions while her comp recorded his words. At least he'd been smart enough not to talk to them while on happytime drugs, or to volunteer information, and had remembered to take notes and invoke his right for an advocate immediately. Some of her clients had all but cremated themselves before calling her, then expected a miracle.

"When do you expect to talk to the OII again?"

"I have an appointment two days from now."

"Good. Scheduled meetings usually mean they aren't trying to play games." She took the last sip of her coffee as she reviewed her notes. "What day is it in Spires now? I can't keep them straight."

"It's Sunday, Star Zero, Sol, whichever you go by." He smiled sympathetically. "It's easy to lose track of planet-based days when you live on a ship."

She supposed he'd know, since his official assignments were often on regular military or CPS ships, with the occasional space station for variety. Damned hard on a personal life, though. He probably knew that, too. Oh well, it wasn't her place to give him the "either you order chaos, or chaos orders you" speech. He was an adult and could make his own choices.

"I see they temporarily assigned you part time to the smaller field office in High Spires. What are you doing for them?"

She made more notes as he explained that he'd been catching the office up on its filing and improving their procedures to make it easier to keep up with the work in the future. It made sense. His cover-story job had him doing similar work for his own field unit. His unit's supervisor had even gone to the trouble of dressing up his personnel record with a couple of commendations for it.

He gave her a self-deprecating smile. "Yesterday, Supervisor Yamazaki rewarded me with the task of doing the same for the CPS Testing Center next door, since they, too, are behind on their filing. Their datasets are more... repetitive."

"Talk about your crappy jobs." She shook her head. "Imagine if you had to do that all day."

"I am thankful that my health doesn't yet permit me such an opportunity." She almost missed his slight smile and wink.

She laughed out loud. She didn't think he had a sense of humor until then. He offered to pour more coffee for her, and she accepted. Watching him pour without spilling a drop, in low-G no less, she had the feeling he'd been trained in tea ceremony. "Do you have any questions for me?"

"Yes." He opened a new file on his percomp. "First, is the investigation taking longer than usual?"

She looked up the dates and saw it had been eight weeks since the flitter crash. "Yes, but the fact that they haven't hauled you in more often, especially considering the recent deaths, is probably good news for you. It means they aren't actively working to throw you off the sky skimmer to balance the load."

"I see." He made a note.

"I probably don't have to tell you, Agent Sòng, but if someone *is* targeting the unit, you should watch yourself. Maybe they'll come back and finish what they started."

"Thank you. I'm glad to know someone else thinks it's a reasonable concern."

She nodded, hiding her amusement at being told, ever so politely, that it was as obvious as sunlight.

"My second question is about monitoring. I'm being electronically monitored in the office and my medical appointments, which is to be expected, but I believe my hotel room, local comms, and transactions are also being tapped. Is that standard procedure?" His tone was mild, but she thought she detected a note of complaint.

She sighed. "Yes, it's standard, but it's not supposed to be. I could call them on it, but it will stir up trouble. Right now, they're distracted, but a request like that would make them look your way again. If you want a little privacy, buy yourself a disposable cashflow percomp and don't do anything stupid with it." She eyed his CPS percomp. "That reminds me. While you're here, let's set up a shared-key secure hypercube. That way, if I have to travel or the CPS reassigns you, we can still exchange data."

"Aren't they supposed to notify you if they move me?"

She snorted. "Agent Sòng, I'm sure you're a model employee, but you're…" She was about to say *dimwitted or chemmed out of your mind to trust the CPS*, but thought he might take offense. "…charmingly confident in the CPS's administrative competence."

He didn't reply, but she could tell from a certain stiffness in his posture that she'd offended him, anyway. It hadn't been her intention, but maybe it would help him wake up and take on the flux, if he planned to keep his career with the CPS. If they let him.

CHAPTER 7

LIÈRÉN DRIPPED WITH sweat like he was in a steam sauna, and his legs and arms shook with fatigue. He still wasn't sure how he'd let Rayle talk him into doing this.

The music was something in Portuguese about defiant love. Lièrén tried to copy the movements of the dance students in front of him, but suspected his attempts were an insulting parody. It didn't help that about half the dancers in the class, including Rayle, were professionals, and knew the choreography well. The song ended, and an extremely well-built and athletic man up front added a spin, a foot stamp, and a flourish, head and one arm held high with pride. He only wore short, tight shorts and was barefoot.

Lièrén gasped for breath, trying not to sound like a bellows.

Up front, the instructor, a tall, tanned woman with shock-white hair tightly drawn back and impossibly straight posture, waved her baton at the athletic man. "*Muito bonita*, Celestin." Confusingly, the dancer looked irritated as he slunk toward the water fountain at the edge of the room.

Lièrén looked to Rayle, who was standing next to him, for an explanation. Rayle's hair was now a rich, dark brown interspersed with subdued gold highlights, with no hint of electric blue sparkles anywhere to be seen. He wore a loose, thin-strapped red top over shaded gray, skin-tight leggings that ended below his knees, and nothing on his calloused feet. He seemed oblivious—or accustomed—to the openly admiring gazes from both men and women in the class.

"*Farruca* isn't supposed to be 'very pretty,'" said Rayle quietly. "It should tear your heart out. If we do *Lágrimas da Lua*, watch Fumiko." He pointed to the middle of the dance floor at a short, porcelain-skinned Japanese woman with midnight black hair and gauzy black clothes that outlined a lithe, muscular body.

The instructor tapped her baton on a waist-high floating bar to get everyone's attention. "No more playtime." Her accent sounded Slavic when she spoke English, but she gave movement instructions in a dozen languages. Lièrén had no idea what most of the terms meant, so he'd just watched the others and mimicked. He felt about as graceful as a newborn kitten.

He stepped back further into the corner. It may have been playtime for the other twenty or so people in the studio class, especially the pros like Rayle, but twenty minutes of "play" was just about killing him.

Instead of moving back into place, Rayle came closer and gave him a sympathetic smile. "Why don't you take a break?" He pointed to the long bench a few meters away along the wall, where another dancer sat shaping a brace to her ankle.

Lièrén shook his head. "It would be disrespectful to Instructor D'Cruze."

Rayle chuckled. "It would be more disrespectful if you passed out. I'm impressed you're even still standing. I hadn't realized how stubborn you are. Come on."

Lièrén reluctantly allowed himself to be led to the back bench, where he slumped back against the wall. He was annoyed that his stamina still wasn't where it should be. Rayle patted Lièrén's bare shoulder. "Give yourself ten minutes."

Lièrén's talent flared on the brief physical contact, and he was startled to realize Rayle was an empath. He didn't know why he was surprised. Empaths were often drawn to the performing arts. There was a fine line between natural acting talent and empathic talent in swaying audience emotions. The regular CPS Minder Corps used high-level empaths in combination with illusionists for crowd control.

The languid syncopation of a well-known classical Second-Wave nocturne swelled, and Rayle rejoined the others. When serving at the Quark and Quasar, he was flamboyantly flirty and pretended to be irresponsible, but in class, he was focused and driven, and it showed in his skill and physical expressiveness. Most of the company was equally good. Lièrén felt like he was being treated to a private performance.

He felt the subtle textures of more talents, empath, exciter, forecaster, telekinetic, finder, and the characteristic blank slate of a shielder. None of them were activating or broadcasting heavily, they were just potential, feathering the edges of his sifter talent. After his sister's visit, he'd decided to stop floating along on the current, and to pay more attention to what his mind, body, and talent were telling him, rather than just attributing everything that was different to the accident and waiting for it to return to normal. This might be his new normal.

He must have still been running hot from using his talent that morning in an interrogation for the local Spires police. From Supervisor Yamazaki's apologetic tone when he'd given out the assignment, Lièrén gathered the local field-office staff considered such requests an unpleasant duty, but to Lièrén, it was a welcome relief from slogging through the badly neglected Testing Center records. Also, though it made him feel disloyal to admit it, the police department's telepath had been more pleasant and easier to work with than his distant and contained partner Fiyon ever had. As a double bonus, the interrogation subject had been innocent of the charges, and because it wasn't a covert investigation, Lièrén had no need to use his twist talent, which would have guaranteed a killer headache for hours afterward.

The dance music changed to an upbeat *romana* with an insistent rhythm, and Lièrén was glad he was still resting. If he'd tried to match the strength and speed required to achieve the precise movements, he'd have ended up in the nearest minder health clinic. Neither of his therapeutic martial arts classes required even half the effort needed for a single dance class. He didn't know how the others survived doing it five or six days a week, plus all the afternoon and evening rehearsals.

Women predominated in the group, and several could put top-class athletes and holovid stars to shame. He liked looking at confident, skilled women wearing clothes that revealed more than they covered, though none of them appealed to him as a potential hot-connect partner. He took a sip of water from the bottle he'd brought and tried to analyze why not. Some of it was his body's weakness and exhaustion, but mostly, and it took him far too long to realize it, he'd subconsciously found each one lacking when compared to Imara Sesay.

Just last night, Lièrén had realized that Imara was a lot smaller than he'd initially thought. Her charisma and quick wit made her seem physically imposing, but when she'd brought drinks to the booth he and Derrit were about to appropriate for the evening's training session, he'd noticed the top of her head only came up to his chin. She'd been wearing wide-legged, high-waisted pants that hugged her hips and a silky orange blouse on top that outlined her surprisingly toned figure when she moved. Her hair had looked different, too—lighter and softer, maybe, though still with a mind of its own. Rayle had praised her, when he could have teased, and a couple of regular customers had complimented her. Lièrén wasn't sure why he'd suddenly noticed her clothes, and couldn't remember what they looked like before. His biggest failing was his poor memory, which had degraded as his minder talents had blossomed. He'd love to have a filer's memory like hers.

He took another sip of water, still slouching against the wall. His eye was caught by a regal, dark-skinned woman with a wide face and close-cropped hair, as she and the rest of the class bent and curved their bodies fluidly like willows in the breeze. She was wearing a colorful bandeau top to bind her breasts, and it made him wonder what Imara would look like in something like that. The image was hot and compelling, and took hold in his imagination. His hormones sputtered to life, and for the first time since the accident, his body responded with awakening sexual interest. It was just Lièrén's luck for it to happen when he was wearing pants form-fitting enough for anyone to see. He didn't even have a towel or a jacket to drape across his lap.

Compounding his embarrassment, the instructor announced a five-minute break, and he was suddenly surrounded by dancers, several of whom smiled when they saw his arousal, and one of them gave him a grin and a thumbs-up. He leaned forward to rest his elbows on his knees, and hoped they assumed the flush on his face was from exercise.

Fumiko, the small Japanese woman Rayle had pointed out earlier, sat next to him and smiled companionably. "I'd be pleased to help you feel less constricted." There was no mistaking the direction of her glance and the invitation in her eyes.

Before Lièrén could respond, several of the dancers chimed in with encouraging remarks.

"Say 'yes.' Fumi is an exciter," said one, and another smiled and nodded.

"Yeah," said an older, sinewy man who'd given him the thumbs-up signal, "and she's joyhouse trained in novo-tantric and kama sutra."

Lièrén had never been around such friendly, touch-happy people who treated sex—or a minder talent for stimulating sensation—quite so casually. He was coming to the conclusion that, for all that he'd traveled across the galaxy, he'd lived a cloistered existence until crash-landing in Spires.

He gave Fumiko a rueful smile. "I am honored and deeply flattered, but regrettably, I am not medically cleared for such activity."

She touched his bare arm with light fingertips and gave him a provocative smile. "The offer is open anytime, *hansamu*." His talent detected the subtle brush of her dormant exciter talent. She leaned under the bench with enviable flexibility to grab a water bottle from her bag, then headed toward the fountain. She went out of her way to avoid Celestin, the well-built blond man who was now standing next to Rayle, his arm draped casually across Rayle's shoulders.

"I've had her," announced Celestin, a little too loudly. "She's not that great." The sharp flare of synaptic disturbance told Lièrén the man was lying. More likely, she turned him down flat.

He caught a quizzical look from Rayle. It was the same look he gave Imara at the bar when asking whether or not to serve a patron. Rayle must have heard about this side of Lièrén's talent from Derrit. He minutely shook his head to indicate that Celestin was not telling the truth.

Rayle half-blinked one eye at Lièrén before ducking out from under Celestin's arm and giving the big man a quick, slightly feral smile. "Sure you have, *hansamu*." Lièrén didn't need his talent to know that Rayle was lying about finding Celestin "handsome."

For the rest of the class, which was blessedly less strenuous, and in the short shower afterward, Lièrén mulled over his response to being approached by Fumiko. Before the accident, he would have readily agreed to whatever she had in mind, pleased that she found him attractive, expecting a no-strings liaison and an enjoyable interlude. Now that he was grounded in Spires, he wanted something more… some*one* more. He'd felt lust before, but it had never felt so focused.

It wouldn't be fair to either of them to start a relationship, assuming Imara was even interested in someone like him. Sooner rather than later, he'd be recovered enough to return to duty, and he'd be gone. The prospect didn't make him as happy as it had just a few weeks ago.

He believed in what his unit did for the CPS, helping stop the worst of what humans could do to one another. He understood that his work could never be publicly acknowledged, but after his short time in Spires, he wasn't looking forward to going back into the isolation required to keep it secret. He missed his family, even his disapproving great-grandfather. He wanted more than just a few distant coworkers, he wanted actual friends, even if they dragged him to an advanced-level dance class or cajoled him into teaching a young minder to wield his formidable talents.

The choice was out of his hands. First, he had to survive the threat to his field unit. After that, he was still under contract, and his skills were needed. For now, all he could do was store up memories of this time for the days and years ahead.

CHAPTER 8

THE TESTING CENTER'S multiple data cubes were assembling in his deskcomp to restore their associations. It was about as exciting as watching hydroponic grass grow, and he was sleepy. He was sure his muscles were stiffening up as a result of the dance class workout.

Lièrén had stopped at his usual restaurant for lunch, only remembering after he got there that he'd decided to vary his routine and schedule more. It would be easy to become paranoid and think every shuttle-docking accident on Concordance Prime—or its space station—was about him. On the other hand, it was neutron-star dense to make himself an easy target.

To keep himself awake, he ran commonality queries against the field-unit case-file data he'd downloaded. The unit's data was in better shape than the Testing Center's, partly because in his cover as the trade office's data admin, he helped keep it that way, but the queries created more questions than answers. What he needed were the personnel, travel, and expense data cubes to make useful correlations. He could get them, but he couldn't think of an innocuous excuse for the OII. Patwardan had been right to warn him they'd be asking.

By all rights, the field unit should have limited his access the day of the accident, but it was typical of them to only clean up when caught. Routine audits always resulted in multiple red flags... which gave him an idea. A technician he'd worked with on a case last year had remarked that the CPS's protections always lagged behind industry standards. Lièrén pulled the prepaid percomp he'd purchased at a tourist shop out of his pocket and considered it. Under its decorative case, he'd added a top-of-the-line security defense and action framework and some customized data divers, all tools of the covert operations trade. His initial download of the case-file data had been questionable but justifiable, but using unauthorized equipment and the auditor account that he was betting was still active, despite his repeated warnings to management, was flat-out defiance of CPS procedure.

It came down to whether or not he trusted the OII or his new supervisor to look out for his interests. He reluctantly decided he didn't.

It only took a few minutes to connect, authenticate, sweep the cubes of interest, and sign off. That done, he moved the case-file data from his CPS percomp to the prepaid percomp, then automated some commonality queries. They'd take awhile since he hadn't rebuilt the associations.

He considered going for a walk to keep his body somewhat mobile, but he was reluctant to leave any of his datasets unattended.

With nothing else to do but wait, he used his CPS percomp to research minder talents, refreshing what he remembered from school. Having accepted the role of teacher for Derrit, he wanted to do the best job he could in whatever time he had left in Spires. He'd had four sessions with the boy, and had been working with him on managing both his precociously strong shielder talent and burgeoning cleaning talent. He'd even cautiously let the boy clean deliberately-created small memories, such as what had been hidden under a napkin, to teach Derrit fine control. The boy was amazingly good already, but especially so, considering he was only eleven. Nearly twelve, he amended with a twitch of a smile, remembering Derrit's insistence.

When Lièrén had been tested and entered the Academy twenty years ago, the CPS had presented the talent categories as accurate and complete for 95 percent of the minder population. He'd been told having two strong talents like he did was rare, but they fit neatly into the existing categories, so he hadn't thought any more about it, and his instructors never said anything else. They ignored his telepathy altogether. From what he was discovering now, he'd been taught a very simplified view, and reality wasn't nearly as neat or classifiable.

For one, there were far more people with dual or triple talents than the official CPS statistics indicated. Maybe the Testing Center data he had access to was anomalous, but multiple talents were common, and even minder polymaths made up a measurable percentage. Which made it more likely that his talent wasn't misfiring when it insisted Imara had multiple talents.

Out of curiosity, he used the deskcomp to look up his own official record and skimmed through it, looking for his minder testing results. He was surprised to discover that his third talent, telepathy, which was admittedly low-level, was mentioned as a brief note in a comments section rather than as an official designator. No wonder the CPS instructors had ignored it.

That made him rethink the work he'd been doing with the Testing Center data. He'd been ignoring the notes because the Testing Center had told him they were unimportant, but in checking a few sample records again, he saw the notes had useful data, if unstructured.

He could see why the CPS might want to keep minder talents easily explainable for the public, especially considering the prevalence of overt prejudice against minders, but he wasn't sure that such a simplistic view did minders any favors.

He wasn't sure it did the CPS any favors, either. He suspected a high percentage of the Testing Center's data mismatch problems centered around trying to use an inadequate classification system to record test results. Even the testing itself was constrained—how could they test something they didn't know about? He'd noticed a surprisingly high incidence of records with "re-test required" flags. Maybe an improved classification system would significantly lower that number.

He stopped the Testing Center build and tried a query on the smallest cubes. When it proved satisfactory, he automated it to run against all the cubes. The deskcomp had a thin matrix, so it would probably have to run overnight.

His prepaid percomp gave him a "task complete" notice through the wire he'd stuck in the high collar of his shirt. He pulled out the percomp and put his ring finger on the biometric reader.

He nearly jumped out of his chair when his office door slid open unexpectedly.

"Are you Agent, uh, Soong... Sing...?" The speaker was a hard-faced, hard-bodied woman named Mateliff, with eerie, silver-edged red eyes and the characteristic nothingness of an active shielder. He remembered her name because of the unique flavor of her talent and her body mods. Her role was security, and her mods also included reinforced and sharpened fingernails and pointed teeth, which gave her the intimidating guise of a predator.

He turned to face her, casually leaving the percomp on his desk. "I am Agent Sòng. How may I help you?" He added warmth to his tone, to tell her he wasn't insulted by her getting his name wrong. She had a thankless job and a talent that isolated her from friends and family as much as his did, though for different reasons.

She didn't relax, exactly, but she didn't escalate, either. "I take it that was you accessing the omicron-level hypercube to look at classified personnel data?" She used her eyes to indicate his deskcomp, not letting her hands get too far from him. From the feel of the strength of her talent, she probably wouldn't need the extra insurance of touching him to shut him down.

"Yes," he acknowledged, then added, "I have clearance."

"Yeah, well, *you* may have clearance, but that deskcomp doesn't. Its encryption wouldn't stop a two-year-old with a Little Starshine babycomp." She shook her head and sighed. "I suppose no one bothered to give you the security briefing?"

"No, but my schedule is unpredictable, and the field office is busy and understaffed." He tilted a hand to indicate the main part of the office. He clasped his hands together non-threateningly and shifted his torso, to draw her attention to his distinctly non-corporate attire. He hoped she'd think he looked too young to be an agent, which was sometimes an advantage.

"What data were you looking at?" Her tone was mild, but her body language said she was testing him.

"My own file." He didn't know what the system alerts told her, and there was no reason to conceal this truth.

She snapped her fingers and pointed at him. "I remember now, you're the twonk doing the Testing Center data tagging." She gave him a crooked smile and relaxed a little more. "I don't know who you pissed off to get *that* job, but I guess someone has to do it."

He shrugged and tried to look chagrined.

She started to leave, then turned back. "Look, kid, if you have to look at CPS files again, use one of the green terminals in the main room, or get Supervisor Yamazaki to upgrade this one." The CPS had fought for years to get their own independent network, but neither the regular military nor the Central Galactic Concordance government agreed, so the CPS had built multi-layered, multi-point security and monitoring methods to protect their sensitive data and communications. He knew them well.

He nodded. "I will. Thank you, Agent Mateliff." She wasn't responsible for the rules, just enforcing them.

"Oh, dead gods, no, I'm a security specialist, not an agent. I leave *that* kind of work to *your* lot." She didn't bother to hide her disdain, but he didn't take offense. He wouldn't want her job, either.

She waved a negligent hand at his parting wish for her to have a pleasant evening.

He waited until he could no longer feel even a hint of her shields before turning back to his prepaid percomp.

He wished he hadn't.

His queries, which he checked twice just to be sure, pointed to the disturbing conclusion that his dead partner, Fiyon Machimata, had been trading favorable interrogation outcomes for cashflow.

Lièrén spent another two hours trying various scenarios that would fit the facts as well, but failed. Official records and his own meticulous notes all pointed to corruption, and decades of it. Which made Lièrén as unbelievably naïve as his CPS advocate Patwardan and his great-grandfather thought he was, if not for the reasons they thought.

Even more deeply distressing, it became glaringly obvious that Fiyon had been cleaning Lièrén's mind of inconvenient memories, probably since Lièrén's first week on the job. It couldn't have been anyone else other than Fiyon, because no one else had the access. Or Lièrén's trust.

Because he'd let Derrit practice erasing specifically created memories, he now knew exactly what it felt like to have unnatural blanks. He had too damned many holes, far more than could be explained by his historically poor memory. Earlier memory holes felt like they'd been clawed out with a garden fork, while later holes were more neatly excised.

The field-office data and his own case notes proved it. Take his birthday, eight months ago. The expense records and his private calendar said he'd had dinner out with Fiyon and Supervisor Uvay Garbey, and his ID was on the receipt along with the others. That evening, the case files recorded an interrogation by Fiyon and Lièrén of a jack-crew captain who had been let go soon after. His memory of the evening wasn't just fuzzy or disjointed, it was totally blank. He'd found dozens of similar examples in the last few years, and almost every time, they correlated with an interrogation subject being exonerated or released.

The most egregious case had been two years ago, when his unit had intercepted a fugitive pedophile in the Con Prime Space Station for a covert interrogation. The pedophile had been one of a pair of predators who had collected children to molest, maim, and murder, then preserve their broken bodies like cordwood in the cryo-hold of their specially modified interstellar ship.

Lièrén remembered with sickening clarity the excruciating texture and stench of the pedophile's mind, and the post-twist headache, but his memory of the interrogation and the twist itself was a black hole. Not moments after Lièrén's memory picked up again, the pedophile had escaped because Fiyon wasn't where he was supposed to be.

Twelve hours later, a shrewd military forensic investigator figured out where the pedophile had gone, but had nearly been killed when he'd cornered the monster in a joyhouse kitchen right there in Spires. Lièrén hadn't helped the pedophile escape, but his naïve blindness had let it happen. He may as well have handed the pedophile the knife.

He numbly closed his files, shut down his percomps, and just sat in his tiny office for a long time, stunned. He didn't know who to trust, and he knew a lot more people *not* to trust. His thoughts spun uselessly, like a tumbleweed in a whirlwind, and his emotions were a chaotic mix of betrayal, fury, guilt, and despair.

How the hell could he have been so willfully, outrageously abused, and so complacently oblivious to it?

Two hours later, he was seated at the end of the bar, nursing his glass of iced lime water like it was 180-proof ice wine.

"I'm tellin' ya," said the long-faced woman in a red tunic who Lièrén recognized as a regular, "Red Shift had a perfect season in '31." Lièrén had no idea what sport she was talking about.

Her companion, also a regular, was an older woman dressed in a casual charcoal-gray jumpsuit. "And I'm telling you, the Event Horizons beat them right before the master levels. Wanna bet?" She held out her hand, palm up, inviting the wager.

The woman in red turned to Rayle, who'd just served them brightly-colored iced drinks with frilly decorations. "Rayle, help me out here. Tell Luli I'm right. I forgot my percomp at the clinic again."

Rayle laughed and held up his hands in surrender. "I don't even know who won the galactic championship last year. Ask Imara." He nodded toward her, then made his escape.

"Sorry, Betz," said Imara, as she dispensed a pink liquid into a shaker. "Red Shift lost to the Event Horizons, six to five, on 3231.144. Red Shift beat them seven to four in the pinpoint pattern round, using trim jets." Based on that, Lièrén guessed it was a space-based competition of some sort, the kind his great-grandfather liked, and had probably competed in himself.

Betz, the woman in red, slumped as her companion Luli grinned triumphantly. "See? Another fan!"

Imara shook her head as she added a powder to the blender, causing the mixture to turn sunset orange. "No, I just have a good memory for trivia."

Lièrén would have smiled at her understatement, but it reminded him too much that his own memory was full of jagged holes. He resolutely focused on the bottles behind Imara, counting them, as a way to keep his thoughts from plunging into deep waters. It wasn't productive, and he was too distracted to keep empathic Rayle from sensing the turmoil. He couldn't talk about his troubles and didn't want to have to lie to either him or Imara. If the CPS Office of Internal Inquiry telepaths ever came snooping around, their ignorance would save them.

Lièrén couldn't prove that the high casualty rates in his unit were related to Fiyon Machimata's corruption, but it wouldn't surprise him. He could easily imagine vengeance from the victim of someone that Machimata had "exonerated."

On the other side of the two women, a balding man thumped a shot glass down loudly on the bar top. The curve of the bar meant Lièrén had a clear view of him and his two friends, and he thought they might be regulars, too. The man, clearly in need of a depilatory for his face and a body shop for his budding obesity problem, cast an ugly look at Imara.

"Oh, frellin' hell, you're one of *those*, aren't you? You're a subbin' minder. You're a whatchacallit, a filer, right? *Cheater* is what I call it."

Lièrén forced himself to remain still and relax. It was nothing minders hadn't heard before. Out of the corner of his eye, he saw the woman in red, Betz, hunch her shoulders a little. Lièrén's talent said she had an animal affinity, maybe birds, judging from the extra padding on her tunic's shoulders and a tiny feather stuck in her hair. None of the other patrons seated at the bar had talent. Imara did, though she was containing it well enough to be a shielder.

The delicate-looking, brown-skinned woman seated next to the balding man shook her head in disgust. The slender black man on her other side leaned in. "Shut up, Tace. You're drunk."

The balding man thrust up his middle finger in a cross-culturally rude gesture. "Wank off, Warner, I ain't drunk yet. Minders ain't like you and me. There's nothin' to stop 'em from messing with every one of us, jus' 'cause they can." He turned to look at Imara. "Or winning bar bets 'cause they're freak *cheaters*."

Imara gave no sign that she'd even heard him as she poured the orange drink into a frosty glass of ice.

With a carefully casual smile, Lièrén said, "I'd love to have a memory like hers. It'd save me a year of penance for forgetting my grandmother's birthday." He nodded his head toward Imara without looking at her. "Besides, it's nice when a bartender always gets your order right."

"Sync that," agreed Luli, the woman in the jumpsuit. She smiled and pointed to her and her companion's mostly empty glasses. "Another round, please." Imara returned her smile and opened the cold box.

Tace grunted and turned to Warner, the man next to him. "That's as may be, but you and Priya here are foolin' yourselves if you think minders don't want to see normal people jacked. You know what they call us? *Nulls.* Like we're nothin'. If you ask me, the lot of them oughta be blank-slated."

Lièrén had to admit that some minders he'd known used that term, but no one liked being called subhuman or a freak, so some defensiveness was understandable.

The pretty brown-skinned woman gave Tace an exasperated look. "And who's going to do the blank-slating? It takes a cleaner—a *minder*—to do that." Her Hindi accent gave a sharp, precise edge to her words. "Or perhaps we should send them all to the frontier, or treat them as if they were old Confederation enemies of the state and just disappear them in uncharted space." She slid off the barstool, keyed her percomp, and waved it at the tab indicator. "You're an unmitigated jackass when you're drunk. I'm not going to stay and listen to your drivel." She nodded to the black man. "Have a good evening, Warner." She grabbed her light coat from the hook and left.

Tace tossed back what was left in his glass. "Lightweight."

"She's right, you *are* a jackass." said Warner. "Did some minder pee in your tea today?"

"No, but how would I know? Anyone in here could be a minder, and we'd never know it." He waved a hand to include everyone in the room, but ruined the gesture by nearly falling off the stool. "They got no moral compass."

Warner's eyes narrowed. "Suck hard space, Tace. My sister's a fixer, and my uncle's a healer. They're just people, like us." He keyed his percomp and paid his tab. "Next time you crack your flitter or get busted up in another bar fight, you can damned well call someone else."

That apparently got home to the drunk man like nothing else had. "Your sister's different," he spluttered, wetting his cheap, sweat-stained shirt. "She's not one of them telepaths that go mucking about in your mind and shit."

Warner shook off Tace's grip on his shoulder and stood. "Nice. All minders are degenerates, except that ones that do you favors. You're just a selfish prick." Warner gave Imara an apologetic shrug before leaving.

Tace hunched his shoulders grumpily and pushed his empty glass toward Imara with a grunt. "Blue Ruin. Double."

She took his glass and gave him a professional smile. "Sorry, Tace. That was your limit. How about something from the kitchen, or a detox or an inhib?"

Tace glared belligerently at Imara. "I only had the two."

Imara snorted. "Plus you drank most of Priya's Superorbital Blitz, and whatever you had at lunch before you came here."

Tace dropped his eyes. "I got nothing for lunch. Got overtime instead." He sounded truly disgruntled, but even through the distortion of the alcohol clouding Tace's responses, Lièrén felt the partial lie.

Imara leaned back and crossed her arms. When her seemingly wandering gaze flickered in his direction, he shook his head once, ever so slightly. She focused on Tace and shook her head. "Nice try, Tace. No more kickers for you tonight."

"It's a free-range galaxy," muttered Tace. "I can have as much as I want."

"Yep," agreed Imara with another professional smile that didn't reach her eyes. "But not here."

To Lièrén's relief, Tace bought a large cup of dark kaffa to go and left.

Belatedly, Lièrén thought to wonder if Derrit had overheard any of Tace's tirade. To his relief, he saw Derrit was still at the small table in back, finishing his school work. Imara had been forced to sternly order him there to get his school assignments done, instead of making friends with the kids lounging around the net terminals, looking for games. He'd been uncharacteristically willful and whiny, reminding Lièrén that Derrit, for all his impressive talent and strong sense of responsibility, was still a boy.

After the other two women left, Lièrén had the bar area almost to himself, with only one other customer at the opposite end who was engrossed in her percomp.

Rayle, grumbling once again about being tipped in worthless lottery tickets instead of cashflow, took a break to get himself something to eat, so Imara had her hands full keeping the several occupied tables and booths serviced and happy. On busy nights, sometimes Derrit would step in and help, but he was probably still sulking.

Lièrén had the impulse to offer to collect dirty glasses, like the Quark and Quasar had somehow become a family kitchen where everyone did his part. He shook his head at the odd feeling. He had no experience, so he'd probably just get in the way. He considered leaving, maybe even going for a walk despite the rain, except he still hadn't had the scheduled session with Derrit.

Rayle returned from the kitchen, holding the last of a sandwich. "You're quiet tonight."

Lièrén felt Rayle's empathic talent energize. Lièrén hastily contained his depression, kicking himself for carelessly broadcasting. "It's been a long day."

Rayle patted Lièrén's shoulder as he went by and headed to the cold unit behind the bar. "I heard old Tace spouting off again. He's usually okay when he sticks to inhalers, but when he's drunk, he's a *testa de cazzo.*"

"Who's a dickhead?" Imara asked as she slid by him to the dispensary cabinet. The door beeped and opened, once it confirmed her fingerprints on its handle. "Order for eight at B-5."

"Old 'valued patron' Tace, with his bullshit about minders." Rayle opened his sandwich to discover all he had left was bread. He threw the crusts in the organic recycler.

"I heard a lot worse when I was growing up." She opened a drawer and pulled out a pill. "Of course, Marmar Coklat is the planet that progress forgot, and they like it that way."

Rayle looked pensive. "It was no better in New Geneva." Lièrén wondered if Rayle's family was related to the Leviso Holdings of intergalactic finance fame, and if so, what they thought about his career choice. "I think attitudes are changing, at least in public. Warner and Priya were honestly defending minders." He looked to Lièrén. "Weren't they?"

"Yes," agreed Lièrén. There had been no vague haze of discord behind their words that would have meant they hadn't believed what they were saying.

Rayle pulled out a tray and set it on the prep counter. "We're lucky we're not on a frontier planet. I've heard it's a lot worse. No CPS or laws to protect us outside the Concordance."

Imara snorted. "No laws to protect us *in* the Concordance, either. The Minder Rights law didn't make it out of review. Again." She filled the tray with a mix of liquids and chems and sent Rayle off with it to the large booth near the entryway that led to the hotel lobby. "Luckily, the bill about making it illegal to deliberately fail minder testing died. How the hell would they prove that? And who would they detain—the parents or the kid?"

Imara leaned her hip against the counter near Lièrén and glanced toward her son. Lièrén followed her gaze. The boy was still working on the portable comp, but his body language no longer exuded resentment.

"Thank Neptune those children left," said Imara, reaching for her half-empty glass of *kelasa*. "If they'd had a kitten or a ferret with them, I'd have had to zip-tie him to the chair."

"He's a good kid. Better than I was at his age. I was rather… indulged." He twitched a smile at her.

She laughed. "Spoiled, huh?"

He shrugged and smiled. "I was my parents' last and much younger child. My first year at the Academy was an eye-opening experience."

"We all have to grow up sometime. I loved my husband dearly, but I let him keep me in a cocoon. When he died, it was either go back to Marmar Coklat or learn to stand on my own two feet so Derrit could have opportunities." Lièrén knew from previous conversations that she had no family on Con Prime, and he couldn't imagine being a single parent in a city like Spires. He admired her courage.

A new customer slid onto one of the empty barstools, and Imara went to serve him. Lièrén's attention was caught by the music, a three-four beat and a tune that sounded familiar, but he couldn't think why until Rayle waltzed into view. "Come show Imara what you learned today in dance class!" He grabbed Lièrén's hand to pull him off the stool. Lièrén gently removed his hand from Rayle's and sat back down.

"No, thank you. I still haven't recovered." He flexed his ankles to relieve the tightness in his sore calves. He'd be lucky if he could walk tomorrow.

"Oh, you're no fun. Imara, come, my dearest darling, and show Lièrén how easy it is." She laughed as he pulled her from behind the bar and into his arms for a dozen steps before she gracefully spun out of his arms and back to the safety of the bar. Lièrén felt a wave of longing and sting of envy at Rayle for his comfortable closeness with Imara, but he squelched it. Lièrén would be gone soon, and he didn't want to be a bad memory for her.

Rayle continued the waltz by himself, holding his arms up for an imaginary partner. "So, Agent Sòng, are you now medically cleared for sex?"

Lièrén only just managed to stop from rolling his eyes. Damn the man. "Yes, Server Leviso. Perhaps you could re-broadcast to the general public your concern about my private health. I'm not sure the people in the lobby heard you." He released containment of his irritation for a moment, trusting Rayle's empathic talent would notice.

If Rayle caught it, he was unrepentant. "Good, just want to make sure, in case some opportunity presents herself." He waggled his eyebrows suggestively at Imara, whose expression was half amusement, half annoyance.

Lièrén couldn't explain the incident in dance class without further embarrassing himself and her, which seemed to be Rayle's intent. He settled for turning away and ignoring him.

"Jackass," said Imara to Rayle. "Go meddle somewhere else."

Rayle seemed to recognize the steel in her pleasant tone and danced gracefully away.

Imara sighed. "Sorry about that." She glanced at the clock, then gave a little whistle to get Derrit's attention. "Dinner," she said.

Derrit bounded up out of the chair toward her as if spring-loaded. "I'm starving. Can I make toad-in-the-hole? Want some, Agent Sòng?"

Lièrén's puzzlement must have been obvious. "It's a fried egg in the center of toast with cheese," she said.

Lièrén ducked his head. "Thank you. I'm afraid my culinary skills are limited to self-heating pouches and reading menus."

"I could teach you," offered Derrit, with pride. Lièrén hesitated, then nodded. It would be good for Derrit to be the teacher instead of always the student. And it would take Lièrén out of Imara's orbit for a while, so he'd quit being tempted by her.

Imara eyed Lièrén up and down, then smiled at Derrit. "Okay, but don't let the kitchen manager see him."

Derrit put his hand in Lièrén's and pulled him toward the kitchen. Lièrén trailed obediently behind him, smiling at Derrit's enthusiasm.

As they entered the large industrial kitchen, Lièrén asked, "Why shouldn't the kitchen manager see me?"

"You don't dress like staff," he said, dragging out a stool and placing it in front of a cook surface. "Customers aren't allowed."

Lièrén glanced down at his dark green cut-and-slash pants and multi-pocket, metallic silver tunic with electroluminescent green piping. He'd grown rather fond of the high style of his new wardrobe, but Derrit was right, it couldn't even pass for trendy corporate wear. When he went back to the field unit, he'd have to order a new, more staid wardrobe for the unit's official, boring cover story.

He watched, bemused, as Derrit scampered all over the kitchen, clearly at home and comfortable with the dizzying array of equipment. Lièrén gathered the employees brought in and stored their own food, so as not to impact the restaurant's inventory. Toad-in-the-hole was as simple as Imara had described it, but Lièrén hadn't exaggerated his lack of experience.

"You really never learned to cook?" Derrit asked, his astonishment evident. "Anything?"

Lièrén thought a moment. "I can prepare and serve Oriental tea."

Derrit patted Lièrén's arm in a consoling gesture. "That's okay. Nanay said my dad couldn't boil water when she met him. If you stay in Spires, she could teach you."

Although Derrit had tried to be casual, it was hard to miss his latest attempt to put Lièrén and his mother together. It wouldn't be good for Derrit to get his hopes up. "I'll be ready for full duty soon, and my job requires constant traveling. I'd never be here for lessons."

It would be irresponsible of him to get any more entangled with Imara and Derrit than he already was, for a whole host of reasons. The cold logic made his chest feel hollow.

CHAPTER 9

IMARA WAS BEMUSED, watching her son.

"Here's more water, Agent Sòng." He placed the opaque glass down in front of Lièrén before sliding back into the booth. He'd just finished clearing the dinner plates and silverware without having to be asked, and had taken the initiative to keep Lièrén hydrated.

Derrit was blossoming, and she knew it was from Lièrén's influence. Derrit had never been rude, but he had been... oblivious, rather like most of her road crew. Lièrén led by example rather than words, and Derrit had picked up a new awareness of the needs of others. Lièrén had mentioned that his latest drug protocol made him feel dehydrated, and Derrit had made it his goal to keep Lièrén always supplied with water ready to hand.

"Thank you," said Lièrén. He took a sip, then cleared his throat. "While you're both here, I'd like to discuss rules and customs for telepaths, since both of Derrit's talents fall in that class. Some of it you probably already know from Torin, but Derrit's cleaner talent brings some added considerations."

He focused on Derrit. "First, it's generally better to disclose your tested talents up front, rather than be accused of it later. Not, 'hello, I'm a shielder and cleaner,' but don't hide them and don't let people assume you have none. Some people will always be afraid of you, regardless, and fear leads to anger and aggression."

Imara appreciated Lièrén's tact. Derrit would run into bigotry soon enough, and she'd help him deal with it, but she didn't want him wearing a chip on his shoulder, either.

"Second, for the most part, we're not allowed in casinos or bluff game competitions, although I've heard of a few telepath-only hyperion tournaments. In the patterner class, forecasters and finders are sometimes prohibited from outcome betting because of the perceived advantage." Imara rolled her eyes. Study after study proved that finders and forecasters did no better than chance, the same as everyone else, but the rumors persisted.

Derrit frowned. "But my dad was in the telepath class, and he worked for a casino. That's how he met mom and saved her from the pirate clan."

Imara smiled at the memory of how Torin had created a tall tale of thrilling intrigue and fated romance out of a chance meeting in the alleyway behind the themed casino on Marmar Coklat where he'd worked at the time. It had been Derrit's favorite bedtime story for years.

"Straight shielders are the exception. As a matter of fact, they're highly valued in security work. Because you're a cleaner, too, you'll likely be encouraged to go into law enforcement."

Derrit frowned, and Imara slipped her arm around Derrit's shoulders. "You have other options, you know." Torin hadn't had much respect for the police, owing to run-ins during his youth, and it colored Derrit's opinions. In Imara's experience with the Spires police, they were just people, good and bad, the same as every other profession.

"Are people scared of you, Agent Sòng?" asked Derrit.

Lièrén sighed. "Yes. Ask your mother what she first thought when I told her I'm a twister."

Derrit's eyes widened, and he looked to her. She now regretted her reaction at the time, but she wouldn't lie to her son. "Twisting is a scary talent, *binata*. Undetectable if the minder is good enough." She looked up to squarely meet Lièrén's gaze. "I trust Agent Sòng to do the right thing." His talent would tell him she wasn't lying.

Emotions she couldn't read rippled across his normally serene expression. She could almost feel him reasserting his control.

He ducked his head once. "You honor me." He took another sip of water. He glanced at her again, then focused on Derrit.

"You're still shielding your mother." It was a statement of fact.

"Yeah," he said, then looked at Imara. When Lièrén had first mentioned it a week ago, Imara had asked Derrit to stop, but apparently, he hadn't listened. It was so like what Torin would have done that she couldn't blame Derrit for his nature, but he'd told her he would, and that hurt. She withdrew her arm from his shoulders and frowned to let him know she wasn't happy.

Derrit fidgeted, then finally said, "But I promised Dad..." There was a half defiant, half beseeching quality to his tone. He looked pleadingly to Lièrén for support.

To Imara's relief, Lièrén shook his head. "This is one of those responsibilities we talked about. It's good that you want to protect her, but it must be her choice, and you must abide by her wishes. Your talent bottles up hers. You dislike it when people treat you like a baby and decide things for you." She gave Lièrén a tiny nod to thank him, then turned back to Derrit.

She kept an unyielding look on her face and waited while her son thought about it. She'd sometimes found that silence worked better with him than arguing. Finally, Derrit's shoulders slumped.

"Okay," he said in a small voice. She resisted the urge to comfort him, because he'd have thought she'd changed her mind. If someone as powerful as Lièrén Sòng thought she could stand on her own, she wanted to live up to that expectation.

She waited, but didn't know how to tell if Derrit had dropped the shield or not.

Lièrén did, though. He touched the back of Derrit's hand. "You don't have to unshield yourself, too."

It took a few tries for Derrit to find the balance. He'd been shielding her for so long that he had a hard time feeling the difference, and Lièrén couldn't show him how, he could only make suggestions and report success or failure.

Imara tried to detect the difference herself, but it was like trying to listen for a song she'd never heard. She was half tempted to ask Lièrén to teach her to feel it, but firmly cut that thought off. It might require a telepathic connection, like she'd only had with the man she'd married, and it'd be one more reason to miss Lièrén when he left for good. Judging from his steadily improving health, his last day would be soon.

She ruffled Derrit's hair. "Thank you, *binata*." She stole a quick glance at Rayle, who was serving a small glass of something blue to a new customer. "I need to get back to the bar before Rayle gives away too many free samples." Rayle, empath that he was and compassionate by nature, liked happy customers. Hotel management liked paying customers.

Derrit started to move, but Lièrén interrupted.

"Would you both do me the honor of allowing me to host you for dinner at Fermat's Last Repast, in celebration of Derrit's twelfth birthday?"

Imara couldn't contain her astonishment at the invitation or choice of restaurant, which was famous galaxy-wide.

"Thank you, but…" she began, intending to turn him down, as she did all invitations from transients, but she hesitated when she saw Derrit's hopeful expression. On her tight budget, they could only eat at a decent restaurant once a year, in the height of the rainy season, when rates were low. Fermat's cheapest appetizer would probably wipe out her solstice day gift savings. "It's a generous offer, but I've heard it takes months to get reservations. Perhaps someplace less, uhm, exclusive?"

Lièrén smiled. "My second cousin and his husband own it. He's been pinging me almost daily, so you'll be saving me from the barrage."

She hesitated a moment longer, then gave in for Derrit's sake, despite her own misgivings. "Then yes, we'll accept." Derrit gave her a big grin as she visualized her calendar in her mind. "How about a week from tomorrow?"

Lièrén smiled ruefully as he opened his percomp's display. "I truly envy your filer talent. Would six o'clock be acceptable?"

"Yes," she said, then added, "We'll meet you there." She didn't want him paying for an autocab, too. He was probably on half-pay while he was on medical leave.

"Excellent. I'll ping Chiu now, before he sends his nightly 'gentle reminder for persons with feeble minds.'"

She chuckled. "Having a good memory is handy, but it also means remembering the bad things with equal clarity." She sighed. "I can think of a few memories I'd prefer to have twisted into something nicer or erased altogether."

Lièrén shook his head, suddenly serious. "No, it would hurt you. Only top-level talents can find all the interconnected threads in a good filer's mind. Otherwise, you'd feel it forever. It'd be like…" He hesitated, then pointed to the travel poster on the wall. "…like that crooked Albion Prime display that drives you crazy. You know it's wrong, but you can't fix it because it's built in." He folded his percomp and put it in his upper chest pocket.

She'd never thought about it like that, but it made sense. "Thank you. I don't know what the CPS has you doing for trade delegations, but I hope it's helping people as much as you've helped Derrit." She thought he flinched, though she couldn't have said why she thought so, because his expression didn't change. "I'm sorry, I didn't mean to embarrass you." She nudged Derrit. "Scoot, kiddo."

Derrit scrambled out of the booth to let her out, then sat back down as Imara headed for the bar.

She kept herself busy while Derrit had his lesson, but she caught herself glancing their direction more than once. Finally, Lièrén and Derrit stood up. Surprisingly, Derrit gave a slight, if awkward, bow to Lièrén, who returned it with more grace. Then Derrit galloped off like a horse toward the fresher.

Imara gave up on doing anything else as she watched Lièrén leave. It would be much easier to ignore him if he weren't so nice. And sexy, even from the back. She resolutely turned away, only to narrowly miss colliding with Rayle.

"You really need a hot-connect with that man. You're practically drooling."

Farkin' A, but she'd like to have a little privacy once in a while. She sighed.

He followed her back behind the bar and winked at her. "I'd hot-connect with him in a nanosecond, in his favorite booth if he likes an audience, but he only has eyes for you."

"Sure, while he's in the bar," she scoffed. "I'm just a geosynced satellite he's passing by. He's a *transient*." She eyed the drink supplies and decided she needed more tangelo peel twists. "It's just asking for broken hearts all around."

He raised his eyebrows in exaggerated surprise. "Oh, so you're *seriously* attracted to him."

Rayle knew her too well. "He's plasma hot, I'll grant you, and I'd like to spend some close-up time with him, but it's not going to happen. It's not *my* heart that would be broken."

They were interrupted by a couple of customer orders, but Imara knew Rayle wasn't going to let it go.

As he loaded a few glasses in the quicksan, he said, "If not Agent Flux-Hot, then take your pick. There's eight million people in Spires, and half of them are men." He winked salaciously at her.

Imara snorted. "Oh, right, because men throw themselves in front of me every day and hope I'll trip and land on their poles."

He gave her a devilish smile. "More than you notice, *bella*. I'd be willing to assume the position if you asked nicely. I'm of similar build to Lièrén. I'll get my hair and eyes done like his and dress like all my clothes came from a skimmer race crew, and you can pretend."

Imara crossed her arms and raised an eyebrow. "I thought you weren't attracted to women."

"Oh, women are all right. I just like men a lot better." He looked at her over his shoulder as he dampened a bar mop with cleaner. "Their naughty bits can do more fun things."

She couldn't help but laugh. "Very self-sacrificing of you to make the offer."

He gave her an exaggerated bow, then twirled away to wipe down the tables he hadn't gotten to earlier.

A few minutes later, he passed by her and whispered, "I could bribe Iggy for Agent Flux-Hot's room number. You could pretend you were just in the neighborhood."

Imara gave him an exasperated look. "You're like a dog with a bone. I'm not going to have sex with the man." She took a fresh bar towel from the stack. "It'll be hard enough on Derrit when he loses Lièrén as a teacher. Derrit's at an age where he needs to talk to trusted adult males about… male stuff."

Rayle laughed. "I'll admit I'm not much help with hetero 'male stuff,' and Derrit feels solidly hetero." Rayle's impish look returned. "I think Lièrén might be a bit more, er, flexible, but I'll wait to invite him to satisfy my lusty lust until after you've had your fun."

Imara shook her head. "Not happening. He'll be long gone before any of that angsty drama can play out." She ran the towel over the countertop where fizzy water had splashed.

Rayle laughed and grabbed a tray. "You're too practical for your own good. Live a little, woman!"

"You're sun struck. What is it with you and wanting everyone to be having sex?"

"*Someone* around here should. It'd make the planet a happier place." He tilted his head toward the couple seated at the table near the front doors, one wearing a torn redball jersey over cartoon-character sleep pants, looking morose, and the other like he'd rather be anywhere else. "You, my dear, could light up the room if you wanted to, and probably double your tips."

She snorted. "And double the hot-connect offers, too."

"My point exactly!" He quickly danced away with the tray, laughing as he barely avoided the snap of her wet bar towel.

CHAPTER 10

ALTHOUGH IMARA KNEW it was an engineered illusion, the deep, rich bass of Chadd Sovereign, a platinum-list actor, almost seemed to come from the just behind her, as though he was close by and murmuring in her ear.

"The education your child receives at the CPS Academy and the prestigious and elite CPS Minder Institute actualizes the social, intellectual, and innate mental talents of each child.... fostering new and empowering connections... helping students learn to approach adversity with strength and leadership. These are the qualities they'll need to deal with the challenges to peace and prosperity throughout the galaxy."

She was glad she'd managed to snag a back seat in the darkened circular immersion room, because she was having a hard time not making rude noises at the slick, expensively produced multimedia presentation offered to parents who were waiting while their children were in minder testing. The presentation was filled with lush images and holos, stirring music, and interactive engagement sections designed to make parents feel as if their child being offered the chance to go to the CPS Academy was better than winning an interplanetary lottery. A younger Imara from a hick town might have bought it hook, line, and fish-finder, but years of bartending and listening to Prime politicians and lobbyists had given her a finely-honed bullshit detector, and the presentation was consistently pegging her detector's red zone. *And this was what I took the whole day off for,* she thought disgustedly.

It was no wonder the CPS was asking for more funding for its Testing Centers, if this one was anything to go by. She wouldn't have recognized the presentation as being high-end if a production company hadn't stayed at the hotel for twelve weeks last year, and the entire crew drank, chemmed, and inhaled like the sun was going nova tomorrow. She and Derrit both had gotten quite an education in the production business.

The immersion room was high-end, too, with adjustable contour chairs and projection equipment that made it seem like each seat in the room had the best vantage point for the holo presentation. The decor and furniture in the rest of the Testing Center office was equally high-end, at least what she'd seen of it. Of course, this was Spires, capitol of the galaxy, not an oasis town on an out-of-the-way planet that embraced its backwater status.

"The Academy steadfastly and unceasingly stresses the total development of each child selected for the program, tailoring remedial curricula to ensure a well-rounded education."

This time, the voice was that of a famous performance artist named Laoreana, known for her distinctive drawl and breathy tone that always made her sound like she was late for something. Imara was beginning to feel insulted by the multiple statements that implied Derrit's schooling was inferior. Not only was this Con Prime, where education was as much a showcase as the city of Spires, but she worked two jobs so Derrit could have extra language, business, and technical classes.

A more insidious undercurrent suggested that top-level talents needed the Academy to teach them morality and responsible behavior, as if those were known failings of minders. She surreptitiously watched the seven other parents in the room to see how they were reacting. Other than the man to the left of the door who was gently snoring, the rest of them ranged from mildly happy to practically worshipful. She decided to keep her opinions to herself.

"...peace of mind knowing a CPS education instills and establishes values that will empower graduates to use their skills and character to help maintain peace and stability throughout the galaxy. Employment with the CPS ensures job security and an ideal working environment that fosters respect and service."

Imara snorted at that last part. If the CPS was such a great place to work, why wasn't Lièrén Sòng happier about it? She'd only recently come to realize it, and he'd never said anything about it, but she'd bet good money that he disliked his job.

A flood of rapid-fire images and sound snips signaled the end of the presentation. She glanced at her percomp to check the time and wasn't sure whether it was good or bad that she'd wasted thirty minutes sitting through that drivel. On one hand, she was now permanently stuck with over-the-top propaganda in her memory, but it was better than sitting in the lobby trying to read trendlines on her near-comatose percomp or worrying about how Derrit was doing. Her own first-round testing twenty-five years ago had been perfunctory, once they realized she was just a filer. Derrit's was taking a lot longer.

Once back in the waiting room, Imara lucked into a plush chair by one of the expensive morphglass windows, farthest away from the front desk and the offices behind it. The whole facility had her feeling wary. The staff had been polite and personable to everyone, and solicitously offered a variety of refreshments, with enough food to make a light meal if need be. Somehow, it all felt like a veneer, like the professional smile she'd cultivated for dealing with the bar's valued patrons when they were being obnoxious or lying. Of course, it could all just be nerves, because her son had been back there more than two hours doing only Neptune knew what.

Remembering her own testing, she realized she didn't know how it had been done. The testers had pointed instruments at her and placed sensors on her temples, then taken her through a series of confusingly random activities, but once they'd determined she wasn't telekinetic or telepathic, they'd seemed to lose interest. She'd been in and out in thirty minutes. From what her sister Piera had said, who'd turned out to have inherited their dad's considerable fixer talent, the CPS hadn't been very interested in her, either. She wished she'd thought to ask Lièrén for details on high-level talent testing, since he'd been through it and was a CPS employee. Although now that she'd seen the presentation, she knew that Lièrén was in a different branch from the Testing Center, so he might not know much more than she did about talent testing for shielders and cleaners.

When the sluggish wall clock ticked over at the top of the hour, she decided she'd waited long enough. As it was, dinner would be late, and growing boys grew cranky when they were hungry. She stood and strode toward the front desk. Either they produced her son, or they'd find out how loud someone used to yelling over road-repair racket could be. She checked herself as she approached, realizing that she'd likely get better results if she was pleasant. She took a deep breath, tamped down her irritation, mentally braced herself, and put on her professional smile.

"Pardon the interruption, but I'm wondering about my son. It's been longer than I expected."

The vapid young man at the front desk gave her an apologetic smile. "I'm sorry, Madam Sesay, but we're short-staffed today, so everything is taking longer than usual." He checked something on his elegant desk display, then stood. "I'll go back myself and see how Derrit is doing." He left his seat and went through a door behind him. Being called "madam" made her feel as old as her grandmother. At least he'd remembered her name and which child was hers.

To keep herself from drumming her fingers on the gold-flecked marble countertop, she mentally rearranged the cluttered mess of electronic devices, styluses, and visible papers on the desk. She was sidetracked into wondering what they used paper for, since the middle of Spires was about as far from a tech dead zone as one could get. The printing was too small for her to read from where she was standing.

The vapid young man returned. "It'll just be a few minutes more. Agent Ghisolfi would like to speak with you and Derrit in the conference room. I can take you there now, if it's convenient." He waved a hand to invite her to a narrow door partially hidden by a tall fern.

"Yes, thank you," she said. He met her professional smile with an equally professional one of his own, then led her through the door and into a long, branching hallway of closed sliding doors. Despite the warm colors and textures, it had a whiff of government office, and the conference room was no better. It was artificially lit and barely big enough for five friendly people. She sat when invited, stifling her inclination to stand and pace. When the door slid shut, the feeling she'd had of being monitored intensified. She didn't like small, windowless rooms. She snorted to herself. It was a government office. Making visitors feel uncomfortable was probably intentional. She took a deep breath and let it out slowly to release her tension.

A few minutes later, the door slid open, and an olive-skinned, dark-eyed man walked in, followed by Derrit. She stood up.

"Have a seat, young man." He turned to her and nodded his head respectfully. "I'm Agent Milo Ghisolfi."

She barely registered his professional smile and slight Italian accent as she watched her son sit. Derrit didn't seem any worse for wear. Ghisolfi sat, so she did. Derrit slipped his hand into hers, and she had to forcibly contain her surprise. He only did that when he was feeling insecure, which was rare. She gave Derrit's fingers a little squeeze, then focused on Ghisolfi, wondering what the hell they'd done to her son.

"Thank you for agreeing to meet with me. I'll get right to the point. As I'm sure you suspected, Derrit has two minder talents in the telepathic classification. He shows promise in both the shielder and erasure, popularly known as 'cleaner,' categories. What we don't know yet is the level of his talents. The tests were inconclusive."

Something about Ghisolfi put her on guard. Imara let her eyebrows rise. "Inconclusive?"

"Yes. I'm sure you appreciate that it's important for Derrit's sake to know how powerful his talents are. Some results were consistent with high-level talents, and others barely registered. Part of the problem is our fault, I believe, because the agent who specializes in testing one of Derrit's categories is out with a family emergency. I'm sorry, but we need Derrit to come back in to be tested again. We'll need you to bring him back in tomorrow."

She didn't even have to think about it. "No, I can't miss any more work this week, and Derrit has five classes. As it is, he'll have catch-up work for today."

He pursed his lips. "How about we schedule it for the day after tomorrow, during Derrit's day off?" Ghisolfi's tone was everything that was reasonable, but Imara didn't miss the slight hardening of his eyes before he smoothed his expression. Derrit must have told them his school schedule, because they hadn't heard it from her.

She shook her head. "I need at least two weeks' notice to schedule time off."

"I'm sorry, Madam Sesay, but the law says we must retest him within five days. We've already transmitted the required rescheduling inconvenience fee to your account." He leaned in a little, edging into her personal space, with a hint of aggression in his expression. "I'm sure someone else could bring him."

Apparently, she was supposed to be intimidated. Ghisolfi had obviously never worked a road crew with Rackkar Horis.

"No," she said flatly, considering her options. Maybe she'd get better results from Manager Klarxon, the woman whose holo was displayed in the lobby.

He seemed to recognize her resolve and leaned back. He brought up something on the percomp he wore on the back of his hand. "It's not our usual practice, but since it's our fault Derrit has to come back, I could authorize a trackable secure cab to transport him at our expense. We have an account with the company the High Council uses."

She looked at Derrit to see how he was handling all this, but his expression wasn't giving anything away. She suspected he was feeling overwhelmed.

Unfortunately, it looked like she didn't have a choice. Involving the manager might delay the retesting, but it would have to be done sooner or later. They were offering carrots now, but sticks were coming. "We'll accept the secure cab option, to and from our apartment. You'll send me the tracking ID and reservation numbers in advance?"

"Of course," agreed Ghisolfi. He fiddled with his percomp. "I've set the appointment for 1430 hours, so the cab will come by at 1330, just to be safe." It was more than enough time, but considering their apartment was in the Rim and low-air traffic could be heavy, the early pickup was a reasonable precaution.

"And should I expect it to take two and a half hours again?" she asked, letting sharpness color her tone.

Ghisolfi's expression slid into chagrin, but it didn't match his body language. He was a practiced liar. If he'd been a valued patron at the bar, she'd have refused to serve him anything but water. "I hope not, but sometimes we get backed up. I should think he'll be home by 1700."

He stood and waved the door open, then led them out to the lobby. Derrit clung to her hand the whole way and didn't even acknowledge the vapid young man's wish for them to have a pleasant afternoon. Her son's closed-off expression made her splurge on a tourist autocab to take them home, rather than spend a couple of hours on the metro. They stepped up to the platform, and she entered the coordinates for their apartment. Five minutes later, a gaudily painted cab glided onto the landing strip, and she and Derrit slid into the open doors and onto the bench seat. The cabin smelled like popcorn and sweet melon, but the lifters sounded well-tuned, and the glass bubble was clear and clean.

Derrit was quiet for a few minutes as the cab slipped into traffic, but Imara knew he'd tell her what was bothering him eventually. Finally, he let go of her hand and sat up a little straighter in the seat.

"I thought I did really well, especially since Agent Sòng has been teaching me. But the lady testing me just kept messing around with some machine and moving the sensor things around on my head. She called in the other guy, Ghisolfi, and they had me do the same things all over again." He slumped again. "I guess I'm never going to be as good as dad was."

"Camel shit." Imara didn't often swear around her son, and it shocked him out of his slumping mood, as she'd intended. "You heard Ghisolfi. The specialist in your talent area was out. It'd be like the hotel sending Rayle to work the front desk. It'd take days to clean up the mess."

Derrit smiled a little at the image, then frowned. "Then how come the measuring divvie didn't show anything? Ghisolfi and that lady just looked kind of… bored."

"I don't know what their equipment does, but I do know that it's usually operator error that causes problems. I tell you what, let's ask Agent Sòng about it over… oh, hell. We're going to have to move the dinner at Fermat's." It completely slipped her mind to check her schedule when setting the retest appointment for Derrit. If today was anything to go by, they couldn't guarantee meeting Lièrén at the restaurant on time, or at all. "I'll ping him right now."

As she worked her ancient percomp, describing to Lièrén what had happened, she seethed inside at Ghisolfi and whoever the other agent was. She'd like to introduce them to her good friend Rackkar and his favorite heavy wrench. How dare those CPS water-wasters be so rudely discouraging to an eleven-year-old boy who'd tried his best?

CHAPTER II

LIÈRÉN'S PERCOMP SIGNALED an incoming static ping from Imara. Glad of the distraction, he read it immediately. He was disappointed that his dinner with Imara and Derrit had to be cancelled, but he found himself more perturbed by the inconclusive test results for Derrit's minder talents. Lièrén knew from personal experience that Derrit was very gifted. Lièrén was pretty sure some of his trained, adult coworkers, selected for field-unit service because of the quality of their talents, were lower level than pre-teen prodigy Derrit.

He tried to remember his own testing at age twelve. He had the vague recollection of being at the Testing Center twice, but he had no idea why. He knew his parents had been thrilled when the CPS had sent the letter and contract for the full-ride scholarship plus family stipend for him to attend the CPS Academy. The rare chance to please his parents kept him at the Academy those first few hard months of bewildering, complex regimentation and no friends. The only plus had been his solid academic background, which saved him from having to play catch-up in that area. Of course, by staying, he'd also alienated his great-grandfather, who still resented Lièrén's choices to this day.

Two anecdotal experiences, one of them twenty years old, didn't mean anything. Lièrén rubbed an idle finger along the CPS deskcomp, full of Testing Center data. It wouldn't take long to craft a multi-thread query to look for patterns related to "inconclusive" test results. It was an ethical gray area, but he could justify his actions under the heading of "looking for process-improvement opportunities," having already earned high praise from Supervisor Yamazaki for how he'd handled the field office's data. It meant he'd once again have to take apart the Testing Center data cubes and rebuild them. No one had mentioned a deadline, but they were probably wondering what was taking him so long. Or they'd forgotten they'd assigned it to him. Either was possible, considering the sad shape the records were in. He pulled up the largest data cube, the one from the most recent year, and cracked it.

An hour later, the pattern he was seeing disturbed him, but he was trying to figure out what a particular notation meant. It was one of the stronger commonalities in records with "inconclusive" test results. He tediously read through the various comments sections of the records, while he ran a separate galnet query about testing protocols in general. Finally, he lucked into a brief note that pointed him to an obscure statute in Concordance military law. Buried deep in the sub-sub-subparts was an emergency conscription provision that allowed the CPS to take custody of minders who posed a threat to themselves or others, or could help the CPS maintain emergency-response capability. The statute was unhelpfully silent about what was legally considered a threat, and impressively broad when it pointed to dozens of other statutes for the definition of emergency-response capability.

With that in mind, the data pattern went from disturbing to ominous. Twelve-year-olds with high-level telekinetic- and telepathic-category talents were retested almost one-hundred percent of the time. "Inconclusive" or "retest required" actions had no correlation with the presence or absence of particular testing staff, specialists or not. An astonishingly high number, close to ninety percent, were offered and accepted a scholarship to a CPS Academy, most often to New Kulam, where he'd attended. Only a few high-level patterner-class talents got the same offer, and they were all forecasters.

Lièrén considered what he knew and didn't. In this CPS Testing Center, evidence pointed to a tacit policy of retesting young high-level talents in the telepath and telekinetic categories, and most ended up in the Academy. What Lièrén couldn't figure out was why they retested at all. Only six percent had different results, usually slightly better. It seemed unlikely that the retests were because of faulty equipment, or assurance that the prospective student deserved to go to an Academy. Without data from other testing centers, it was impossible to determine if this was a bigger pattern or just a local anomaly.

Lièrén rubbed his temples, wondering when his headache had started. Being stuck in Spires had more than just upended his ordered life, it had upended his faith in the institution to which he'd devoted two-thirds of his life.

If he'd stumbled across this data six months ago, he'd have discounted it as an isolated aberration, and been certain that CPS oversight would discover and correct it. But they'd missed his own partner's long-running, deep corruption, and now at least five years of very questionable procedures from a testing center in the galactic government's capitol. He had to wonder what else the CPS was missing.

A glance at the clock made him realize that either someone was tampering with the building systems, or he'd spent nearly three hours in his deep data dive. No wonder his head hurt. And now his stomach was complaining about being empty, and he realized he'd forgotten to take his drugs again. The latest regimen called for midday doses, and since he'd forgotten to eat lunch, he'd also forgotten to take his drugs. He couldn't take them without food, or his stomach rebelled violently.

The current drug protocol didn't seem to have any noticeable talent-regulation aspects—his sifter talent, especially, felt constantly powered, like a low-level speaker hum, and he had to consciously remember to contain it when in crowds so as not to exhaust himself. He was grateful for the thick, dense walls of the CPS building, which were designed to give minders some relief. At least the current drug side effects were limited to temporary nausea and the occasional vivid dream if he slept too long. He didn't know whether to report it to the medics or not. He definitely wouldn't report forgetting a few doses, unless he was in the mood for another twenty-minute lecture.

He looked at the data analysis on the deskcomp display and decided not to do anything one way or the other with it until he was more clear-headed. In his present surly mood, he was liable to overlook long-term consequences of his actions. He encrypted the queries and results, then disguised and buried them with boring transaction data, a trick learned from a jack crew his field unit had intercepted. The stealth was probably unneeded, but covert field-agent habits were ingrained.

He set the Testing Center data cubes to rebuild overnight, then locked down everything as usual and pulled on his coat. The main office area was deserted, but he thought he sensed a tendril of human presence toward the back rooms, near the utility stairs and lifts. He'd only been through that part of the facility once, when he was still disabled and being shepherded by the physical therapists from the adjacent clinic. Although the CPS buildings looked architecturally separate, a set of connecting hallways deep in the bowels of the third floor linked the field office, the Testing Center, and the clinic. He'd gotten the impression that it was frowned upon to use the connecting doors for ordinary traffic, but the therapists had been ordered to bring him to the field office to meet Supervisor Yamazaki, and hadn't wanted to take him and his gravchair around through a rainstorm.

As he often did lately, he ended his metro ride one platform early, deciding the solo walk would be better than dealing with the gaggle of noisy tourists headed to the glitzy joy palace district. A small Mediterranean restaurant on his path was happy to prepare takeout, so he could silence his stomach.

He wished he could silence his thoughts as easily. Derrit Sesay gave real and personal meaning to dry statistical trends. It was highly likely the CPS would offer Derrit a full scholarship to New Kulam, and Lièrén knew Imara would ask him about it, since she knew he'd been there.

If he told Imara the CPS Academy would be good for Derrit, it would be a lie by misdirection, because while the training was rigorous and thorough, the warm, nurturing, funny kid Lièrén had come to know would be miserable in the rigidly structured environment. Even if Imara moved to New Kulam to be near her son, the CPS required students to live in the dorms with other students, and limited outside communication as too much of a distraction. She'd be lucky to see him once every three weeks.

On the other hand, if Lièrén told Imara to refuse the scholarship offer, it was appallingly likely the Testing Center would invoke the "emergency" statute and simply take Derrit, leaving Imara to guess which of the twelve academies throughout the galaxy he'd been assigned to. Lièrén remembered something about an appeals process in the statute, but that would take time, money, and an advocate as good as Patwardan. He'd gladly pay for the advocate, but he doubted Imara would even be speaking to him at that point, much less accept assistance from him, considering who his employer was.

He turned a corner toward the restaurant and was surprised to see the overhead lighting strip on his side of the street was dark. Infrastructure failures were rare in Spires. From what Imara had said, the local government had road crews on call twenty-four hours a day to maintain the "City of Light." He crossed at the intersection to the well-lit side and picked up his pace. He hadn't heard about any more casualties in his field unit lately, but reasonable caution never hurt. He stepped around what looked like a crate that had fallen off a ground hauler, taking him closer to a narrow alley.

He was surprised by the sudden awareness of someone behind him, and then pain as his arm was grabbed and forced behind him, and a sear of pain on his neck, accompanied by the sizzling sound of a powered shockstick.

"Comps, jewelry, chips. *Now*," growled his large attacker, dragging him sideways into the darkness of the alley.

While Lièrén's brain froze, stunned, his body at least knew to elbow back into what felt like flesh-covered concrete. The man grunted in reaction before jabbing Lièrén's shoulder with the shockstick. Lièrén yelled in pain and tried to twist away, stomping on the man's instep, powered by the weight of his pilot-style boots. The man grunted again and forced Lièrén's arm higher, sending Lièrén's shoulder into a cascade of agony. "Quit!" snarled the man, as the flange of the shockstick scraped Lièrén's jaw and ear.

Lièrén's mind finally engaged. Adrenalin fueled his anger and fluxed his sifter talent. He swamped the man's cortex with a flood of conflicting brain chemicals, causing him to involuntarily relax and sink, twitching, to his knees, then fold over and down to sprawl sideways on the mud-spattered walkway.

Lièrén stumbled away several steps. He turned to look at his attacker, who was even larger than Lièrén had guessed. The loose black clothes did little to hide the extreme musculature that probably owed a lot to body shop mods. Lièrén could feel the man's brain struggling, like an upended turtle, to right itself and regain equilibrium. At least he had no minder talent to get in the way. Lièrén reached out with his sifter talent and adjusted the chemicals so the man would stay down and happily oblivious. Lièrén was surprised it worked from that distance, but he pushed that thought aside for now.

With someone gunning for members of his field unit, it would be foolish not to consider the possibility this was an attempt to kill him. The other deaths had been made to look like anything except murder, so a "random" fatal mugging fit the pattern. Someone could have been watching Lièrén and arranged the attack based on Lièrén's stupid-in-hindsight tendency toward routine.

On the other hand, it was equally plausible his attacker saw an opportunity in the streetlight problem and used the fortuitous alley to waylay any solitary tourist that came by, counting on surprise and his size to subdue his victims. The thickness of the building walls effectively muted the man's mental signature from most minders. From what the local police had said when he'd worked with them, mugging inattentive tourists was the criminal element's unofficial pastime.

Ignoring the agony of his abused shoulders and burned neck, Lièrén energized his telepathic talent. Mind delving had always been Fiyon's job, but Lièrén at least knew techniques. He took a half step closer, but was distracted when his foot nudged something. He cautiously stooped to pick up the shockstick. The long, slender tube felt cold in his hand.

He didn't know what to do. He was an interrogation specialist, not a retriever, and unused to physical fights in dark alleys. *Think*, he ordered himself. He needed to know if the attack was random or targeted. He needed to manage the attacker, because he needed skin-to-skin contact to use his low-level telepathy.

That decided, he used his sifter talent to keep the man feeling safe, content, and unfocused. He gripped the shockstick in his right hand and primed it, then slowly and carefully moved closer to the man's prone form. If anyone came into the alley, Lièrén could honestly say the man had spoken, then passed out. He touched his fingertips to the inside wrist of the man's outstretched hand. He resisted the reflexive habit to close his eyes, willing himself to stay aware of his surroundings. He'd be safely in the restaurant if he'd done that a few minutes ago, but better late than never.

It was a tricky balance to keep his subject dopey, but coherent enough for a low-level telepathic probe to be effective, all while warily watching for passersby. The man's recent memories had him waiting impatiently in the alley, just beyond the light, with a powerful anticipation that someone would walk by. Lièrén floundered a bit, trying to find a time or association thread. Finally, he found one that led back to a memory of a meeting with a shadowy figure in a dark pub. Vink, as he thought of himself, slid the figure something of value, maybe a cashflow chip, and the figure... Lièrén was startled to realize Vink's memory had been twisted. Lièrén might not have noticed, but the join between the twist and the normal memory web was rough. He examined it with his own twister talent, hoping the other twister had left dangling strands to trace, but unfortunately, that part of the twist had been thorough.

Lièrén heard multiple voices and laughter in the distance and knew he was out of time. Getting caught in the alley with a sifter-doped mugger wouldn't do his CPS field career any good. Lièrén twisted Vink's memory so he'd think he'd over-chemmed and passed out before ever seeing Lièrén. Not elegant, but it would do. A louder shout from the street made him hastily use his sifter talent to knock the man cold, which would last fifteen or twenty minutes, followed by another hour of grogginess. Vink would wake with a nasty headache and be hung over for a day, both of which Lièrén thought were richly deserved.

As he got to the alley entrance, he realized he was still carrying the shockstick. He considered leaving it in the alley, but didn't want to take the chance of children finding it. He ducked back into the shadows long enough to switch it off and collapse it, then stuck it in the cargo pocket of his pants. Even those simple movements made his wrenched shoulder scream. He couldn't go into the restaurant and not cause a stir with his battered appearance, so it was either summon an autocab to go to the CPS clinic for a healer, or walk to his hotel room for a self-heating pouch of soup. It was the return of the rain that swayed him. The hotel was two short blocks away, and his hotel bed was warm and soft.

He pulled the asymmetric lapel of his fitted overcoat closed and hunched over as much as his abused shoulders would let him and walked more slowly than he wanted to, aware that the glass walkways were always slicker with rain, regardless of the city's claims to the contrary.

Too bad he hadn't learned anything useful from his probes. Vink's altered memory was suspicious, but he likely had dangerous associates with dangerous talents and secrets to protect. He could have been telepathically tricked into attacking Lièrén. Shocksticks weren't lethal, but maybe he'd had a second weapon. Lièrén kicked himself for not thinking to check Vink's pockets.

He was feeling muddled, probably because he hadn't used all three of his minder talents at once since he left the Academy. The rain became a deluge, and his coat was feeling heavier with each step, as if it was absorbing instead of shedding the water. At least the rain took some of the sting out of the scrape on his face.

After what seemed like an endless trek, Lièrén gratefully walked through a familiar doorway, but the carpet color was wrong. He looked up, confused. Instead of the hotel lobby, he realized his feet had taken him straight to the Quark and Quasar's street door. He stood, blinking against the lights, taxing the floor mat's capacity to soak up the puddle he was leaving. He needed to go to his room, but his coat was wet, and it was raining outside.

CHAPTER 12

* Planet: Concordance Prime * GDAT 3238.218 *

IT WAS AN average night at the bar, with a dozen customers spread out among the tables and booths. Imara scrubbed a tabletop, wondering how one of their valued patrons had managed to permanently discolor the supposedly stainless surface. The side door opened and closed, and she glanced up to see who it was. It took her a moment to realize it was Lièrén Sòng. Instead of moving, he just stood there, dripping like he'd been swimming, looking almost as pale as he had the first week he'd been out of the medical center. She left the cleaning towel on the table and moved closer.

"Lièrén? What's wrong?"

He blinked once. "I tripped," he said. "I should go to my room." His words were a little slow, like he'd chemmed with canab, but his diction was as precise as always and his pupils were normal.

"Let's get you out of that coat." She unfastened the top clasp. Lièrén fumbled at one of the lower clasps, but she had all the rest undone by the time he finished the one. She started to push the coat off his shoulder, but he hissed in pain. His neck was burned and bleeding sluggishly. A cut on his jaw and earlobe oozed more blood.

She raised an eyebrow and started to ask him what the hell was going on, but hesitated. He wouldn't appreciate being the center of attention. Not taking her eyes off of him, she yelled over her shoulder. "Rayle, take over for a few minutes."

She gently finished pulling the sodden coat off, then hung it on the hook and switched on the solardry. His black resilk tunic, shiny with dampness, clung to his chest like a second skin. The color hid the blood.

"Come with me," she ordered, in a tone that left no room for argument. She turned and headed toward the bar's storeroom, glancing back once or twice to make sure he was following.

As she passed Derrit, she said, "Help Rayle, please."

Derrit took one look at Lièrén and his eyes grew round. "Sure."

Imara led Lièrén into the narrow storeroom, then had him sit on the stepstool.

"What else hurts besides your neck and face?" she asked, as she opened the first-aid kit and looked through the burn patches, trying to find the long, skinny ones.

He straightened up a little from his slump. "I'll be all right."

"True, but you aren't now," she said with asperity. "What is it with you men not wanting to admit you're in pain?"

She selected the longest patch and handed it to him. "Hold this." She pulled open the top magnetic snap of his tunic and gently peeled it out of the way. She pulled the burn patch's activator strip, then laid it gently on the brown-edged oozing burn. "It'll beep when it's ready to come off."

He gritted his teeth as the burn patch did its job. She belatedly remembered that he'd said painkillers didn't work on him. The patch was designed to numb first, then scrub. It probably hurt like farkin' hell.

"Sorry," she said softly, suppressing an impulse to touch him, as if that could take away the pain she'd caused. She shoved her tingling fingers in the pockets of her vest.

"It's okay," he said. "It needed cleaning, regardless."

"Want us to dry your tunic? It's sopping."

He started to shrug, but winced instead. "Dry would be nice."

She carefully undid the rest of the tunic's snaps and peeled it off his right shoulder, which turned out to have a nasty red welt, likely from whatever had caused the neck injury above it. Any number of things could have caused the scrape along his jaw and across his ear. She pushed the shirt down his arms, slowing when she heard him breathe in sharply. His skin was cool where her fingers brushed it, and she had the feeling his back and shoulders were stiffening up.

Despite the fact that she was annoyed with him for hiding things, Imara found part of her mind was memorizing every detail about Lièrén's nicely shaped shoulders and chest, and the lean taper to his waist. *Focus*, she told herself sternly as she hung his wet tunic on a nearby cabinet handle.

A burn patch wouldn't help the red welt. He was starting to shiver. She looked around the storeroom for something he could wear, but there was nothing.

"Stay," she ordered, then stepped back into the bar and caught Derrit's eye. He came to her immediately, with a serious expression.

"Is Agent Sòng hurt?" he asked. Derrit was unhappy when adults in his life were unwell.

"A little scuffed up. Right now, he's cold. Bring him a cup of hot green tea, and ask Rayle to heat one of the orange knit tablecloths. Oh, and re-hang Agent Sòng's coat so it dries faster." That would give him something to do instead of worrying.

Derrit took off, and she went back to her patient.

Lièrén gave her a brief, tired smile. "Thank you for… this."

She crossed her arms. "Want to tell me what happened?" she asked, unable to keep the annoyance out of her voice.

"Wrong place, wrong time," he answered, meeting her gaze, then looking away.

She snorted. He was certainly the master of the true-but-unhelpful statement. Still, she'd take that over the zombie-like responses from a few minutes ago. Water was dripping from his wet hair onto his bare chest. She followed a rivulet down, fascinated, then looked away before he noticed. *Transient,* she told herself. *Wandering star. CPS minder hotshot and way out of her spectrum.*

A thought struck her, and she snapped her fingers. "Fluxback. You overused your talent. That's why you were so dopey." She caught herself reaching out to touch his temple and dropped her hand. "How's your head?"

He took a few seconds to answer. "Not bad." He sounded almost surprised. She noticed he didn't deny her diagnosis.

At the sound of Derrit's shuffling footsteps, she moved away from Lièrén. It was crazy, but she could still feel… something from him, like she was at the edge of his heat field. She shook her head. She'd been unsettled lately, distracted by phantom sensations like that. Lièrén wasn't the first, but it was stronger with him right then. Crazy.

Derrit had smartly put the full mug on a little tray to catch spills, but he held it too close to his body, slowing his progress. Imara removed the bright orange tablecloth that he'd slung around his neck and draped it over Lièrén's shoulders, hoping it was soft enough not to irritate his burn. She snagged a shelf hanger clip to secure the ends together as a makeshift cloak. Not pretty, but it would do.

"Thank you," Lièrén said sincerely, taking the proffered mug and holding it near his chest for a moment before taking a sip.

"What happened to your neck?" asked Derrit, staring at the distinctive burn patch.

Against her better judgment, but because she knew Lièrén didn't like to lie, she did it for him.

"Oh, just a little run-in with a cash-and-carry. He'll be fine, *binata*."

Derrit's expression went from distressed to intrigued, but Imara headed off his questions. "Best thing you can do for him right now is help Rayle, so I can finish getting Agent Sòng patched up. You can escort him to his room in a few minutes. Here, take this to the solardry, with his coat." She handed him the damp tunic.

Derrit chewed on his lip and looked at Lièrén once more, then left.

Lièrén was giving her an odd look, and started to speak, then looked down to the floor. "What's a 'cash-and-carry'?" he asked.

"Street thief." She remembered the Mandarin word. "*Fěi.*"

He looked up at her sharply, and she felt a flare of something that she ignored. "You mean I was right? Oh, for Neptune's sake, why didn't you call the... oh." If he'd used his minder talent on the thief, he was guaranteed a trip to the local police lockup, CPS agent or not. "Will the CPS healer keep it confidential?" She narrowed her eyes at him. "You *are* going to see a healer, aren't you?"

He gave her the ghost of a smile. "Yes."

She sighed, suspecting she wasn't going to get any more out of him. And she needed to get out of his orbit, because she was having weird reactions around him, beyond the undeniable physical attraction. She took a step back as she pushed her hair back over her shoulder and re-tightened the elastic ribbon that corralled it. She'd get Rayle to help him.

"Have you ever heard of a minder polymath?" Lièrén asked suddenly.

She pulled the definition up out of her memory. "Full spectrum of talents. Rare, according to the CPS propa... uh, presentation." He'd already admitted to three talents, and whatever he did for the CPS, it was patently more than just administrative work. "Are you a polymath?" she asked quietly.

The corner of Lièrén's mouth twitched. "No, but you are." Before she could react to that, he continued. "I've been distrusting what my talent has been telling me for weeks. First because of the accident, then because of changes in drug protocols. I felt all your talents when Derrit stopped shielding you, but I thought it was my mistake."

"You think *I'm* a polymath?" She shook her head. "You're sun struck. Testing would have caught it."

"Polymaths usually don't develop their full range until they're in their late twenties or early thirties. Your filer talent was strong, and that's all the testers noticed. The others came later, I'd bet. They're low-level, but they're there. All classes."

She gave him a sharp, skeptical look, but he seemed to be serious. "I see. And I didn't notice all these wonderful extra talents because…" She trailed off, challenging him to explain that one.

"Because you were shielded by Derrit until four days ago, and your husband before that. Blocked."

She thought a moment. "Nice theory, but Derrit would've had to have been shielding me since he was five."

He shrugged, then winced, clearly regretting the movement. "You didn't know to look for them."

"Look, you're hurt, I've got a long shift ahead of me, and the storeroom isn't exactly private. We can talk about this later." *After you've seen the mind shop therapist about your delusions.* "Finish your tea, and I'll send someone with your shirt." She gave him a teasing smile. "That tablecloth would ruin your style cred forever."

Actually, he could be wearing a space exosuit, and she'd still think he was plasma hot. Which is why she needed to keep her distance more than ever. She left the storeroom quickly and went to find her son.

* * * * *

There may have been a worse time for Lièrén to tell Imara about her polymath talents, but he couldn't think of one off hand. She obviously thought he was addled, and he couldn't blame her. Up until the attack and its aftermath, he'd still been distrusting his talents, clinging to what he thought he knew about them. He pulled the tablecloth up on his shoulders a little and finished the last of the tea.

He'd used all three of his talents simultaneously that evening, and the only consequence had been temporary exhaustion, the dopiness that Imara had noticed. No killer headache, no hypersensitivity to synaptic haze from other people, no light sensitivity. Even when contained, his sifter talent was detecting far more nuances and details, like the angular margins and strength of Derrit's natural shields, or the soft and subtle texture variations of Imara's multiple talents. Using his telepathy on the attacker had been comfortable, and the twist had been easy. It seemed unlikely that the physical and stress trauma of the accident had improved his minder talents, and the only other major change in his life was the drugs.

Contrary to all he'd been told, all he'd believed, it was glaringly obvious that the CPS minder drugs gave him control but interfered with his talents. Tonight had inadvertently proven the case. He'd forgotten to take his current drugs for the past two days, meaning his talent was unhindered by anything, and it had saved him. Even if he could have used all his talents while on his old drugs, he'd have been huddled in a dark corner somewhere, riding out the after-effect agony.

He felt someone approach and knew without looking that it was Rayle, with the unique signature of his empath talent firing up as he walked in holding Lièrén's dry but now wrinkled shirt.

"I'm fine," Lièrén said, hoping to preempt any questioning. "Just a little worse for wear." He made an effort to contain his roiling emotions. Rayle was close to a high-level empath, and if motivated, could find out anything from Lièrén if he wanted to.

Rayle raised an eyebrow. "And prickly, I see." He held out the shirt.

"Thank you." Lièrén didn't have it in him to be more gracious than that. Most empaths where congenitally nosy because they wanted people to be happy, or at least calm. Lièrén didn't have those in him, either.

He unclipped the hideously bright tablecloth and stood to pull on his mostly dry shirt. His boots, which had turned out to be more decorative than waterproof, made his feet feel like he was standing in a swamp.

Rayle gave him a searching look, then sighed. "Come on, then, *hansamu*. Prove to Imara and Derrit you're functional so they'll quit worrying." He led the way out of the storeroom.

Lièrén followed, folding the tablecloth as he walked. He was uncomfortably aware of his chilly wet pant legs with every step.

Rayle was sidetracked by a customer, so Lièrén continued by himself around to the end of the bar where Imara stood. He offered the tablecloth to her with a brief bow.

"I am very grateful for your kindness," he said, hoping she'd understand he was thanking her for both the first aid and her discretion. The bar's ambient glowlights made her eyes sparkle and highlighted her beautifully intelligent face and wide mouth. Her expression softened as she met his gaze, and he wanted to kiss her senseless. He really had the worst timing.

"You're welcome," she said. Several of her talents—sifter, empath, and healer—stirred, like sudden sparks, then quieted. She'd probably think it was ordinary intuition. "If you don't mind, I'll send Derrit with you to your room. He needs to see you're all right." She hugged the tablecloth to her chest as she watched Derrit carefully take Lièrén's coat off the hook near the door. "He's had a disappointing day."

Lièrén had completely forgotten the "inconclusive" test results, and what his data dive had discovered.

"Yes, of course," he said, despair crashing into him. The CPS Testing Center had already set its hook in Derrit, and would reel him in, one way or another. And the Academy would make sure he stayed in the CPS fold, one way or another, as they'd done to Lièrén himself.

He looked away, fighting to keep from broadcasting his feelings or letting them show on his face. It was almost a relief when Derrit approached, carrying the still damp coat. His naturally strong shields dampened Imara's sparking empathy. Lièrén desperately wanted to tell Imara what was coming, but he couldn't prove any of it without destroying his career and getting himself blackholed, and the CPS would still have her son. He wasn't a violent man, but he had a growing urge to kick something.

"I appreciate your assistance," Lièrén told Derrit. "Shall we?"

Derrit led the way through the wide doorway that led to the hotel lobby, and Lièrén followed without a backward glance at Imara, unable to look at her without feeling guilty.

Derrit carried the coat so carefully that Lièrén felt like he was part of a procession of two as they traveled the halls to his first-floor room. He could have moved to a more desirable upper floor once he was no longer an invalid, but he'd enjoyed the illusion of stability that staying in the same suite had created.

Derrit turned around to face him while walking backward for a few steps. "If you tape something opaque on the shower door sensor, it'll stay open, and you could put your coat on it so it'll hang over the solardry." Derrit turned back around, so Lièrén moved faster to catch up with him.

"I'll try it. Did you come up with that?"

"Rayle. He comes in all stinky from rehearsals." He lowered his voice. "Staff isn't supposed to be in the guest rooms, but…"

"He probably heard about it from a guest," Lièrén said firmly, to stop Derrit from saying anything more. Since the hotel was approved for CPS staff, Lièrén had no doubt that the premises had comprehensive security monitoring, beyond the obvious security eyes that littered the hotel public areas.

Derrit caught on right away. "Oh yeah, I'm sure *that's* where he learned it," he said, delighting in the small conspiracy. Lièrén nodded and winked, but couldn't enjoy the moment for long. If the local CPS Testing Center ran true to form, Derrit would be on his way to the Academy at New Kulam inside of ten days. Lièrén doubted he had the clout, even as a covert agent, to be allowed to visit Derrit any more often than his mother would.

When they arrived at the door to his suite, he unsealed it and accepted the coat from Derrit. Though it felt like another small betrayal, he held out his hand for a handshake. "Thank you, Master Derrit, for your excellent care."

Derrit shook hands with enthusiasm. "My pleasure, Agent Sòng." He turned away, then turned back. "We're synced for tomorrow night, right?"

Lièrén nodded and waved as Derrit skipped away.

In the suite, Lièrén found the shower door trick worked well, and ten minutes later, he hung the dry coat in the storage wall.

Although it was tempting to just dowse the lights and crawl in bed with the covers over his head, he pulled out his prepaid percomp and started a list. Tomorrow would probably be the last training session with Derrit, and he wanted to tell him as much as possible to help him fit in at the Academy faster than Lièrén had.

CHAPTER 13

LIÈRÉN STARED AT the deskcomp's display without really seeing it. He'd been tinkering around the edges of the final Testing Center dataset, ostensibly to spot check normalization, but mostly as a cover for his spiraling thoughts. He should be hypercubing the datasets for transfer back to the Testing Center, but he was strongly averse to doing anything to make it easier for the staff to identify and target any other minder children.

He'd spent a sleepless night, trying and failing to come up with a way to prepare Imara and protect Derrit. Painstaking, anonymous searches of the net had brought a tangled jungle of opinions and a barren wasteland of facts. What few friends he'd had at the Minder Institute were ten years gone. He'd have once said Fiyon was his friend, which was painfully laughable in light of his betrayal. He had no relationships with the rest of his coworkers, in part, he suspected, because Fiyon had deliberately kept him isolated. His sister Nàiměi was too practical, and Rayle was too impractical. He'd be willing to put up with his great-grandfather's disapproval to ask his advice, except with the CPS involved, Sòng Tiān Cì's prejudices would get in the way.

And on top of everything else, Lièrén's life was about to change again. At his morning checkup, after the healer had repaired his assault injuries from the night before, the coordinating medic announced he'd been medically cleared for return to duty, and had notified the CPS. She'd told him he could eat, drink, or do anything his body would let him, and gave him a list of CPS-approved body shops that could remove the last of the scars. She even waived his final drug tests, saying his regular medic would set up a new schedule, and would most likely be adjusting his drug protocol yet again. The medic's demeanor said she expected Lièrén to be happy, and he'd sincerely thanked her for the excellent care she and her staff had provided. Even three weeks ago, it would have been good news. Back when Lièrén was complacently ignorant of several unpleasant truths.

By the time he'd arrived at the office, he'd already received a formal memo from Talavara, the field unit's acting supervisor, welcoming him back, but saying that because of the recent "staff transitions," an appalling euphemism for four deaths, the unit's next interim base of operations hadn't yet been selected. Lièrén was instructed to stay in the hotel but be ready to leave at a moment's notice. Talavara's memo didn't mention the Office of Internal Inquiry case, and he realized he hadn't heard from them since they'd canceled the appointment scheduled for a few days ago."

He dutifully filed a report of the previous night's robbery attempt and worded it to imply his escape had resulted more from the assailant's incompetence and Lièrén's physical skill than from his minder talents. He omitted his possibly paranoid and certainly unprovable suspicion that the assault might have been targeted at him, not random. Covert field agents were expected to take care of small matters themselves.

The walls of his tiny temporary office were closing in on him, and he was repeatedly distracted by his awareness of the synaptic activity of the staff in the main area. He was having to re-learn how to control and contain his talent without the drugs. It was a price worth paying if it made him safer because his talent wasn't impaired. Making a snap decision, he locked the deskcomp and headed out of the building to a public comm center, planning to leave a message for Advocate Patwardan.

He avoided the closer comm center that catered to noisy tourists, choosing instead to walk a few blocks farther to a less crowded corporate center. He took advantage of its premium service offerings and paid for a silenced booth with real-time secure-link vid capabilities and sent the ping. Just as he was composing a message in his head, Patwardan unexpectedly answered in person. The high-quality holo made her look and sound almost real.

"I thought you might be in touch, though not quite so soon," she said. "I got a copy of the return-to-duty notice." The slight disarray of her short hair and shirt suggested she was in low-G, probably on her ship.

He thanked her for taking the call, then told her about the internal memo from Talavara, and the lack of anything at all from the OII.

"It's probably good news," she said. "Your supervisor wouldn't take you back if the OII wasn't satisfied."

Lièrén wasn't so sure about that, considering Talavara's antipathy toward the OII. "Is there some way to be assured of official closure?"

"Yes, and no," said Patwardan, her distinctive Hindi accent giving her a lilting tone. "Policy requires the OII to issue a determination of findings, which is supposed to mean they're done with you, but unofficially, they'll probably keep an eye on you for as long as they feel like. Any more deaths in your unit?"

"No," he said, then twitched the corner of his mouth. "But the day's not over."

She grinned. "You're an unexpectedly funny man, Field Agent Sòng." Her hand lifted into view holding a coffee cup, and she took a sip. "You need to be thinking about what else you want to do in the CPS, in case you can't return to your field unit."

He took a sharp, shallow breath. "Have you heard something about my case?" He tried to keep his face calm.

She shook her head. "No, it's something I tell all my clients. The CPS can be like a two-story megatank rolling down your path. You'll have to get out of the way, regardless, so it's better to plan the direction of your new path, rather than jump and hope for the best."

He nodded, marginally relieved. "Wise advice. I'll give it some thought."

"Anything else?"

He was strongly tempted to ask her if she knew anything about the CPS's use of the emergency conscription clause for minder children, but he remembered her pointed comment about telepaths illegally fishing in her head if the CPS was sufficiently motivated. He didn't want anything on record, and he didn't want Patwardan to be vulnerable because of him. It was his dilemma to deal with.

"No, but thank you for your time," he said. After promising to send a copy of Talavara's memo, he signed off.

He took the long way to walk back to the office, since it was good practice in containing his talents, while he considered alternative career options. He'd once imagined he'd be offered an Academy instructor position, but his twist talent had sent him into field work. If he'd just been a high-level sifter, he might have ended up at one of the thousands of minder clinics throughout the galaxy, or perhaps been assigned to the Kameleon program, about which he'd heard more rumor than fact. He was overqualified to work in a Testing Center, but even if he could miraculously swing a transfer to that division, he wouldn't be able to save Derrit.

And if he couldn't do that, it didn't really matter where the CPS sent him.

The wind picked up, a harbinger of more rain. Lièrén pulled his light jacket closed and hurried along the walkway toward the field office's nondescript front door. Wherever they sent him, he wouldn't miss the rain.

Back in his temporary office, which hadn't become more spacious in his absence, he was surprised to receive yet another memo. After six weeks of no contact, he'd suddenly become quite popular.

The Minder Corps division chief directed him to report to the High Spires CPS office in three days to meet with a regional CPS supervisor named Jane Pennington-Smythe regarding a "routine audit" of Fiyon Machimata's records. Since "audit" was the OII's code word for investigation, it looked like the OII had finally discovered Machimata's corruption. The memo didn't say whether or not Talavara would be there.

If it wasn't a formal OII action, he couldn't request Patwardan's presence, but he sent her a copy, anyway. He spent some time researching "Jane PS," as she'd informally been referred to in the memo. Her official record and unofficial rumors in the employee back channels said she was a powerful CPS manager with an insistence on correct procedure and a reputation for seeing justice done. He wanted to believe she'd do the same for the victims of Fiyon Machimata, but Lièrén's faith in the CPS was shaky.

For his own protection, he needed to know if the field unit had been working on any of his and Machimata's cases since the accident. He activated his CPS-issued secure percomp to access the covert field-unit files, only to discover his permissions had finally been revoked in all but a few administrative areas. Fortunately, when he used his prepaid percomp to try, he discovered they'd once again overlooked the auditor account.

Not wasting any time, he made an innocuous-looking package of the unit's current case notes, manually encrypted it, then hid it deep in one of the administrative areas his regular account was allowed to be in. To cover his tracks, he copied the package into the administrative areas of random employees. Lièrén altered the audit account credentials before signing off. The account could eventually be recovered, but he hoped the transactions would be discounted as routine audit tests. He used his CPS percomp to sign back in as himself and downloaded all data he was allowed. From there, he transferred the files to his prepaid percomp, with its better security and data divers, and applied a second encryption scheme that would require his cooperation to unlock.

There were dozens of other covert field units across the galaxy, but he was of the growing conviction that the CPS wouldn't be putting him in any of them. He couldn't admit, even to his advocate, that he'd been manipulated and assaulted by his partner, unless he wanted to fatally compromise his credibility. No one would believe he was blameless, even if he permitted a parade of telepaths to rummage through his mind at will. With Fiyon dead, Lièrén doubed he'e ever get the full story. The CPS probably wouldn't, either.

The old adage that where there was gravity, there was mass, was as true as ever. There would always be people who would suspect Lièrén's chief ability was being too clever to be caught. About the best he could hope for would be to take Patwardan's advice and influence his place of exile. After Spires, a desert planet might be an improvement.

What made it all so galling was that he still believed in the mission of the CPS Minder Corps, to deploy minder talents to help keep the galactic peace, where planetary governments had no jurisdiction and the brute force of the military was counterproductive. With the twelve years left on his present contract, he could either endure, or he could use the time to look for opportunities to improve the CPS from within.

All things considered, he wasn't sure he'd want another field-unit post, if he had the choice. The loss of the excitement and seeing the galaxy would be replaced by a regular schedule, a real home base, and actually helping people who needed it.

Which brought his carousel of thoughts back to Derrit and Imara. He dreaded the session with Derrit, because he'd have to be very careful to hide his knowledge and worries from the boy. Not to mention from Imara, with her flaring multiple talents, several of which would detect his turmoil right away. He abhorred the thought of having to lie to her, even by omission, but telling her everything would change nothing.

He was selfish enough to want to keep her good opinion of him, even if he would never see her again after tonight.

* * * * *

Imara glanced toward the bar's netcomps, where Derrit was collaborating via the net with two classmates on a school project. He was animated and happy, making her glad he'd taken after his father in enjoying working with people. Some of Torin's shielder friends had been one step up from sand lizards as far as social interaction skills.

Derrit's tutoring session was usually around eight, and Lièrén had requested her presence for part of it. She wondered if he was going to offer to teach her, too, considering he claimed she was a minder polymath. After thinking about it for a day, she was cautiously ready to entertain the possibility that he might be right. It would explain the weird sensations she'd been noticing, like feeling a foggy heat wave when Rackkar Horis, her volatile road-crew chief, lost his temper, or the comfortable coolness of Derrit's natural shields. The effects were distracting. Most likely, her extra talents would end up being about as useful as screen windows on an interstellar transport.

From her vantage point behind the bar, Imara covertly watched Lièrén as he nursed a chilled barleywine, the first kicker she'd ever seen him indulge in. He was wearing all black, though the back-cinched grey tunic with its wing shoulders and high collar saved him from looking like an off-duty gunnin from CGC Military Command. He'd arrived at his usual time and spent a few minutes chatting with her and Rayle before snagging a big booth near the outside door, the only one available. He never sat at tables, she'd noticed, even when plenty were available. He'd said all that was polite, and laughed at one of the odd music selections that slipped in via the bar's overly-broad music selection algorithm. For all that, something was off about him, and it wasn't just her supposed talents telling her so. She was annoyed to catch herself watching him again, and sternly told herself to look somewhere else.

Rayle brought a tray around to the large sink and gave it a quick spray. "All anyone wants to talk about is the Mabingion Purge thing." He shook the tray to get the water off, then stored it in its slot. "That, or the TSAC march."

"Tell me about it," said Imara, feelingly. "But you have to give that news magazine credit for putting it together." She admired the stubborn persistence it must have taken to track down the facts on so many planets.

Rayle leaned against the end of the bar, where he could see any patron who might need him. "Yeah, no way the CPS can get away with saying it was just coincidence that *thirty* some-odd planets had riots that just *happened* to kill a few hundred Minder Corps veterans in each one."

Imara nodded. "At least it wasn't thousands killed, like on Mabingion. 'Isolated procedure failure,' my ass." Imara finished loading the quicksan with glassware and started it. "I've heard Ridderth is a city-planning nightmare and rotten with corruption, so I might have believed that one, but thirty-eight 'riots' in a two-year period isn't a procedure failure, it's institutional policy."

"I bet the Spires journos are fluxed." He gave her a sharp smile. "Nothing like an exploding newstrend to get politicians to improvise on planet-wide broadcast. Like that High Command general this morning who said the dead were all part of a terrorist minder uprising."

Imara snorted. "Oh, I hadn't heard that one." She put the paring knife back in its slot. "I don't know if it was luck or planning that put the TSAC march on the one-year anniversary of the Spires' riots, but they're genius at exploiting newstrend bandwidth."

She noticed Lièrén stand and head their way. She signaled Rayle with a quick glance. He turned and smiled. "Hey, *hansamu*, what can I get you?"

A corporate-suited, dark-haired man at the bar who'd been following their conversation chimed in. "I'll tell you who's a genius. That dobber who wrote that book on the Collectors. He's been selling billions." His distinct Scots accent sounded exactly like the singers of the some of the piped-in music.

"Water with lime, please," said Lièrén quietly.

"Is that the book from last year with all those grisly pictures and vids?" asked Rayle with distaste, as he efficiently filled a glass with ice, then water, and added two lime twists, the way Lièrén liked.

The fit-looking corporate man took another pull from his canab inhaler. "No, it's recent. The author's gliding the trend, same as the TSAC. Claims the CPS knew about those pedophile wankers for years and did nothing, and even let one of those putrid pugs escape. You know, the one that nearly killed that military detective."

Imara nodded. "We met the man—Foxe, the investigator that got stabbed. He stayed here at the hotel when he was presenting findings in High Court. He was healed by then, of course, but he still seemed… fragile."

"If even half of what that book said is true," said corporate man, "then I'm thinkin' the frellin' CPS needs a freighter's worth of frontier justice visited on their heads."

Imara felt a sudden wave of emotion, maybe distress, coming from Lièrén. Rayle glanced at him curiously but said nothing. She hadn't thought Lièrén was so sensitive about his employer. She glanced at the clock and saw it was nearly time for the tutoring session.

"I'll send Derrit now and be there in a few minutes, if that's all right."

"Yes, of course." Lièrén nodded to her, then gave Rayle murmured thanks for the water and headed back to his booth. The wave of feeling was gone as if it had never existed. Her talents were ruled by chaos, because they certainly weren't ruled by her. She had no idea how to use her empath talent, or any of the others Lièrén had mentioned. She hadn't told Derrit or

Rayle yet about being a polymath, in part because she still only half believed it herself.

She went around to the net terminals where Derrit still sat and put a hand on his shoulder. "Agent Sòng is waiting for you." She pointed to the big booth next to the street door, in case he hadn't noticed where Lièrén was sitting.

Derrit grinned up at her as he pulled off the earwires and stuffed them in his pocket. "Maybe he'll show me how to do better on the test tomorrow."

"I bet you'll do well, even without his help." She ruffled the pointed locks of his determinedly springy hair. "I'll be over soon."

She went back to the bar to get a mixed fruit juice blend for the young girl at Table C-2 and to tell Rayle she was taking her break.

The corporate man stood. He was taller than she'd thought, and had a willowy build. "It's a nice place you have here," he said to Rayle as he settled his tab. "The restaurant still open?"

Rayle angled himself away from the security camera. "Yes, until eleven," he said, but subtly shook his head and drew his hand across his throat. Imara had a hard time keeping a straight face.

The corporate man gave Rayle a sly grin and a wink. "Thank you, laddie." He crooked an eyebrow suggestively and rested a thumb on his belt with his fingers pointed downward, drawing subtle attention to his crotch. "I think I'll have a short lie-down first. Care to help me find my room? I might get lost."

Rayle smiled regretfully. "I'd get just as lost, I'm afraid, and management wouldn't be happy. How about a token for the Red Blossom just up the walk?"

"No, that's too far. Another time, then," said the man with a wink.

Rayle sighed dramatically as he watched the attractive man leave. "Just how I like them, too. Comfortable in their own skin." He took the glass of fruit juice from her and waved toward Lièrén's booth. "Go see what Agent Flux-Hot wants. Find out what's got him upset and fix it."

He often teased her about her penchant for problem-solving. She didn't mind. It was better than wailing and moaning or hoping someone else would do it.

She poured herself a glass of spicy tomato juice to tide her over until she got a chance to eat. "Don't give away the store," she said, smiling. He curled his tongue at her in exasperation as he walked away.

CHAPTER 14

* Planet: Concordance Prime * GDAT 3238.219 *

LIÈRÉN WATCHED IMARA approach and did his level best to keep his emotions contained and his attention focused. Serenity wasn't in his repertoire that evening. Neither was enjoyment in what he needed to tell her.

"I'd like to talk to you about the CPS Academy, in case Derrit is offered a scholarship." He should have eased them into the subject, but he only had that evening. His plan, if it could be called that, was to convince Imara that she had to give up everything and go to wherever Derrit was sent, without admitting the other choices were worse.

Derrit's eyes rounded in surprise. "But I failed…" He glanced at his mother. "The tests were inconclusive."

"I had to go back a second time, too," Lièrén said. "Perhaps it's common with high-level talents."

Imara looked thoughtful and attentive. He activated his sifter talent so he'd know if her talents flared. He couldn't hide his turbulent emotions from an experienced empath like Rayle, and good sifters would notice the vague haze of discord about him, but he was hoping Imara hadn't worked out how to use her talents yet.

The downside was that it opened him to feeling the presence of everyone in the bar, and the unique signatures of the three people in the booth behind him, in addition to Imara and Derrit. Not to mention the brushes of all the latent talents in the room. It was almost like being back in school, struggling to control his untamed talents.

"The Academy will offer a contract. I remember my parents negotiating, so the CPS can be flexible."

She tilted her head slightly. "What's not negotiable?"

As usual, she'd jumped right to the heart of the matter. He needed to pick his path carefully, because she was smart and quick. "Derrit will have to live on campus with the other students for the first three years."

Derrit frowned, looking at his mother. Lièrén guessed he was remembering his promise to look after her, which would be impossible if he was in the Academy. She was quiet for a long moment, then gave Lièrén a considering look. "How often did you see your family?"

"Twice a year. My closest relatives were three interstellar days away."

She gasped. "Three *days*? What were your parents thinking?" She instantly looked regretful. "Sorry, that was rude."

The outside door behind the booth side where Imara and Derrit were sitting opened. Lièrén's sifter talent was suddenly overwhelmed by a shockwave of violence from the tall man who'd entered. The characteristic rising shriek of a beamfire weapon assaulted his ears.

"Down!" he hissed, throwing himself sideways and sliding under the table. He pulled Derrit's ankles down and shoved his smaller body against the wall. Imara was already rolling under the table with them when the room reverberated with a hail of projectile impacts. Did the man have two weapons?

"Motherfucking CPS!" shouted the man. The continuous waves of violent haze felt like howling wind as Lièrén struggled to control his sifter sense. The acrid smell of beamfire residue made his nose sting, meaning the shooter had a combo-gun. He pulled Imara up against Derrit and huddled over them as best he could. He heard hot debris rain down on the table above them. He felt Derrit's shielder talent expand to his mother, and hers, though weaker, did the same for her son. For a half second, their familiar synaptic harmonies touched him at the deepest level, and he wanted to be a part of it. The shooter's yowl of rage shattered the moment.

"You want a riot? I'll give you twisted fucks a riot!" The combo-gun spat again and people screamed. Lièrén tried to focus his sifter talent on the shooter, like he'd done with the street thief, but the man was too far away. He whipped his talent back quickly when he realized the shooter was a strong telepath and maybe a ramper.

"You tell the CPS they reap what they sow!" The man opened the door, fired one more burst that shattered and burned the glass above the bar, and ran out into the rainy night. Silence prevailed for a few heartbeats, and then something in the back crashed. Voices began to rise.

Imara tried to shift under him, but he kept her immobile until his sifter talent confirmed that no one else was broadcasting violence. He retracted his sifter talent as he eased his body back enough to let her move. She partially turned to him and gave him a questioning look.

"It's clear now," said Lièrén.

"Rayle?"

"Near the storeroom, I think." He'd felt Rayle's unique synaptic signature and the flare of empath talent at the edge of his sifter range. He indicated Derrit with a quick warning flick of his eyes. "People were hurt."

Concern and determination warred in her expression. "I have to help."

"I'll stay with him." He crawled out onto the floor, then turned to help Imara slide out.

When her body was only centimeters from his, she paused, her breath warm against his cheek. "What should I tell the police about you?"

Her unexpected protectiveness made him want to close the distance between them and just hold her, but it wasn't the right time or place. "Tell them what you know," he whispered. She only knew his official cover story of being a functionary in a CPS trade office.

She nodded and rose to her feet. Voices were clamoring, accompanied by wailing from the back corner of the bar.

Lièrén, still crouched, held out his hand to Derrit. After a long moment, the boy crawled out. In the light, it became apparent that he had a bloody nose.

Lièrén stood and grabbed a recyclable napkin from the table. "Please accept my apologies for injuring you." He watched to see if Derrit needed help standing, but he had no trouble.

Derrit rolled the napkin into a fat tube and stuffed it up his right nostril. "It's okay. I've had worse. It's easy to fix." He was starting to look around, and Lièrén moved to block his view of the back. Young boys didn't need visions of blood to fuel their nightmares.

"We may as well sit here for a while." He indicated the booth bench facing away from the trouble area. "We can't go anywhere until the police release us."

Derrit sat and slid back toward the wall. "What happened?"

Lièrén grabbed a cloth napkin from the nearby large table and sat next to Derrit. He dipped the napkin in his abandoned glass of water and began carefully wiping the blood from Derrit's face. "You haven't had good luck with your nose lately."

Derrit snorted, and a little blood splattered out of his left nostril. His chin was also scraped.

"I'll get you an ice pack. Stay still so you don't bleed so much."

Lièrén surveyed the situation as he made his way carefully toward the bar. The decorative glowlights had shattered, leaving halos of glass on the floor. A crooked burn traced up the walls and onto the ceiling to his left. Rayle was comforting a woman and her daughter, his empathic talent burning bright. Imara emerged from the hallway with the first-aid kit and placed it on the edge of the bar where it met the wall.

"Cold packs?" he asked her.

"Under the sink to the right. Bring them all out."

He shut down all his talents and steeled himself to turn right to go around the end of the bar. It was worse than he'd imagined. The shooter had been close, and the burn was wide. It curved from the ceiling and dipped to table level in the back two booths. Three people were dead, burned beyond recognition, and another was badly injured. Someone huddled under the table where Derrit sometimes did his schoolwork. The two men in the large booth closest to the door had escaped with only minor injuries from burning fragments blown out by the beamfire.

He spun quickly to a crouch when he heard running feet from the wide lobby entrance behind him. He stood again when he saw it was the hotel's security staff, the same pair who'd handled the chemmed telepath a couple of weeks ago.

The slender, black-skinned man took charge as the short, stocky woman crossed to the street entrance where the shooter had been.

"I'm Security Okonjo, and she's Security Poltorak." He spoke loudly enough for everyone to hear, and made eye contact with several of the patrons. "The police are on their way. The first two medevacs are two minutes out, and our on-call healers and medics will be here any time. Who's not a hotel guest?"

One woman raised her hand, and Okonjo started toward her. Lièrén picked his way through the debris around the end of the bar and stopped near the figure under the table. A black-haired teenage girl was rocking herself, and her plain face was distorted in anguish and wet with tears. He energized his sifter talent and was buffeted by waves of synaptic distress pouring off her. He crouched, so as not to crowd her, and slowly extended his hand to her.

She looked at his hand, then met his eyes. "He burned them," she whispered in Chinese-accented English. He noted a flare of healer talent and realized she'd not only seen the deaths, she'd felt them in her mind.

"What's your name?" he asked softly. He repeated it in Mandarin.

"Sh-sh-sh… Xiàlìng Leung Lǎo." She shook like an exosphere re-entry capsule.

"Xiàlìng, *ràng wǒ lái bāng nǐ.* Let me help you." He infused as much warmth into his tone as he could and moved his hand closer to where one of hers was tightly gripping her knees. She put her trembling hand in his, and he energized his sifter talent to help her brain deal with the flood of conflicting responses to her traumatic experience. Although he wasn't trained, he'd learned some of the technique from his own therapist.

He gentled her transmitters as he helped her to first kneel, then stand, keeping contact with her hand the whole time. He blocked her view of the corner as he took her around the bar and straight to the booth where Derrit sat.

"Xiàlìng, this is Derrit. He's a shielder. I'm going to ask him to help you contain your healer talent until you can control it yourself, all right?"

Derrit's eyes grew round, then he nodded determinedly. He was very much his mother's son.

"Hi, Xiàlìng," he said, moving his legs so she could sit next to him. Lièrén nudged the girl's dopamine levels as he helped her sit. It would take a little while for the adrenalin to flush out of her system. Derrit's shielder talent energized, and the girl visibly relaxed.

Lièrén caught Derrit's eye and gave him a respectful nod of thanks, then turned to go back for the ice packs and see where he was needed next.

CHAPTER 15

"ALL RIGHT, LISTEN up, people. Any filers in here, raise your hands."

Imara sighed and raised her hand. In the larger booth near the entry, an older man wearing exercise gear did the same.

The police had arrived in force thirty minutes ago. Guns were strictly controlled in Spires, unlike other cities and planets, and whoever had shot up the bar had carried a damn big gun. One officer each guarded the three exits, another two were setting up forensic equipment to survey the damage, and three had commandeered the only undamaged corner and brought over a table and chairs. Commander Arfan, the man yelling at them like they were road-crew noobs, was of indeterminate heritage, and his English had a slight Arabic accent.

Imara was glad that Lièrén had already identified himself as being in the CPS Minder Corps and provided the name of a Spires police detective he'd worked with. With luck, neither the obnoxious Arfan nor the much nicer Detective Hǎinán would ask her anything about him.

Arfan glared at everyone in the room. "I'm taking statements from the filers first, so the rest of you will know not to lie about anything."

She barely stopped herself from rolling her eyes. People disliked minders enough already. If he was worried about lying, he should have brought in a sifter. She glanced to where Lièrén sat at the end of the bar, then looked away. He had done as much as Rayle in calming people down. An empath and a sifter made a good team.

After the medevac autocabs had come and gone with the three bodies and the severely injured, and the emergency healers had treated the remaining bar patrons, Arfan had separated everyone and ordered them not to talk to one another. He'd made a grudging exception to let Derrit and Xiàlìng stay together in the booth, if only to keep the girl from sobbing uncontrollably. Two of the dead had been her parents.

Imara approved of Lièrén asking Derrit to help the girl, and she knew

Lièrén had done something to help her, as well. At her suggestion, Lièrén had quietly asked one of the medics to send an advocate and a trauma specialist for Xiàlìng as soon as possible.

"You, tender, behind the bar," Arfan barked, and rudely pointed at her with a stabbing finger. "Come with me." He pointed to the corner table.

"Sorry, I have to stay here." She tilted her chin toward what was left of the dispensary door. Beamfire had sheared off the top right corner, and the door was hanging precariously by one deformed hinge. She'd already cleaned up the spills as best she could. She'd have to do a detailed inventory later. It would be safer to replace everything, but the hotel might not want to pay for it.

Arfan glared at her. "The server can watch it." He jabbed a thumb toward Rayle, seated at the middle of the bar, a couple of chairs away from Lièrén.

Rayle, acting relaxed and bored, though she knew he wasn't, shook his head. "Can't. I'm not licensed."

"Your pardon, Commander," said Lièrén, his head respectfully lowered, "but perhaps you might direct Bartender Sesay to protect the chems and alterants, so no one can get warped or fluxed before their testimony is recorded."

That possibility apparently hadn't occurred to Arfan, and it clearly annoyed him even more than being defied. Imara had been privately gratified to note that Lièrén's polite deference in the face of Arfan's bad manners had even caused his coworkers to help rein him in.

"Stay," Arfan ordered, as if she were a trained dog. He motioned to the other filer and pointed to the corner, where Detective Hǎinán was, then followed.

Imara mouthed a soundless "thank you" to Lièrén, then leaned against the counter again.

About ten minutes later, the police set up the recording equipment so Imara could stay near the dispensary. She told them everything she'd seen and heard, including the exact words the shooter had yelled. They didn't ask how it was she was already under the table by the time the first shots were fired, and she didn't volunteer it. She owed Lièrén a great deal for protecting Derrit first.

Since they were there, and Lièrén was seated at the end of the bar, they recorded his statement next. He led the police to infer that it had been the noise, not his minder talent, that had first alerted him to trouble.

As they were moving the equipment back to the corner for the rest of the interviews, Detective Hǎinán turned back. "Where will you be if we have more questions?"

"Regrettably, I am unable to say. I am moving to a new duty station in a day or two, but I don't know where yet." He fished his percomp out of his pocket. "I can provide a universal ping ref."

A sharp stab of deep dismay took her by surprise. She tightened her arms around her ribs and made hidden fists to keep anything from showing on her face. It was her own damned fault. She'd reminded herself over and over that he was a transient, and to keep her distance, but obviously, it hadn't stopped her foolish heart from hoping. Derrit wasn't going to take the news well, either.

Rayle turned to look at her. His expression softened in sympathy momentarily before he smoothed it back to boredom and swiveled his chair away. She needed to do a better job of keeping herself contained, if only so she wouldn't drag her empathic friend into her personal drama. She tried to imagine walls of one-way glass around her mind, like the Spires roadways, letting out only what light she chose. She thought she felt something, but for all she knew, it was an incipient tension headache.

Two hours later, the police finally left, and Imara found herself in the bar with Rayle, Derrit, and Lièrén who had insisted on staying to help clean up when the restaurant staff had categorically refused.

Xiàlìng, the traumatized girl who'd seen her parents murdered, was claimed by her older brother, who'd been in his room at the time of the shooting. He'd whisked her away to meet with the advocate and therapist, much to Commander Arfan's disgruntlement. Imara doubted even a skilled interviewer, which Arfan certainly was not, would get anything useful out of Xiàlìng for a while.

The bar was closed for now, but the hotel manager had already arranged for an overnight temporary restoration, with the ambitious goal of being open again by tomorrow evening. To her surprise, he'd authorized the emergency purchase of a whole new dispensary and supplies, and sent the hotel's maintenance crew to secure the damaged dispenser until it could be properly recycled. Maybe the Quark and Quasar really was the hotel's cashflow magic, like Rayle kept telling her.

Derrit was subdued, in part because of the aftereffects of his healed bloody nose, and in part because Lièrén had told Derrit he was shipping out, and this was his last night. When Derrit asked if he was coming back, Lièrén said he didn't know, but Imara privately thought it was a snowball's chance in hell. She couldn't fault Lièrén for anything—he hadn't once hinted he would stay, or even wanted to—but she could fault the universe for unfairness.

Even now, the universe taunted her as they all worked together efficiently and easily, like a family. Not that Rayle didn't have family of his own, but she'd met a couple of them and wasn't surprised Rayle had run away as fast as he could. Caring, mischievous, empathic artists didn't thrive in the hushed, hallowed halls of high finance. Her own family was far away, and determinedly content to scrape out a living from a dry planet. She knew Lièrén had family, too, but what kind of parents abandoned their child to a school for years?

The shooting and its aftermath had made her emotional, wanting to cling to the people she liked and loved. That was why she'd accepted Lièrén's help instead of shooing him out like she should have, especially when she'd had to explain to him what a pry bar looked like. She mentally shook herself to get her head back in the game. She could cry later, in the shower, after Derrit was asleep. She pulled another reclamation container off the stack and activated it so it would stand on its own, then marked it for petroplastics. Rayle and Lièrén were prying what was left of the broken travel poster off the wall after a jagged edge had caught Derrit's hair twice.

"Hey, Imara," said Rayle. "Maybe this time they'll install the poster so it's straight."

She smiled. He'd been valiantly trying to cheer them all up. "I'll add it to the repair list so they do."

Derrit paused the cleaning robot so he could replace its collector, which had filled up quickly with splinters of wood from the back booth. "Agent Sòng, looks like you'll need a new favorite booth when you come back. This one's slagged to zero."

Imara ruthlessly cut off any thoughts of what would have happened if Lièrén and Derrit had been there as usual. Dwelling on might-have-beens was a quick trip to hysteria. She focused on sorting the undamaged bottles into an even display, knowing she'd have to do it again tomorrow night if the promised re-supply came in on time.

Out of the corner of her eye, she saw Lièrén stiffen, as if he was just now realizing how lucky he'd been. She watched as his eyes traced the burn pattern that started high, dipped into the last two booths, then rose again.

His fingers tightened to a death grip on the handle of the pry bar. Rayle suddenly staggered back a step, and a sudden white-hot wave of fear and guilt blew past her. She flinched, then re-imagined her glass walls, which seemed to help. This time, she didn't discount what she'd felt… what her *talent* felt. Lièrén looked down, and visibly forced himself to relax.

He drew a breath to speak, hesitated, then let it out slowly as he looked to the ceiling. "I am not at my best this evening. Please forgive me." He looked to her, then back to Rayle.

"You can't blame yourself." Rayle stepped in closer, a compassionate look on his face. "Whatever it is you just thought of, you can't have known this would happen."

Lièrén shook his head and looked at Derrit, then at Imara. The raw distress on his face made her heart ache. "I should have."

"No," she told him firmly. "You saved us. Not even Ayorinn himself could have predicted this."

"Who?" asked Lièrén.

"Legendary forecaster." Lièrén looked miserable. She was torn between shaking some sense into him and pulling him into her arms. Rayle looked as conflicted as she did. The tension in the room was tangible.

"Mom, I'm hungry."

And with Derrit's complaint, the tension eased. Chaos might rule her life at the moment, but growing boys were ruled by their stomachs.

Rayle put the multi-tool down on a table and wiped his hands of the dust a couple of times. "Come on, kiddo, let's clean up and raid the kitchen." He sidled closer to him conspiratorially. "I know where they hide the good stuff."

Derrit looked intrigued. Thank Neptune for her son's resiliency, and for Rayle's sensitivity. She watched them leave, then turned to Lièrén.

His head was down, shoulders hunched, and his free hand was in his pocket. She couldn't tell if tonight's drama was responsible for his visible unease, or if he'd just hidden it better in the past.

He looked up to meet her gaze. "Please understand there are things in my life I regret, but teaching Derrit will never be one of them. I know he's formed an attachment to me. I am humbled by it, and hold him in high regard, but… would you prefer I leave now, before he gets back?"

She sighed, and an errant coil of her hair tickled her face. "I don't know if there's a right answer to that." She removed her hair clip, felt for and gathered all the stray coils of hair that had escaped, then secured them with the clip again. "He was strong enough when he was five to say goodbye to his father, but he had nightmares about medical centers for months. He's older now, and you're not his father. And you're not dying, you're just leaving." *Like transients always, always did*, she reminded herself. "What do *you* want to do?"

He started to say something, then clamped his mouth shut and looked away. "I'd like to say goodbye to him."

She didn't need wayward talents to sense the discipline he was exerting over himself.

"All right," she said warily. However much she liked him, she was prepared to hurt the man if he made promises to her son he couldn't keep.

He put the pry bar next to the other tools. "I know you don't believe what I said about your minder talents…"

She held up a hand to stop him. "Actually, I do believe you. It explains… weird stuff I've been noticing." Not elegantly phrased, but she didn't know how to describe it any better.

He quirked a brief smile. "Good, because that means you can start learning to use them. Get Derrit to teach you shielding, because it'll give you time to work on the others. Only work with people you really trust, like Rayle. Right now, you're vulnerable."

"I know, I know." She knew she had to deal with her new talents, but she didn't have to like it. She had her hands full with two jobs, putting food on the table, and raising a kid on her own. She didn't have time to contemplate her navel, or whatever it was going to take.

He shoved his hands in his pockets and rocked back and forth on his heels. "Since I'm imposing on you with unsolicited advice, two more things. First, most polymaths find it hard to stay focused because they have input streams coming in from all their physical senses and talents. You already cope extraordinarily well, from what I've seen."

"Thank you, I think." She wasn't sure she wanted him to remember her for her coping skills. "Have you known many other polymaths?"

He shrugged. "A few. Second, you should look up 'mental mesh.' It will help you understand why you… get along with some people better than others."

She gave him an amused smile. "You mean beyond the fact that some people are nice and some are *húndàn*?" Thanks to her road-crew coworkers and her perfect memory, she could call someone an asshole in dozens of languages besides Mandarin.

"Yes," he said, matching her smile, but it faded quickly. He eyed the clock, then surveyed the bar. "Is there anything else to do here, or may we join Derrit and Rayle?"

She glanced at the clock and saw it was nearly eleven, the end of her shift, and much later than Lièrén usually stayed. There was plenty she could still do, but no need to do it right then. She knew she'd be glad tomorrow to have something to keep her busy. "Let's go see if they've set the kitchen on fire yet."

He blinked in surprise, drawing a chuckle from her. He really wasn't at all domesticated. It only reinforced her opinion that whatever he did in the CPS Minder Corps, it wasn't ordinary office work.

Fortunately, the kitchen was none the worse for wear. Rayle, wrapped in an overly large apron, had affected an outrageously bad French accent while instructing a giggling Derrit how to properly plate and garnish flash-grilled sandwiches.

"*Vous êtes arrivé* just in time," Rayle announced. "What would *la dame et le monsieur* care for on their culinary creations?" He waved the tongs toward the sideboard, where meats, cheeses, and vegetables were arranged.

"Ham and Swiss with red mustard," said Imara, because it was quick. Now that she was smelling food, her stomach was growling.

"Thank you, but nothing for me," said Lièrén. "I can't stay any longer."

Rayle pulled a hot sandwich out of the griller and plated it, then wiped his hands on his apron. He put his right hand on his heart and gave a little bow. "It's been an honor to serve you, Field Agent Lièrén Sòng."

Lièrén returned the bow. "It was an honor to see you dance."

Imara smiled. It was the perfect thing to say to Rayle. "Safe travels," she said. "The CPS is lucky to have you."

"Your son is lucky to have you for a mother." He turned to Derrit. "I'm glad I was able to open a door for you, Master Derrit. I hope you are as patient with future teachers as you have been with me."

He gave them all a warm, sincere smile. "I am grateful for the kindness you've shown me in these past weeks, and it has been a pleasure getting to know you." He bowed respectfully to each of them in turn. "May your friendship for one another last a lifetime."

Derrit did what she didn't have the courage to do, and launched himself into Lièrén's arms to wrap him in a tight hug. "Thanks for everything, Agent Sòng." Derrit stepped back.

"You're welcome," Lièrén said with a smile. He gave them one last look, then turned and headed for the hallway that would take him to the hotel.

"Ping us if you can," Derrit called after him.

Lièrén waved, but didn't turn around, and with that, he was gone.

Imara hoped Derrit knew better than to expect anything. If she had a deca-credit for every hotel guest that had promised to ping, or call, or come back, they'd be living in a High Spires penthouse.

CHAPTER 16

THERE WERE NO windows anywhere nearby, so the man stared moodily out the door of the office he'd called home for the past two weeks. Not nearly as nice as the office Field Agent Lièrén Sòng now occupied.

This one had become his by the simple act of dusting it and adding a few personal-looking items on the work surfaces and a generic deskcomp he'd easily smuggled in. Security was more tuned to catching equipment leaving. Since the office was small and inconveniently located, the few people who walked by assumed he was on someone's shit list. He was amused when they avoided meeting his eye, in case his bad luck was contagious. Throw in typical corporate lack of communication, and the one or two people who might have been curious wouldn't even know who to ask.

He wouldn't have chosen to be within a kiloparsec of the bloody fishbowl that was the government capital city of Spires, except that's where Sòng and the rest of his unit had gone to ground. Quite literally, in Sòng's case, considering the flitter crash.

Even perfect plans became vulnerable if loose ends were left dangling, and now everything was in disarray because *someone* had gotten paranoid. He'd been one day—one bloody day!—from getting Field Agent Lièrén Sòng right where he wanted him, where he wouldn't know what hit him.

But thanks to the moronic mugging attempt, followed the next day by the over-the-top performance art of the bar shooting, Sòng had finally woken up to the fact that he was a target. He may have been naïve at first, but he wasn't stupid.

He'd entered the CPS building at the crack of dawn, wearing comparatively nondescript clothes and carrying his coat and exercise bag as usual, but hadn't budged since. Given time, even that could be worked around, but time was in short supply and getting shorter by the hour. Sòng had been cleared for duty and could be gone tomorrow.

The hotel was still his best shot, but he didn't want to endanger the woman or the kid that Sòng spent so much time with. Unlike some other people he could mention, *he* wasn't a monster. Innocent bystanders weren't acceptable collateral damage, whether on a metro platform or in a tacky hotel bar. Neither were the victims of the sick twists that the field unit let escape. The whole field unit had become a corrupt, stinking nest of vipers that needed to be exterminated.

When it served their interest, the CPS could deploy competent corporate fixers, but who knew how long that would take, and how many others would become collateral damage in the interim. No, the only sure solution was to burn the nest out once and for all. They'd started it, but he would bloody well finish it. He always paid his debts, as they'd find out to their cost.

He tapped a stylus rhythmically on the stained desktop. He'd originally planned to take care of Sòng, then pick off the rest one by one, but never let it be said he wasn't flexible. Besides, two of the idiots were in the same location. They liked their creature comforts, and he knew the perfect bait to reel them in quickly. He could be back in his homey little office by early afternoon.

Decision made, he stood, collected his cheap raincoat and headed out. As he walked, he used his oversized percomp to set another part of his plan in motion. Doing so also saved him from having to make eye contact with anyone.

It would take more finesse and preparation to get to the clever and deadly agent who'd set him on this path. Monsters like that got others to do their dirty work, and had an innate caution that kept them alive long after good people, innocent people, were dead, flamed, and made into memory diamonds.

CHAPTER 17

LIÈRÉN WAITED JUST inside the CPS office building's entryway, watching for the secure autocab that had pinged him of its arrival. He pulled his coat closed and tied its attached scarf. Dusk had faded into night, and the lights of Spires were at full brightness. He'd packed essential clothes and toiletries in his gym bag, and planned to select a random restaurant, then a random hotel in which to stay that night. Regardless of what Rayle had asserted yesterday evening, Lièrén's predictable routine and longing to be among friends were responsible for the deaths of three people. He'd be damned if he'd let that happen again. He was grateful he'd had the chance to say goodbye, though it had clogged his throat and hollowed out his chest like someone had taken a cryoblade to it.

The cab dropped down and glided to a stop. He replied to its arrival ping, then waited until its doors slid open before exiting the building. He waved the doors closed as he sat, then gave the cab coordinates to a restaurant district he'd never been to. He settled back in the contour seat and watched the low-air traffic go by without seeing it.

He didn't know whom to tell about his conviction that he was at the top of someone's deletion list. CPS procedure said he should go to his supervisor, Talavara, but if his theory was right, she was on the same list. It'd be stupid for them to be in the same place, and a memo wasn't the appropriate medium for saying "*I think someone is trying to kill me, and you might be next.*" Yamazaki, the field office's supervisor, didn't know any of the background. Lièrén didn't know Jane Pennington-Smythe at all, and he didn't trust the Office of Internal Inquiry to act in time.

The whole situation was, he realized discontentedly, partly his own fault for allowing the austere isolation of the field unit's cover story to overwhelm his personal life. He'd always blamed the job for his failed relationships, because it was easier than admitting his loneliness or taking responsibility for his own happiness. He'd cut himself off from his whole family because he was tired of never being good enough and not measuring up to his great-grandfather's expectations. Now he was paying the price for deliberately pushing himself out into hard space with only an exosuit to protect him.

A ping chime from the prepaid percomp interrupted his thoughts.

"Rayle, good evening." He used the wire in his collar slot to activate the holo, and Rayle's face and shoulders appeared.

"Thank the gods I found you. Are you still on the planet?" He rubbed the side of his face. "Of course you are, because you gave me a local ping ref. Derrit never came back, and Imara's missing. I tried everyone else I could think of, and then I remembered you work for the CPS." He bit his lip. "Maybe I shouldn't have called you…"

Lièrén smoothed the shock from his face, because it wasn't helping. "It's fine. Details, please."

"Derrit went in for testing again, and he didn't come home when he was supposed to. Imara knew I took an extra shift, so she pinged me three hours ago to see if he'd come to the bar, but he hadn't. She said she got zeroed when she called the Testing Center, so she was going down there in person, and to let management know she might be a few minutes late for her shift. She never showed, hasn't pinged." Rayle's expression wavered between anger and worry. "She doesn't miss shifts, and she's *never* late without telling us."

"Who else did you call?"

"Road-crew dispatch, Horis—he's one of her road-crew chiefs—and the neighbor couple she trades child-watching with. No one knows anything."

As a covert field agent, he should stay out of this, but he wasn't going to be that person anymore. He was entitled to a life outside the CPS. "I'll see what I can find out."

Rayle sighed with relief. "Thank you. I'll ping you if they show up, and it's all just miscommunication."

Lièrén didn't need his sifter talent to tell him Rayle didn't believe that. Lièrén didn't, either.

He didn't know what he'd be able to do, but he'd be flailing in the dark without information. Fortunately, he could cure that. He ordered the cab back to the CPS building. The threatened rain finally made its appearance with a roll of thunder, making the lighted city shinier than ever.

By the time he got back to his tiny office, he'd formulated a plan and a cover story. He cracked the Testing Center datasets for the third time, then used his temporary access to comprehensively collect current Testing Center data, which accounted for the last eight days since he'd been given the original hypercube. If asked, he'd imply it was in the name of doing the most thorough job he could before shipping out, since it was unlikely that the regular employees would be keeping it up.

As soon as the data began filling in, he ran "data integrity" queries, tweaking them to return results that would bring up records similar to Derrit's without having to explicitly search for the name. He wanted no inappropriate inquiries traceable to him. Derrit's first visit came up in the first batch, and he skimmed through it, but it was the same as all the other retests. High scores by the subject, and no reason given. They'd lied to Imara about the "inconclusive" results—Derrit was already high level in both talents. And in his ignorance, Lièrén had helped ensure Derrit got those high scores by training him.

He stood up at that, with a need to pace, and realized he was still wearing his coat. He took it off and hung it on the hook by the door. As a bonus, it covered the office's tall, narrow window, making it difficult for anyone in the main area to see what he was doing. He kicked his gym bag into the corner to keep from running over it with his chair, then sat again.

The current data unfortunately didn't include Derrit's record from today, probably because it was still in use. He wished he'd thought to find out more about the daily operations of the Testing Center when he'd discovered the pattern, but he'd been focused on the trends. It would take too long to create the query and search through the main hypercube to look for patterns related to custodial parents in the other inconclusive records.

He was a planner, not a strategist like his sister, or a resourceful quick thinker like Imara. He snorted to himself. He needed Imara to help him find her son, which was probably exactly what she was doing. He assumed Derrit had made it to the Testing Center, because she'd have known a lot sooner that he was missing. The only thing he could think of was to look at the open record.

He probed the Testing Center data space, trying to get a feel for the structure without stumbling into the intruder protections. He set up a harmless routine that activated at random intervals, hoping it would mimic a glitchy segment that the network AI would come fix. He triggered a tiny query that would hitch a virtual ride on its data integrity checks, which would lead him to open records. In the meantime, he found the data staging areas and began to delicately feel around for activity. Luckily, the only open and active record had Derrit's unique identifier. When he tried to open a copy, though, the system denied his access.

Dammit, he didn't have time for all this. In the worst-case scenario, the CPS had already invoked the emergency draft statute and was in the process of hauling Derrit off planet, leaving Imara with an uphill fight to even find her son, much less assert custodial rights.

He stared at the screen, suddenly remembering the Testing Center had skirted procedure to give his temporary account the ability to change ownership of files, after he'd had to call them about thirty times on the first day for access to old records. It was dangerous, because it could trip multiple alarms if he made a mistake. He took a deep breath and did it, then quickly sent a copy of the file to his deskcomp. He immediately reset the original ownership. If he...

"Agent Sòng."

He jumped, then turned around to face Security Specialist Mateliff, the hard-edged woman with silver-red eyes and a ferocious shielder talent. She looked tense and alert. Once again, he'd been an idiot, so focused on his work that he hadn't paid attention to his surroundings, or his sifter talent would have felt the moving void of her shields a lot sooner. He fought to keep his face serene and his body relaxed. "Hello. I'm sorry, I didn't hear you come in."

"Come with me, please. Supervisor Yamazaki wants to see you." Despite the phrasing, it was not a request.

"May I lock the comp first?"

She hesitated, then nodded.

He swiped his thumb over the sensor, and the deskcomp went inert. They'd need his cooperation to figure out where he'd hidden things.

His heart was pounding as he followed Mateliff through the halls toward the center of the building, past the lift and the stairs. He disciplined himself to contain the frustration and despair that accompanied every step that took him farther away from the information he needed to help Derrit. He consciously relaxed his shoulder muscles and kept his gaze steady.

"May I ask what this is about?"

Mateliff grunted. "Interrogation."

"Who's?" he asked.

She shrugged. "Yours, I imagine." She frowned.

He didn't know what they'd found out, but he clung to the hope that he still had wiggle room. If they were certain, Mateliff would have zip-tied his wrists and locked down his talents tighter than a radiation containment field.

She led him into a room that was unmistakably used for interrogations. He'd seen hundreds of them. Yamazaki and one of the other office agents he vaguely recognized sat in two of the chairs, leaving the third for him. Mateliff nodded once to Yamazaki, then stood next to the door at ready ease. Lièrén's sifter talent said MacPenn was a cleaner, and he already knew Yamazaki was a telekinetic and a telepath of the illusionist variety.

"Have a seat, Agent Sòng." Yamazaki pointed to the chair, and Lièrén complied. "MacPenn here saw you come in after dinner and remembered your background and showed me your file." He tilted his head toward the narrow-faced, pale blond man. Yamazaki sighed heavily. "We need you for an emergency interrogation and twist."

Lièrén blinked. "What?"

"The recruiters next door created a clusterf… uh, situation, and now they want us to help clean it up." Yamazaki shook his head and frowned.

"Bunch of farkin' lopars," muttered MacPenn. Mateliff snorted from the doorway in apparent agreement.

Lièrén was too busy feeling relieved that he wasn't in the hot seat to care that they thought the Testing Center staff was reckless and careless, and sublimely oblivious of it.

"Our office is spread really thin with the TSAC march tomorrow. We need to find out what the subject did today, what she knows, and who she told, then make her forget about it. All we have is MacPenn, and while he's a mid-level cleaner, that's all he can do. We'd rather not use a sledgehammer when all we need is a good multidriver."

Lièrén had never thought of himself as a hand tool. "I'll be happy to be of assistance."

"No time like the present," said Yamazaki. "We need this off our plate." He stood, and MacPenn did the same.

Lièrén stood and followed them down the hall and into the next room, which was full of displays showing bird's-eye views of empty rooms. Mateliff stopped in the doorway. Yamazaki touched a control, and the multi-room display was replaced with one large one.

Lièrén's breath froze in his lungs and spread to the rest of his core. The subject was Imara Sesay.

He turned to Yamazaki. "Why is she being detained?" He managed to keep his voice even, and not gasp for air.

Yamazaki frowned sourly. "The Testing Center says she refused to believe they didn't have her son, and that she assaulted the intake admin and broke into the testing area looking for him." He crossed his arms in front of his chest. "Instead of talking her down out of orbit, or calling the local police to have her detained, one of their gung-ho tekes immobilized her, stripped off her percomp, and locked her in a conference room to let her cool off."

"Farkin' lopars," said MacPenn darkly. Both he and Yamazaki were speaking what they believed to be the truth.

Yamazaki gave MacPenn a quelling glance, then continued. "They couldn't call the police afterward, because the ziftheads used minder talents to detain her illegally. And the capper is, when they went to check on her, they discovered she'd jacked the deskcomp and was sending out encrypted pings." Yamazaki took a quick breath, then let it out slowly. "Now they want us to figure out what she knows, who she contacted, and to 'fix it.'" He made air quotes with his fingers.

Lièrén fought to keep his expression neutral and his tone even, despite his raging emotions. "Where is her son?"

Yamazaki and MacPenn exchanged a look. MacPenn finally answered. "Every once in a while, the recruiters have to use… extraordinary measures to do what's best for the kid. He's got two top-level talents, and he belongs in the Academy, where they can teach him how to handle them. We need skills like that working for the galactic peace and not against us." His synaptic haze said he wasn't lying, but his tone and expression said he was conflicted.

Yamazaki looked up to the ceiling and sighed. "They probably took him offsite somewhere, until the parents calm down."

"That's legal?" asked Lièrén. He couldn't keep outrage out of his voice.

Yamazaki and MacPenn exchanged another look, and out of the corner of his eye, he saw Mateliff clench her jaw. She lost control of her shields for an instant, and he felt the synaptic haze of nascent violence that went with deep anger.

"It's a gray area," Yamazaki said after a bit. "Anyway, what's done is done. I got orders from regional to cooperate, so this is me, cooperating. Well, you, actually." MacPenn shook his head but said nothing.

Lièrén rolled his shoulders. "What memories do you want the woman to have?"

"I don't know," said Yamazaki with exasperation. "Whatever it takes to get her to do the right thing for her son. We can make the records match later."

Lièrén needed more time to think, but wasn't going to get it. He shook his head. "Since you checked my record, you know I'm barely a mid-level twister, so it may take me a while to get it right. Does she have any minder talents?"

Unexpectedly, Mateliff spoke up. "She's a mid-level filer." When Yamazaki gave her a surprised look, she put her hands on her hips and glared at him. "What, you think I'm letting some stray woman into our perimeter without checking that?"

Yamazaki put his hands up in a show of surrender.

Mateliff relaxed and turned to Lièrén. "Her name is Imara Sesay, she's thirty-seven years old and works two jobs. Her twelve-year-old son is Derrit. The father's dead." She shook her head.

Lièrén sighed. "That'll make the twist harder. Filer memories have long association threads."

MacPenn nodded his agreement.

Yamazaki rolled his eyes impatiently. "I don't care if it takes all night, just do it."

If Lièrén wasn't careful, Yamazaki would decide to make use of his sledgehammer instead. Lièrén bowed his head respectfully. "I'll do my best." That seemed to satisfy Yamazaki.

Now all Lièrén had to do was figure out how to save his career, his integrity, Derrit, and Imara, all under the watchful eyes of three experienced CPS field agents.

Chapter 18

ONE, TWO, THREE...

Imara started counting to one thousand for the nineteenth time, in an effort to keep her thoughts from scattering like a startled herd of sheep. She clasped her hands in her lap, where she used minute twitches of her fingers to count by ten. The only furniture in the room was the softly padded, low-backed bench she sat on. She wondered what the room was for when it wasn't being used as a detention cell.

...four, five, six...

She'd made a tactical error in losing her temper in the Testing Center and trying to take them on by force. Their teke had taken her down so fast, she hadn't known what hit her, and now she was stuck in a glorified closet to which they'd hastily added temporary camera eyes in every corner to monitor their rebellious detainee. After the incident with the conference room's deskcomp, she had no doubt those piss-drinking water-wasters would be sending in a telepath to crack her brain. She was pretty damn sure what they were doing was six different kinds of illegal, but her sporadically sparking talents told her they weren't feeling guilty or even regretful, only annoyed.

...seven, eight, nine...

Her biggest fear was that they'd hurt Derrit. She couldn't think about that, or about what a good cleaner or twister might do to her, so instead, she made half a dozen plans for what to do once she got away. Until she did, her best bet was to delay the CPS as long as possible, and hope her messages got out to the right people. If delaying them meant pretending she was now calm and harmless, then she'd count for as long as it took.

Because she'd been trying like hell to keep her talents open and active, she felt a brush of something a moment before the door slid open. When she saw the familiar face of Agent Lièrén Sòng, she knew in a sharp spike of terror that she was well and truly farked.

Between one heartbeat and the next, he closed the distance between them and put his hand on the back of her neck. She tried to raise her shields, but knew it was too late when she suddenly felt really relaxed for the first time since Derrit hadn't come home. She was still worried, but it wasn't as mind-numbing as it had been. Despair and fear tried to tear into her, but their claws melted away.

She was confused when she heard her name, because it wasn't coming from her ears.

Imara… Imara… the not-voice said patiently, and she realized it was in her mind. *Huh,* she thought. *So Agent Flux-Hot is also a telepath.*

She felt a momentary twitch of amusement that wasn't hers. *Flux-Hot?*

Rayle's nickname for you. A new terrible thought threatened her new-found peace, which she knew wasn't real, but couldn't do anything about as long as Lièrén's sifter talent controlled her. *Have you come to twist me?*

No. His thought was forceful, and rang true. *But the agents observing us think that's what I'm doing, and we'll have to fool them.*

We? Of all the scenarios and plans she'd imagined, Lièrén hadn't been in them. She'd thought he'd be in interstellar transit by now.

In response, he sent her a quick burst of memories that showed her what the CPS agents wanted. *I'm not fast and clever like you are,* he said. *This is the only thing I could think of to do. It may still be too late.*

Why? More fear bubbled up, but floated away with a gentle ripple that must be his sifter talent working on her.

Because the Testing Center is determined to have Derrit. He sent her another quick burst, this time of the damning pattern of behavior he'd uncovered about the Testing Center, and the emergency conscription clause it fell under. *I don't know where they've taken him, or if he's still on the planet. He scares them.*

What? He's a twelve-year-old boy.

Whose full shields are already unbreachable by anyone in their staff, and whose cleaning talent could blank-slate anyone who tried. Like MacPenn said, they want him on their side.

Her mind felt muzzy and disconnected, like she'd combined fortified brandy and canab. *Why can't I feel my toes?*

He sent her a wordless apology, and the difference was noticeable almost immediately. She could feel his active talent, too, now that she thought about it.

You can feel all of them, but you don't recognize what your sifter talent is telling you yet.

I have sifter talent?

Yes, but that's not important now. If I relax too much control, it'll show in your face to the people watching. And since I'm supposed to be twisting you, MacPenn will expect to see pain because he knows you're a filer.

Would they believe it if I fell sideways into you, so they couldn't see my face?

Yes, but let me do it. I know what they're expecting to see.

She thought he meant he'd adjust her brain chemicals again, but instead, he took temporary telepathic control of her body. It was weird and made her want to giggle, which she knew was wrong but couldn't do anything about. She felt herself slump into his arms and against his chest. He smelled really good, and she liked the solid warmth of his chest on her cheek, the comforting weight of his arm across her shoulders.

Sorry again. Your sifter talent is trying to fight mine. I'm having a hard time keeping you balanced.

The need to snuggle into him drifted away, and her body was her own again. A rebellious part of her said that enjoying being held by him had nothing to do with whatever he was doing to her.

Yes, it does, he said. His thoughts were accompanied by musical notes of sadness and guilt, as she'd come to think of the emotions her empath talent picked up.

Focus, he gently chided her. *We're running out of time. We need a plan.*

Right, she thought. *Get me out of here intact, find and liberate Derrit, and avoid the emergency draft. Easy as free fall.* Her sarcastic comment triggered a synaptic flash and a memory in Lièrén's mind, and she had a brief glimpse into pain and fear like she'd never imagined. She wanted to soothe him, but didn't know how. *Okay, one step at a time. What do the field office people expect from all this?*

The names of the people you pinged, no memory that you were detained and illegally handled, and that you'll release your son to the Academy when the time comes.

She liked how crisp his thoughts were when he sent them to her. Hers were probably a muddy mess by comparison. *I don't want to get the people I pinged in trouble.*

Create an image in your imagination and show it to me. Use your filer talent for detail to make it real.

He was telling her how to twist him. She tried to pull back from the connection. She didn't want to twist anyone.

He sent her a soothing wave. *I'm telling you how to lie to me.*

Oh.

She called up her memory of secure-pinging her lawyer, Rackkar Horis, and Rayle before the really annoyed CPS woman had caught her. Figuring they knew how many pings she sent, she imagined the ping refs of the police, the TSAC office in Spires, and the constituent help line of an agitator politician who despised the CPS. She sent the constructs to Lièrén one at a time, because she couldn't figure out how to bundle them into memory packets the way he could. She felt his amusement at the politician "memory."

If you don't twist me, will the cleaner guy, MacPenn, be able to tell if he checks?

Yes.

Then we'll have to give him no reason to check. What would convince them everything is fine?

She could feel him thinking, but he was better at limiting what he shared with her. It was like being in a walled garden outside a house. No way was he a simple admin staffer for a boring trade office.

You apologizing for causing a disruption, and trusting them to know what's best for Derrit. You should still want to see him or talk to him, but not be worried that it won't be until tomorrow.

She twitched in sour amusement. Farkin' assholes didn't want much, did they? *What if I offered to sign the release tonight?*

She felt a flare of alarm from him. *Giving the Testing Center custody...*

I said 'offer,' not actually do it. I'd need my lawyer to review the content.

The field office would consider it a bonus.

Will they let me walk tonight?

I think so. A bit of doubt accompanied the thought.

She'd have to take the risk. She had one more favor to ask. *I don't want to get you in trouble, but can you help me find where they took Derrit?*

She felt him take a deeper breath, and it sent a shimmer of warmth through her, which she shared with Lièrén. She barely stopped a soft vocalization of pleasure. *Sorry, you need to re-balance me again.* The wave of desire eased off, leaving her feeling empty.

Yes, I'll help you find your son.

* * * * *

The hardest thing Lièrén had ever done in his life was to watch Imara leave. She'd played her part supremely well, and now he had to play his.

As he walked down the hall with Yamazaki, MacPenn, and Mateliff, he concentrated on keeping his mind serene and his body mimicking the post-twist headache his file said he should have. If he didn't, Mateliff was sharply observant enough to note the discrepancy and mention it, and MacPenn would suspect what it meant.

"...saved us a planet's worth of trouble. I'm going to write a commendation memo for your record," Yamazaki was saying. MacPenn looked relaxed and satisfied.

Lièrén bowed his head briefly. "Thank you for the recognition, but it would be better if you didn't." He gave them a small smile. "Trade negotiation administrators rarely get noticed for such things."

Yamazaki looked puzzled for a second, then nodded. "Oh, yes, I see your point. Well, if you ever need an informal reference, send them my way. It was pure genius, getting her to go for the release." Lièrén agreed wholeheartedly. Imara had timed her offer just right, and it had her out the door fifteen minutes after he'd left her in the quiet room, lying on the bench, supposedly napping.

They arrived at the intersection that would take him back to the main operations area and his office and he stopped. "If you have no further need of me, I would like to finish what I started with the Testing Center datasets."

Yamazaki waved it away. "That can wait until tomorrow. After a forty-minute sift and twist, you deserve a good night's rest. Or come out with MacPenn and me now, and I'll buy you a drink."

Lièrén shook his head. "I'd rather finish tonight, if you don't mind. I may be off-planet by tomorrow." He clasped his hand behind his back and set his jaw, the picture of a dedicated staffer.

Yamazaki smiled. "No wonder your supervisor wanted you back so fast. Be my guest, then. Do you need Mateliff to show you the way?"

"No, thank you." Lièrén looked to Mateliff. "Unless it's required by protocol?" he asked deferentially.

She twitched a smile, acknowledging his subtle rebuke of Yamazaki's disrespect in treating her like a lackey instead of a peer. "Nope. You're clear. I need to get back to the control center. Physical system's been glitchy lately."

Lièrén nodded his thanks once again, then made sure to rub his neck as he left, as a reminder of his supposed headache. His brain did feel like it was wrapped in wool, but that was the result of straining to keep his thoughts contained while speaking mind-to-mind with Imara. She was a fast learner, and toward the end, had been unknowingly eroding the barrier of his "walled garden" by her openness and instinctive desire to make a deeper connection with him. The desire wasn't real, it was an artificial side effect of modulating her brain chemicals to make her receptive. He knew once she was away from his influence, and figured out that he hadn't planned to do anything about the Testing Center taking Derrit until he'd been sent to interrogate her, she would never trust him again.

He felt the pressure of the seconds slipping away, but forced himself to keep a steady pace as he walked the empty halls. He didn't have a teke's natural sense of spatial awareness and direction, but he'd paid attention to the turns when following Mateliff, in case he needed a quick escape. A good habit for covert field agents, even ones that worked in corporate offices.

The deskcomp was as he'd left it. He quickly disguised the metadata and location of Derrit's file, then opened it in an encrypted workspace and skimmed through it. As of ninety minutes ago, the Testing Center had prepared a declaration of emergency conscription, but it was incomplete. The file said he'd been authorized for transport to an auxiliary location and helpfully gave exact coordinates.

Lièrén swiveled his chair and bent over to dig through his bag and retrieve a water bottle. Under cover of that movement, he subvocalized the coordinates into the wire of his prepaid comp, encrypted the packet with the passcode he and Imara had agreed on, and sent it to Rayle. Any direct contact with Imara would have been dangerous.

And that was supposed to be the end of his involvement. Imara had badgered him into agreeing because committing career suicide wouldn't help anyone. He'd let her win the argument because he was still a target, and whoever wanted him and his covert agent coworkers dead didn't mind collateral damage. Every time he left the building, he put anyone near him in danger.

He had deliberately not asked Imara what she planned to do, and she had deliberately not volunteered it, but because she wasn't good at containment yet, he had the gist. Unsurprisingly, it was clever, flexible, and bold. Since he had to wait for the Testing Center data cube to rebuild for the final time anyway, he set about doing a few things that would help shore up some weak spots in her plans and give her some additional options.

Twenty minutes later, the deskcomp signaled that the cube was finished.

He'd dutifully included the current data, to cover his recent forays into their data space, but he'd also introduced several tiny corrupt seeds that would burrow into the cube and introduce subtle anomalies that would make it more difficult for recruiters to find the records of high-level targets of interest. It felt like a tiny bit of justice to use covert CPS agent skills to hinder the misbehavior of a rogue Testing Center.

He transmitted the completed hypercube, then as his final act, launched a custom query he'd developed to systematically alter the deskcomp and data spaces he'd used that would make security passes ignore them as already reviewed. It was the electronic version of twisting.

He rocked back in his chair and stretched. The squeak of the chair echoed in the main office area, and it reminded him to check for the synaptic haze of other minds. It annoyed him that doing so wasn't yet an automatic habit. He was pretty sure no one was in the main office or nearby, probably because they were deployed in the field in preparation for the TSAC march.

His talent felt a little sluggish, which was understandable, considering how much he'd used it that evening, but it would have been much worse if he'd still been on the enhancement drugs. That was something else he needed to deal with, now that he was about to go back on active duty. Advocate Patwardan had mentioned several workarounds that he wanted to research once he got to whatever new hotel he'd end up at that evening. It would keep him from worrying about what Imara was doing, or fretting about his upcoming meeting with the CPS regional supervisor. His stomach growled, reminding him he hadn't eaten that evening, either.

He leaned forward and pulled his gym bag from the floor onto his lap, then slid his water bottle inside and sealed the bag against the rain. As he slung the strap over his shoulder, he felt the brush of haze against the edge of his sifter talent. He quickly stepped out of his office and focused. Someone was approaching from the direction of the core of the building. Low-level telepath and cleaner talents, which ruled out the agents he'd already been introduced to.

A few seconds later, a youngish-looking, long-limbed man with reddish brown hair and a narrow face emerged from the hallway. He stopped and smiled when he saw Lièrén.

"Thank chaos, someone's still here. I'm new here, and I need some help…" He trailed off when he saw Lièrén's bag. "Oh, are you leaving?"

Lièrén nodded.

The man glanced at the room. "I don't suppose you know if anyone else is around? I need to secure one of the small offices on the third floor, but the door won't seal. If someone could hold it, I could get it back on track. It'll just take a minute, but I can't do it by myself." His shoulders slumped and he sighed. "Looks like I won't be going home anytime soon."

Lièrén couldn't fault him for wanting to go home, and he wasn't lying about anything. "I can help you."

"You can?" The man's sunny smile was back. "You're a lifesaver!"

Something about the taller man triggered a sense of familiarity, but his synaptic haze signature was an odd texture that Lièrén would have remembered. He mentally shrugged and started toward the hallway.

"I'm Henry Nothenil, by the… Hey, is that yours?" He pointed to Lièrén's coat hanging in the office.

"Yes," Lièrén said. He went back for it and waved the lights off as he draped the coat over his arm. "Thank you for noticing."

Nothenil led the way to the stairs, and Lièrén dutifully followed. Nothenil seemed distracted by something on his percomp, so Lièrén started making a list in his mind of the things he still needed to do that night, and was sidetracked by noticing that ever since the accident, his memory had improved. He didn't used to be able to hold lists in his head for long, which was why he'd relied so heavily on taking notes. The only thing new was that he was no longer on his original drug protocol. That, and no one was regularly erasing chunks of his memory.

He began to wonder where, exactly, the small office was, because it seemed like they were walking through a lot of halls. He wasn't surprised when Nothenil slowed to a halt at an intersection.

"Uhm, we might be turned around." He looked left and right. "Do you know which way the connecting door to the central core is from here? You know, the one that looks like a closet?"

Lièrén had to admit it was easy to get lost, because the third floor was carved up into a confusing tangle of odd hallways with closed doors, but the favor was taking longer than he'd hoped. He'd been checking from time to time for synaptic telltales from others, but the floor seemed to be deserted. Nothenil followed as Lièrén backtracked one hallway and found a room number, then used his percomp to tell him which way was east. "Left at the next intersection, down the short hall with the orange corridor light, then right. It's in the middle."

Nothenil beamed a smile. "Excellent. I'm glad not to have to ping security and tell them I'm lost." He took off again, his confident body language restored, with Lièrén following.

The final hallway was as he'd remembered it, about fifteen meters long and very plain. He was amused to note that all of the doors were numbered except the central core door, as if not numbering it made it less visible. Nothenil's problem door turned out to be around the corner at the far end of the hall.

He motioned to Lièrén and opened the door to the first room on the left. "I've already set this one up. Why don't you put your stuff in here?" Lièrén put his bag and coat on the desk, then followed Nothenil back to the stuck door. The problem was easy to see, but not so easy to fix. Nothenil kept going back to the other office for various tools, and after about fifteen minutes, was growing more irritable by the second.

"Come on, you *zelenooký fena*," he muttered, working a varidriver back and forth in the track, "we haven't got all night."

Lièrén didn't recognize the language and didn't much care at that point. He still hadn't eaten, and the chances of getting to a hotel before midnight were fading.

Nothenil froze a moment, then smiled and put down the driver. "Come with me."

Just as they rounded the corner, Nothenil tripped and stumbled into Lièrén… and Lièrén was suddenly Nothenil's puppet as his telepathy talent flared hard and fast.

He was compelled to kneel, looking down the long corridor. The unmarked connecting door opened. *So this is how I die.*

From down the hall, another flare of white-hot telepathy talent flooded his sifter sense, with an undercurrent of healer. From his peripheral vision, he saw Nothenil's arm extend with a handbeamer at the ready. Someone hurled into a tumbling roll on the floor and came up with a needler pointed directly at Lièrén, but Nothenil's beamer was faster and didn't miss. The needler flechettes went wild, but not wild enough. Lièrén felt searing pain in his right shoulder and heard Nothenil grunt behind him.

In that moment of distraction, Lièrén flared and focused all his talents on Nothenil, hoping at least to take the *húndàn* with him into death. The telepathic body control broke, and Lièrén crouched and slammed Nothenil's knees to knock him off balance. Lièrén scrambled back to keep the distance, then angrily flared his sifter talent to disable Nothenil.

"Stop! Stop!" shouted Nothenil, staggering back. "I'm on your side!"

Lièrén gritted his teeth and continued the assault, fighting to overpower Nothenil's telepathic talent. "*Fèihuà.*"

"It's not bullshit. Look at who was shooting the needler if you don't believe me." Nothenil's blue jacket and pink shirt were starting to show spots of blood where the needler flechettes had stitched a pattern up the left side of his torso, with a few hitting his arm.

Lièrén snatched the beamer from Nothenil's hand and pointed it at him, then eased back on his sifter assault. "Why don't we both go see?"

Nothenil kept his hands visible and took a step toward the prone figure.

"Slowly," snapped Lièrén. Nothenil's mouth tightened, but he nodded.

As they got closer, Lièrén saw long, dark hair, and a woman's figure. A sickening smell of burned flesh and blood made his stomach roil. Synaptic haze told him she was still alive. She was curled on her side, with her hair covering her face. Her hands clutched her midsection. The needler had fallen about twenty centimeters away, so he kicked it toward the wall, away from both her and Nothenil.

Carefully keeping an eye on Nothenil, Lièrén crouched slowly to push the hair aside. He glanced down.

The woman who'd tried to kill him was Agent Cini Talavara, his field unit's acting supervisor.

He glared at Nothenil. "Explain."

Nothenil suddenly looked alarmed. "Don't let her touch you. She'll kill you!"

Lièrén leaned away and stood, narrowly avoiding Talavara's fingers, which had only been centimeters from his calf.

She was clearly in a lot of pain, but she had enough energy to look at Nothenil. Her telepathy flared laser-hot, and her expression changed from puzzlement to anger. "You're dead."

"Not yet," he said softly, with a smile that had a haze of violence behind it. "But you are."

A sudden flare of low-level telekinetic talent surged from Nothenil. The needler on the floor spun and emptied its clip of flechettes into Talavara's throat. Blood welled quickly from the dozen needle wounds. It only took a few seconds for her synaptic haze to flatline and dissipate as she died.

CHAPTER 19

LIÈRÉN THUMBED THE beamer and focused on Nothenil, who stepped back in alarm, one hand high, the other arm drooping, as if not in his control. "I saved your life."

"You used me for a shield." Nothenil's odd behavior fell into place, making Lièrén want to grind his teeth. "I was your *bait*."

"It was either that or let her start hiring mercs to shoot up a bar, or mug you, or take out a fucking metro platform that killed dozens, since she used up all the unit's agents."

"What?" Lièrén was stumbling over the implications, but Nothenil believed the accusations he made.

"Look, could we play jack trade somewhere else? I disabled the security eyes back here, but they'll send someone to check. I'd rather not be here when they find this." He tilted his head toward Talavara's body. "We can buy ourselves some time if we move her into the connecting corridor. No eyes in there, since it's not supposed to exist."

Lièrén sighed, then nodded. "I'll hold the door, you drag her."

"I can't." He pointed to his drooping left arm. "Anesthetic needler. She wanted you alive, at least for a while." Needlers were one of the very few legal weapons in Spires. Politicians didn't like being shot.

For once, the fact that sifters were immune to chemical painkillers worked in Lièrén's favor. His shoulder hurt, but he could feel and use it. He picked the needler up off the floor, then gave Nothenil an uncompromising look. "Do it one-handed."

Nothenil sighed and shook his head, then did as ordered while Lièrén kept the beamer on him and his sifter sense watching for any other hidden talents. They couldn't do anything about the bloodstains in the porous plascrete flooring or the line of tiny flechettes that had pierced the ceiling tiles.

Lièrén considered his options. He wanted answers, and he didn't trust

Nothenil out of his sight. The ideal place would have been the connecting corridor, except it now had a murdered agent's body. Not something they wanted to be caught with. A memory surfaced of what was at the other end of the corridor.

"I want my bag and coat, and then I know a place we can talk."

"Leave the scarf. That's how she tracked you tonight." Lièrén frowned and added that to his list of questions.

With the bag slung over his shoulder, he directed Nothenil back through the corridor, then to the left and down another hall that took them to the door he'd remembered. They were now in the CPS medical center and the plethora of oddly shaped and clearly abandoned offices that had bemused his surgery-addled imagination the first time he'd seen them.

He did a cursory pat-down of Nothenil, who rolled his eyes and sighed the whole time, then had him sit in the far corner before dragging up a chair. He carefully sat out of Nothenil's reach, but close enough that they could talk quietly.

"Tell me your given name."

"You already know it." Truth, but shaded. He let it go for now.

"Why was Cini Talavara tracking me and trying to kill me?"

Nothenil smiled humorlessly. "She thought you were betraying her to the Office of Internal Inquiry."

Lièrén schooled his face to hide his surprise. It was bad technique to let the subject see what an interrogator knew and didn't. "Interesting. What did she think I knew?"

"That the 'Trade Assistance' field unit was selling interrogation outcomes to the highest bidder, and doing special favors for CPS brass. When you downloaded the files, she thought you were turning them over to the OII." Truth.

Lièrén kept his expression neutral, but inside, he was reeling. He'd thought it was just his partner who was corrupt, and now Nothenil was claiming seven other people were just as bad. How had he not known?

He knew the answer before he even finished his own question. Fiyon Machimata, the man he had been so monumentally naïve to trust and admire, had been erasing his memories.

"And the flitter accident?"

"A falling out among thieves. Machimata was the target. You were collateral damage." Truth.

"How do you know all this?"

"I'm an agent." Shaded truth. The measured hesitation before each very short answer proved Nothenil had experience with sifters and interrogation, but maybe he didn't know that Lièrén didn't need skin contact. Hadn't since he stopped taking the CPS drugs.

To cover his action, Lièrén chose not to force Nothenil into uncomfortable areas just yet. Instead, he sighed and let his shoulders droop a little. "What's in this for you?" He carefully extended a tendril of talent and gently nudged a few receptors at a time in Nothenil's brain. The man's oddly textured synaptic haze began to smooth out.

A smile ghosted across Nothenil's face. "Payback."

"For what?"

"A life for a life. Talavara was a psychopath."

Lièrén stimulated Nothenil's transmitters, a few at a time. "That's hard to believe. The CPS evaluators would have caught it."

"What makes you think they didn't? Psychopaths can be useful tools." Nothenil sneered. "Their mistake was thinking they had her leashed. Apfel, the teke, wasn't much better. Bloody CPS thinks drug protocols are the answer to everything and always work." He didn't seem to notice that he was beginning to volunteer information.

Lièrén raised an eyebrow. "Why am I still alive?" He tweaked a few more neurotransmitters. If he went too fast, Nothenil would notice and start fighting, and his telepath talent was much stronger than Lièrén's.

"Luck. And an angel." Nothenil's smile was almost a smirk. Lièrén let that go for now, too. Nothenil's synaptic haze was smooth as glass, but the shape kept changing in subtle ways. It was very odd.

"Why did Talavara come after me now? Tonight?"

Nothenil rolled his eyes. "I told you, she had no one left to do it for her. She had a secret healer talent, and she knew how to make murders look like natural causes. Heart attacks, cerebral accidents… Cini was clever, I'll give her that. Most healers don't like death, but she lived for it." He seemed pleased with his own joke. Lièrén continued to nudge his receptors.

"Uvay Garbey." No wonder the unit's late supervisor's family was surprised by her death.

"And you, after she compelled you to spill. Or tried to, anyway. Her biggest fault was impatience, and details bored her. A needler on a sifter." He shook his head. "Loved money, though. Not spending it, just having it. CPS will probably never find it."

Something about the time line was bothering Lièrén, and he finally figured it out. "I didn't download any files until recently. Why the sloppy metro platform attempt?"

"I don't know. Maybe you were a loose end." Lie.

Not for the first time, Lièrén wished his talent would tell him whether or not the lie was a deliberate distraction. He used to rely on Machimata for... he was struck by a wild thought. "Who are you an agent for?"

Nothenil met Lièrén's gaze, but a corner of his mouth twitched with humor. "Myself." Truth.

"Are you an employee, agent, or contractor of any other organization?"

"No." Truth.

That killed Lièrén's notion that Nothenil might work for the OII. It suddenly occurred to him to wonder why Nothenil was willing to answer any of Lièrén's questions. The brain chemical adjustments were too subtle to make Nothenil that relaxed and disposed to be cooperative. Nothenil was toying with him.

"What do you want from me?" He was tired of the games.

Nothenil was silent for a long moment, then said, "Your goodwill." And with that, he struck, his telepathic power blazing even as his teke talent pushed Lièrén's hand holding the beamer toward ground.

The pressure in Lièrén's head was nearly overwhelming, cajoling and compelling him to relax and just go with the flow. It made him mad. Lièrén was through letting anyone think for him.

He dug in behind his eroding containment walls, and desperately threw everything he had into swarming around Nothenil's telepathic resistance and swamping his synapses with a flood of conflicting instructions. The synaptic haze had gone sharp and jagged with the attack, but now started to go chaotic under Lièrén's assault. Lièrén concentrated on stimulating Nothenil's gamma-amino butyric acid to convince his body and talent to ignore the brain's orders, as if he were in a sleep state.

The pressure in Lièrén's head was so strong, he started seeing spots, and he had to drop the beamer or have his hand crushed. Lièrén's low-level telepathy wasn't enough to control all of Nothenil's body, but he compelled him to close his eyes. Lièrén hoped that without sight, Nothenil wouldn't know where to direct the teke talent.

Lièrén felt Nothenil's cleaner talent activate, meaning he could start ripping into Lièrén's already damaged memory. Panic spiked. He couldn't afford to lose any more. In desperation, all he could think to do was flare his own twist talent. He went after the first pleasant memory he could find, that of a man in a bathhouse pool. Nothenil's telepathic assault faltered as Lièrén smashed the memory together with the recent death of Cini Talavara, twisting the bathhouse memory to leave a burning, jagged hole in the man's chest. Lièrén pulled on a memory of a pretty woman…

STOP… Lièrén… stop… There was despair in the thoughts.

Nothenil's cleaning and telekinesis talents deactivated. Lièrén cautiously let go of the memory, but kept his twist talent ready, not trusting.

I didn't want it to be this way. Ineffable sadness and guilt accompanied the thought.

In the new quiet of their mind-to-mind connection, Lièrén finally saw the truth that he should have recognized a lot earlier. The man in front of him might be Henry Nothenil now, but the mind and the memories were of his former partner. His supposedly dead partner. Fiyon Machimata.

Behind his battered containment, Lièrén was rocked by a flood of impulses. Congratulate him for cheating death. Flay him alive for the years of wrenching betrayal. Find out the truth. Get away as fast as he could. Knowing he was vulnerable, he pumped Noth… Fiyon's abused receptors with enough sleep hormones to keep him sluggish but awake.

Why did you attack me? demanded Lièrén.

I just wanted to control you long enough to get the beamer. You were getting angry.

Lie.

Fiyon mentally sighed. *Okay, okay. I also wanted to clean your memories of me as I am now. I didn't realize how strong you'd be. You're off the CPS drugs altogether, aren't you? No wonder you threw off the compulsion.*

Lièrén ignored the attempt at sidetracking. *I didn't recognize you… not even your synaptic signature. Why not just let Talavara kill me?*

Glad to know my funds weren't wasted. When I got the full body makeover, I paid a hell of a lot extra for a permanent brain chemical changer so even top-level sifters wouldn't recognize me. Not an approved procedure. As to why I saved you… I owe you.

Lièrén remembered Fiyon's favorite saying. *And you pay your debts.*

Yes. Pride accompanied the thought. *Talavara and Garbey were at war. After Talavara compelled me to let that pedophile go, I knew dying was the only way they'd let me leave. I found out the flitter was sabotaged to kill me, so I used it. I couldn't tell you to stay off that flight because you'd have asked why. You surprised everyone by surviving. While you were in recovery, I used your credentials to download the unit's entire hypercube, in case I ever needed leverage. Talavara ordered Baretti to send Apfel to arrange a 'metro accident.' I don't know how Baretti and Apfel died, but I do know Talavara had no patience for failure. I doubt she cared about the hundreds of casualties Apfel caused when she crashed that metro platform, only that you weren't one of them.*

Lièrén sent a dark, bitter thought. *If she killed me, how could I be the team's sacrificial lamb?*

It was the only logical explanation for why he'd been kept on the team for so long. Otherwise, they would have had him die in an "accident" years ago.

Fiyon went completely invisible behind his containment, the way high-level telepaths could. After a long moment, he answered. *It was the only way I could keep you alive.* He thinned his walls a little to let Lièrén see a complex coil of selfishness, greed, guilt, and remorse. *Garbey and I had a good little business going, long before you were assigned to the unit. Just the occasional "mistake" or altered record, and our cashflow accounts were fluxed. When she got promoted, the CPS sent you as her replacement. I knew after the first time you and I connected that you were too... idealistic to be a part of it. Garbey made the mistake of bringing in Talavara, who brought everyone else in, even the new transfers. It went slowly chaotic after that. Cini was a binary thinker—if you weren't her friend, you were a waste of carbon and oxygen. The only way to save you was to convince them we needed a scapegoat for the OII or whoever else came looking.* He sent a mental wave of affection. *I always liked you.*

Lièrén couldn't suppress the physical snort that statement elicited. *You liked me so well you gouged gaping holes in my memory. Why didn't you just get Garbey to transfer me?*

Talavara would have killed you, anyway. Did I mention she was psychotic? I kept you as isolated as I could... Garvey kept us all... on the move...

Lièrén felt Fiyon slipping away and realized he'd kept him under so long that all his body wanted to do was sleep. Lièrén adjusted the receptors to ignore the sleep hormones. He also released control of Fiyon's eyes, since he didn't seem intent on doing more harm. After a few seconds, he blinked, as if the lights had suddenly come on.

Fiyon shared his amusement with Lièrén. *Weird to be on the receiving end of your sifter talent. My brain'll be mushy for weeks. You're top-level, better than Garbey ever was.* Truth.

Lièrén hated that he still liked Fiyon's praise. *Cleaning isn't on your record. Neither is telekinesis. I get how you hid them from me, by simply erasing inconvenient memories, but how did you hide them from the CPS?*

I didn't, exactly. My cleaning talent was so low when I was twenty that the recruiters thought it was an equipment fault. The CPS leashes cleaners really tight, so when my talent got stronger, I didn't tell them. Garbey discovered it when we were still the interrogation team, and she agreed to keep it secret if I used it to make sure no one remembered us. I still wasn't very good when you came along. I made some… mistakes with you that I regret.

Truth, but little consolation. Lièrén hid behind his containment so as not to distract Fiyon from his story.

Two years ago, I finally decided to stop taking the CPS's bloody 'enhancement' drugs because they were killing me. He sent a quick bundled memory packet of increasingly unreliable talents, debilitating pain, and bad news from the medics. *No one else in the field unit was taking them by then, either, except you. After I recovered from the withdrawal, the teke talent showed up. Bloody drug protocols had been suppressing it for fifty bloody years. It's like your telepathy, which is a lot stronger than it was. You probably still think the CPS is all things good…*

I don't anymore. Lièrén sighed. *I still believe in the mission, and a safe place for minders, but from what I've seen, the Service has grown… careless.*

He was tempted to tell Fiyon what the local Testing Center was doing, but that would have exposed Derrit, and he didn't trust Fiyon that far. His ex-partner had forgotten more about surveillance than Lièrén ever knew, and had obviously been watching Lièrén and the rest of the unit for weeks. He undoubtedly knew something about Derrit and Imara, but Lièrén refused to put them any closer to Fiyon's unpredictable orbit.

Lièrén glanced at the clock and was surprised to see it had only been forty minutes since he'd followed Nothen… Fiyon down the hall.

What do you want to do now? Lièrén asked.

Get out of here, replied Fiyon promptly, *then vanish, like I'd planned. I've paid my debts. Except for you, everyone in the field unit is dead.* Truth.

Fiyon was right about needing to leave. Lièrén picked up the beamer from the floor where it had fallen and put it in his pocket. It was disconcerting watching lanky, narrow-faced Nothenil as he stretched cautiously, but feeling Fiyon's mind.

Lièrén picked up his bag and coat. With luck, anyone finding the scarf he'd abandoned would assume it was left behind by some previous occupant of that office.

I assume you have a plan for leaving? Fiyon always had a plan. Usually plans within plans. He was admirably crafty and thorough.

I fractured the central security monitoring system, and every vid of me and most everyone else in the field office side is farked beyond recovery. If we're out of here before someone flashes the system or finds Talavara, all you'll need is an alibi. He sent a flash of amusement. *I don't know what you did for Yamazaki tonight, but he's definitely a fan.*

One side of Nothenil's body sagged, and Lièrén remembered the needler shots. *The needles will dissolve on their own, but I could burn out the anesthetic for you, if you'd like.*

There's the polite Lièrén Sòng I remember. Yes, please...

Lièrén directed Fiyon's brain to flush out the anesthetic with a counter-agent. After a few minutes of annoying pins-and-needles tingling, Fiyon should be fully in control of his body again.

By tacit agreement, Lièrén led the way through the medical center's corridors and down the stairs. With Lièrén wearing his coat, he and Fiyon... Nothenil... the man by his side... looked like anonymous mid-level admin staffers going home after a long day.

Lièrén had one more question. *Did you kill the others?*

Nope, they killed each other. Heavily shaded truth. Lièrén decided he didn't need to know.

He wanted to tell Fiyon that he would never forgive him for abusing his trust for ten years, but that he was glad Fiyon hadn't died, because he'd also been Lièrén's only constant friend. He wanted Fiyon to feel how much he'd been hurt, but it wouldn't change the past.

In the end, as they walked out the door together, all he said was "goodnight," then turned and walked away.

It took Lièrén several blocks of randomly going with the pedestrian flow, looking for a secure-cab platform, to realize that if he was the only living member of the unit, no one was left to want him dead. His shoulder still hurt from the needles, but he'd be fine by morning. His stomach growled at the smell of sizzling pork coming from the street stand. Too bad he didn't already have a reservation somewhere that would put him far away from the CPS building...

But he did. Sort of. He'd never canceled the reservation for celebrating Derrit's birthday at his cousin's fancy restaurant. The original reservation time was hours ago, but while Chiu might grumble, he always came through for family.

CHAPTER 20

LIÈRÉN READ THE frustratingly brief notation again. "Recruit cooperating without assistance."

It was the first update to Derrit's record since yesterday, when the CPS Testing Center had moved him to the alternate location, the one for which Lièrén had sent the coordinates to Rayle.

The last place Lièrén had imagined he'd be after leaving the CPS building the previous evening was in the CPS Testing Center, but an excellent meal and a few hours of sleep in a quiet luxury hotel gave him time to think.

Once again, he was temporarily adrift, between one assignment and the next, with no responsibilities other than the upcoming meeting with the regional supervisor. That left him free to do as he pleased, and he chose to spend that time volunteering to help the Testing Center, which would allow him to serve as a silent backup for Imara's plan to find and free Derrit.

His idea had worked out far better than he'd hoped. The three-building security system was still a complete shambles. Most of the able-bodied staff had been dragooned into helping keep the peace during the TSAC march. Yamazaki had been happy to recommend him to Klarxon, the harried Testing Center manager. Evidently, she was long overdue for Mateliff's security briefing, because she'd seized on his administrative experience and security rating as being good enough to make him the sole data manager for the day, giving him access to every record, data stream, and communication of anyone on the staff.

By mid-afternoon, the TSAC march was in full swing, with full-spectrum coverage on broadcast news. With the recent publicity from the Mabingion Purge story, the number of marchers had swelled by an order of magnitude beyond the original estimates of either the police or the organizers. Reports had begun trickling in that the police were having trouble in the Rim. The military—including the CPS—had officially been brought on board as observers only. Lièrén didn't know about the regular military, but he knew the CPS would step in if minder talents were used, official permission or not. He thought it very likely that by the time the marchers got into High Spires, the whole situation would be chaos cubed. Imara was counting on it.

After finding his way around the Testing Center's ridiculously outdated netware and hopelessly convoluted data streams, Lièrén concluded it was a wonder they could find any testing records at all, or even knew who worked for them. The digital clutter made it easy to add a few "auditing" routines that would send any data points of interest to an encrypted interceptor he'd set up, which was how he'd seen the record update for Derrit.

"Recruit cooperating without assistance."

That last word bothered him. It could be benign, but he was afraid it was code for CPS drugs. As Fiyon had said, the CPS's first answer to most minder problems was drugs. Use of any of them required monitoring by a medic. Some of the drugs were very dangerous, meant for out-of-control adult minders, or, if the darker rumors were true, to keep powerful minders addicted and therefore leashed. The CPS didn't put twelve-year-old children on permanent drug protocols. But as MacPenn, the field-office agent, had said, the Testing Center recruiters were a bunch of farkin' lopars who wouldn't even think to worry about any harm even temporary use of the drugs might do to a twelve-year-old boy.

At least the record update gave him another name to add to the list of recruiters who might be holding Derrit. Most of the staff with that title seemed to be low- and mid-level talents. Milo Ghisolfi, the man who'd updated the record, a low-level shielder and mid-level ramper, was listed as the primary recruiter. When Lièrén looked up his file holo, he recognized Ghisolfi from Imara's memory—he'd been the man who'd lied to her about the "inconclusive" test results. Shelo Yoo, a mid-level empath, and a genial man he'd been introduced to that morning, was listed as secondary recruiter. The record updater had been Paz Élmaléh, a mid-level shielder with no image on file. Lièrén hoped that meant they were taking solo eight-hour shifts.

Lièrén was just about to use his prepaid percomp to send that information in another encrypted packet to Rayle when he saw an incoming ping from the man himself. He took the call audio-only.

"Good afternoon, my friend." He'd been left alone in the hub office most of the day, but it never hurt to be circumspect.

"Hi there, hansamu," said Rayle. *"I need a big favor. Remember my friend who's moving? I promised to help, but the timetable has moved up, and I can't do it. I was hoping you could sub for me."*

Lièrén didn't hesitate. "When?" He'd nearly failed Imara and Derrit once before, and he refused to do it ever again. Imara wouldn't be happy to see him, because she didn't think it was worth his CPS career, but that was his choice to make.

"As soon as possible. She doesn't trust the landlord's new security guard not to damage her stuff."

Lièrén looked at his CPS percomp for the time. "Where should I meet her?"

Rayle gave him the coordinates of a restaurant near the offsite location where Derrit was being held.

"Please tell her I'll be there in forty minutes."

"You're a nova-class star. I owe you one. Thanks!" Rayle ended the call.

Lièrén hated to leave the Testing Center hub, where he had access to their digital ecosystem, but it couldn't be helped… or could it? He eyed his CPS-issued percomp. That crafty *húlí* Fiyon had controlled—and shattered—the entire security network from a percomp.

Lièrén quickly created a new hub account, then through a quick series of associations, gave it the virtual keys to the kingdom, and locked it with his percomp's unique ID. He tested it a couple of times, and it seemed to work. He pinged for a secure cab, left the hub station powered but secure, grabbed his gym bag, and told the man at the front desk he was going out to a restaurant, then for a workout, and would be back later.

The cab glided to a stop. Lièrén got in and shut the door before transmitting the coordinates from his prepaid percomp. Once the cab went airborne, he darkened the canopy and changed into flexible boots, loose pants with multiple pockets, a knit shirt and vest, and slash-layered, waterproof jacket with a deep hood, because as usual, rain was in the forecast. He hesitated, then put the shockstick he'd taken from the mugger into one of his thigh pockets. He hoped it wouldn't come to that.

* * * * *

Imara walked with Lièrén hand-in-hand down the walkway, like a couple out for a stroll. She knew she should have been upset with Rayle for involving Lièrén yet again, and upset that Lièrén was jeopardizing his career, but all she could feel right now was relief. She'd examine her other, more complex feelings for him later.

She tilted her head toward the bland-looking office condo at the end of the row. It was mostly a small-business commercial neighborhood in Half Spires, with cookie-cutter buildings carved up into narrow cookie-cutter spaces. "That's the one," she murmured. "There's a balcony and collapsible stairs in back. Air pad up top, inside lift to get there. Biometric lock."

"How did Ghisolfi enter?" His voice was equally quiet.

"Roof, with the pilot."

She'd been up there scouting, so thank Neptune the warning ping from her friend in traffic control had given her time to hide when the flitter was cleared to land.

Then things went from manageable to farked. The flitter had taken up the entire pad, leaving no room for anything more than an airsled. The pilot and that oily jerk, Ghisolfi, had entered the lift and hadn't come out. Imara hadn't liked the feelings coming off of Ghisolfi. His body language and her talents said he was dangerous. She'd thought she was totally farked when Rayle said he couldn't come early, but would try to find a substitute.

When Lièrén had walked into the diner, she'd just about cried. Instead, she paid her bill, slid her hand into his, and led him out the door.

She explained her original plan as they walked. Once the TSAC march came streaming by, she'd pound on the door and tell the guard that someone was trying to break into their condo from above. Meanwhile, Rayle would land a borrowed aircar and try to get in the lift, making the guard think it was an attack. While the guard ran upstairs, she'd take Derrit out the front door and melt into the marching TSAC crowd. Rayle would take off in the aircar and return it to the city's hangar.

"That CPS flitter is the problem. If Ghisolfi even smells me, the flitter is their ticket to blue skies, and Derrit will be gone." She realized she was squeezing Lièrén's hand like a vice and let go. "Sorry."

He caught her hand again. "You didn't hurt me." She felt a distortion in his aura.

"Liar."

He smiled faintly and ducked his head. "Much."

She smiled back. "Truth." She couldn't do the sifter's trick with everybody, but it worked with her friends. She'd been practicing.

His eyes widened for a moment before his expression smoothed again. "I have... Let me try something." He moved her hand to just above the crook of his elbow, then bent his arm so he could rest it across his waist and use the corporate-style percomp on his wrist. As they continued walking, she smiled contentedly, in case anyone was looking, and pretended he was looking up some nice, touristy show to take her to. She hadn't been to a show in years.

Focus, she ordered herself. Even though Lièrén had twice come back after saying goodbye, he was still a transient.

If she couldn't remove the flitter, maybe she could disable it. She had enough tools in her backpack to do it. That only left the street as an exit point, unless they had a secret way into the adjacent condo. It would be harder to elude two men on foot, but not impossible. The trick would be in luring them both away from Derrit. She had some ideas for that.

Sensing that Lièrén was on autopilot as he walked, and not paying attention to his feet, she gently steered him around the walkway corner, out of sight of the condo, and toward the nearest bench. She gave a silent nod of appreciation to the city planners who'd taken pedestrians into consideration, even in the more industrial parts of Spires.

She sat him down on its textured glass surface, then sat next to him and stared at the sky, as if looking for the rainbows Spires was famous for. She had plans for staying under the CPS's radar, but it wouldn't hurt to have alternatives.

"I can't do anything about Ghisolfi, but when would you like the flitter to leave?" Lièrén's voice was calm, as if he'd asked if she wanted a cup of tea.

She couldn't help but look at him in startled surprise. "How can you… Forget I asked. The sooner the better. I want Derrit away from Ghisolfi. He… doesn't feel right."

Lièrén went back to his percomp for a few more moments, then closed the display. "The flitter and pilot should be leaving in about five minutes. They've been ordered to report to the Rim to assist with crowd control."

"You're the best!" she said, patting him on the thigh. "Remind me to kiss you later." She pulled out her brand new percomp, the one she'd emptied her solstice presents fund to buy. She pinged Rackkar Horis and told him to execute Plan B. As Lièrén' stood to leave, she gave him a sunny smile. "I love a good parade, don't you?"

Channeling the TSAC march in the west had forced it to spread north. The leading edge of the TSAC march was finally visible, so she pinged Lièrén's local percomp. A few very long minutes later, he pinged her back.

She got up from the bench and walked purposefully to the condo's front door, which opened as soon as she approached. She stepped inside, and Lièrén quickly sealed the door behind her. From what she could see, the ground floor was decorated like a corporate office. In the main area, Agent Ghisolfi was slumped over a desk, as if he'd fallen asleep. Lièrén had told her he could neutralize the man, and she'd believed him, but it was nice to see it for herself.

He pointed toward the curving stairway. "Second door on the left."

She took the stairs two at a time.

She found her son asleep on a narrow cot, and her eyes and her talents said he was all right. Relief swamped her so strongly that she had to hang onto the door frame for a second before she could cross to him.

"Derrit," she said softly, touching his shoulder.

He woke, groggily. "What time is it?" He always asked that if she woke him, because it usually meant he was late for school.

"About four. Come on, let's go." She ruffled his hair.

He sat up and looked around, then frowned. "Agent Ghisolfi said you couldn't come."

She bit back a curse as she took Derrit's hand. "Of course I can. I'll *always* come for you. It's time to go home."

Watching him closely, she led her sleepy son down the stairs. He smiled when he saw Lièrén, but faltered when he saw Ghisolfi on the desk beside him.

Derrit's eyes filled with tears, and he pulled his hand away. "I can't go."

"Why not, *bata*?" She tried to focus all her talents on him, but his shielding made him a black hole.

He backed away toward the corner of the desk. "I'm untrained. I'll hurt someone." A tear leaked down his cheek. "I already did."

She stilled. "Who did you hurt?" she asked carefully.

"One of the testers at the center, Recruiter Yiu… Yoo. He wanted me to show Agent Ghisolfi what I could do, and I told them I didn't want to, but he said it was okay. I thought I did it right, just like Agent Sòng taught me, but he passed out. They said I slated him." He was openly crying now. "I don't want to hurt people, awake or asleep. I need to be at the Academy, where they'll teach me not to be a monster."

Imara closed the distance between them to gather him into her arms. "You will *never* be a monster," she said fiercely. She gave Lièrén a desperate look.

"Derrit," asked Lièrén, "did they tell you that you could unintentionally use your talents while you were asleep?"

Derrit looked up toward Lièrén and nodded.

"I… heard the same thing when I was young, but it's a spacer's tale." Lièrén shook his head. "Your brain makes chemicals that keep you from sleepwalking, or wrestling alligators in your sleep. Those same chemicals prevent your talent from operating while you're dreaming. Did they also tell you that when you're mad, you could lose control, and become a danger to anyone nearby?"

"Yes, but it's true! I *was* mad at that tester, just like with that guy from the bar, because he said I was faking it. I hurt him."

Lièrén shook his head. "No, you didn't. He was perfectly fine when I talked with him this morning. It takes more than a momentary push to blank-slate someone, no matter how good you are."

"But he…" Derrit looked at Ghisolfi, still slumped on the desk, then up at Imara. The despair on his young face nearly cratered her. "He said one of them had to be with me at all times, 'cause otherwise I might hurt *you*."

"Derrit," said Lièrén, "have you ever hit your mother when you've been mad at her?"

"No," he said, then looked down and added in a small voice, "but I've thought about it."

"Remember what we talked about with the guy at the bar? Thinking isn't doing. If you don't hit her, why do you think you'd use your talent to hurt her?" She was grateful for how patient Lièrén sounded.

She felt Derrit relax a little in her arms. She stroked his back and tried to project her love to him.

Derrit looked at Lièrén. "You said my shielding bottled up Nanay because I didn't know what I was doing…"

Lièrén nodded. "That's true, but you were keeping your promise to your father. You can learn to do better, but it doesn't have to be at the Academy."

The distant sound of a police warning horn startled them all. She looked to Lièrén. "Could you see if the marchers are here yet? They should be coming from the north."

He nodded and moved quickly toward the side window to peer up the street.

She loosened her hold on Derrit, but kept her hands on his shoulders.

"They were lying to me, weren't they?" The heartbreak on his face nearly made her cry.

"Yes, *binata*. They're like used aircar sellers. They'll tell you anything to get you to buy their camel shit." She brushed moisture off his chin with her thumb. "Where's your coat?"

He nodded and pointed with his chin. "They put it in the closet."

She turned to look and was startled by a loud crash. She spun back around to see Ghisolfi surging toward them. He grabbed Derrit's shirt and yanked him back. Before she could reach him, Ghisolfi put a needler to her son's temple.

"Freeze!" he snarled, dragging Derrit away from the desk and fallen chair. "One twitch from either of you, and I'll lobotomize the kid." He glared at Lièrén, who'd stepped in from the window. "Your career is flatlined, *compagno*. I hope you got great sex first, or you'll have thrown it away for nothing. Shift change will be here any minute."

Lièrén's face gave nothing away, but she could feel his anger coming in harsh hexanic waves.

"Derrit can't go to the Academy if you shoot him. You won't get your commission, or whatever it is you get out of this." She put as much challenge in her tone as she could muster, willing him to make eye contact with her. He did, and his expression hardened at the disdainful look on her face.

"Better that than let him go. You think I'm doing this for money? *Tu femminile ignorante. Non lo sai che è un mostro?*"

"Hey. *Stronzo*." She glared at the asshole as she took a deep breath and tightened her hands into fists. "I'm not ignorant, and my son is not a *monster*." She channeled all her anger and fear into the telekinetic push that forced the tip of the needler toward his own face.

The astonishment on his face was gratifying, but not as gratifying as seeing a thunderingly enraged Lièrén grab the man's throat and make him drop like he'd been poleaxed. She lunged forward and pulled Derrit away so he wouldn't be taken down, too.

Lièrén stayed crouched a few seconds longer, then looked up at her. "We have to go. He wasn't lying about the shift change. I can twist away our little visit, but I don't have time to do anything more."

"Do it. Derrit, get your coat." She gave him a quick squeeze, then nudged him toward the closet. She stepped around Lièrén to look out the window. The previously empty street and walkways were filled with people walking, some carrying flags and signs, and some banging on drums, although the condo's soundproofing made it look like silent newstrend footage. At least that part of her plan had worked.

The condo's wallcomp started blinking with a message announcing the approach of an air vehicle. She touched Lièrén's shoulder. "Company coming." She bent to pick up the fallen needler, and started to pocket it, but hesitated. Maybe it would give them a few extra minutes if Ghisolfi didn't notice it was missing. That didn't mean she had to leave it functional, however. Needlers were finicky little weapons that often jammed, especially if their delicate tips were bent.

Lièrén stood up. "Help me get him into the chair, like he was before. He'll think he's sleepy, maybe coming down with something." They wrestled him into the chair and draped his upper body across the desk, with his arms for a pillow. She put the disabled needler in his left pocket.

"I'm sorry, I didn't think to check that he had a weapon," Lièrén said, looking abashed.

"Me, neither." She patted his hand. "We lived, so we learn."

A double-thump on the roof told her they were out of time. She grinned when she saw her clever son had raided the tiny kitchen, and was carrying flatbreads, a package of sliced meat, and three pouches of juice. Thank Neptune for resilient boys who were ruled by their stomachs.

They quickly exited through the front door, making sure to seal it behind them, then went out to join the march.

CHAPTER 21

LIÈRÉN SMILED AS Derrit, still holding his mother's hand, talked animatedly with the slightly taller boy who was walking with his parents. Lièrén had tucked Imara's other hand into the crook of his arm, as a cover for him using his percomp to monitor the Testing Center's communications. He'd seen lots of other people using their percomps from time to time, so his behavior wasn't remarkable. It was distracting to have her so tantalizingly close, but he didn't want to chance getting separated. The news from the Testing Center wasn't so good.

He tightened his arm muscle twice to get Imara's attention, then took a chance and sent her a thought. The proximity made it easy. *Imara, can you hear me?*

Yes.

The bad news first. They've discovered Derrit is missing and figured he has to be in the march. They're launching a swarm of camera drones. It was a delicate balance, watching where he was going, reading the percomp, and connecting with Imara. *The good news is they're looking for a boy alone, not with parents, but all it will take is one face-match, and they'll have him located.*

Imara digested the information, but still appeared confident. *I've got transpo waiting for us in the next sector block. It was stupid of me not to bring a hat to hide Derrit's hair, though.*

She was the most resourceful woman he'd ever known, and she was kicking herself over little things like that. He looked to the sky, which was still overcast and cloudy.

"Looks like rain," he said to Imara, as if he'd just noticed. "Want to borrow my rain hat for the kiddo?"

She met his gaze with amusement. "Sure."

He fished it out of his gym bag and handed it to her. She made a game of putting it on her son, pretending his hair would lose all its curl if it got wet. It gave him a distinctly piratical look.

They couldn't walk any faster without drawing attention to themselves, so he concentrated on the percomp and watching for the flare of nearby talents. He'd been more than a little surprised at how many non-minders were in the crowd. Friends and family, probably.

"Stupid frickin' adbots ought to be outlawed!" a woman's voice from behind them declared. Her comment brought a chorus of vocal agreement. The surveillance swarm of camera eyes had caught up with them.

Imara must have heard the comment, too, because she let go of his arm to pulled a bandanna out of her pocket and turn Derrit to face her. "You've got sandwich spread all over you," she said, using the bandanna to effectively cover his face. She pulled him closer and whispered something in his ear. His eyes widened, but he kept the bandanna up, as if scrubbing a sticky spot.

Lièrén felt a flare of mid-level teke to his right, and the swarm of cameras flew out and aside like they'd been caught in a stiff breeze. It was the mother of the taller boy who Derrit had befriended. It took superb control to be able to handle so many small targets. Lièrén met her glance and gave her a small nod of thanks, then went back to his percomp.

"I hate to say this, but I'll need a fresher pretty soon" said Imara apologetically to Lièrén, louder than was strictly necessary. "Have you seen any?"

They must be close to the sector block she'd mentioned earlier. "No, but we could try that street coming up." He waggled his wrist. "I'll check for public stations."

He busied himself on his percomp, monitoring the incoming reports. He took the opportunity to insert a false record of someone reporting they'd found a lost twelve-year-old boy with brown skin who said his name was Seezay. He added coordinates that were north of the condo, hoping they'd think Derrit might have been going against the crowd.

"Let's try this way." Imara pulled on his elbow. "I think there's something behind that ground hauler." As they turned down the walkway, she held out her hand to Derrit. "I think your face is clean enough, *matalino binata*."

Derrit put the bandanna in her hand, grinning. "Clever, huh?"

"Yes, you are." She folded the bandanna and put it back in her pocket. "Let's see what Uncle Rackkar's done for us." She slowed a little and looked back, so Lièrén did, too. All he could see was the angled side of the big ground hauler that had the Spires city logo. With a wave of her hand across the biometric reader, the forward cab door opened, and she motioned Derrit to get in. Lièrén hesitated, then followed.

She dropped her backpack in a bin and threw herself into the center driver's seat. Her hands moved like lightning across the control panel. Lièrén looked around for some place to sit, but it wasn't intended to be a passenger vehicle. He didn't think he'd ever been in a ground hauler.

"Agent Sòng, back here," said Derrit. He grinned gleefully as he flipped down two panels that turned out to be jump seats, similar to those found on interstellar ships. "Strap in, 'cause it's gonna be a fusion ride."

Lièrén shoved his gym bag into a holdfast, then pulled the seat's webbing across him, barely getting it connected before the ground hauler accelerated quickly. He hadn't known ground haulers could move that fast or quietly. He'd always assumed they'd be as slow and noisy as they looked.

Two smooth turns, and they were on surprisingly clear roadways. They must be headed north, or they'd be running into the TSAC march. He checked the time. He'd been away from the Testing Center office for close to two hours. He sent an apologetic ping from his prepaid percomp to tell the front desk he was delayed by the TSAC march and would be back as soon as he could.

On his CPS percomp, he caught up on the recent communications. "Trouble," he said loud enough for Imara to hear. "Ghisolfi figured out Derrit left the march. They're getting traffic pattern analysis now."

"Damn. We're off grid, but only for six more blocks. Anyone smart will see the hole."

Presumably, the unnaturally clear course they were taking. She waved a hand on the console. "Rackkar, I need Plan C in five… make that six minutes. Sending coordinates now. Backfill behind me if you can."

"Rackkar's bad with numbers," said Derrit. "That's why she always sends them direct."

"Who is Rackkar?"

"One of Nanay's crew chiefs. They started on the same day. He looks scary, like he wants to detonate you, but he's got a melty center."

Lièrén nodded, then went back to his percomp. He was dismayed by the number of resources the Testing Center was freeing up to hunt down one twelve-year-old boy. The data manager hub received an automated request from Ghisolfi to append Imara Sesay's address in a tip to the Spires police, telling them a fugitive was holding her at gunpoint. It was clever—even if Derrit wasn't there, it would keep her pinned down.

"Imara, the Testing Center wants the police to visit your home," he said. "What coordinates should I send them?"

"Hell, don't…. wait, I know." She rattled off coordinates, and he dutifully entered them.

"Where did we send them?"

"You remember that High Command general who said the minders killed last year in the riots were part of a terrorist minder uprising? He's got a home office in Half Spires."

Lièrén's smile faded when he went back to monitoring. "More trouble."

"Dammit. What now?"

"They're sending a traffic override to stop all ground haulers. One of the surveillance cameras caught Derrit's back. They think he's with a man in a hooded rain jacket. Me."

"Farking hell!" She was still a moment, then waved the console again. "Rackkar, I need two aircars at the transfer point." She listened a moment. "No, Derrit's staying with me."

"Imara," Lièrén said urgently, "I only know how to fly interspace shuttles."

She gave him a startled look, then turned forward. "Rackkar, change of plans. One aircar and as many cabs as you can route. I'll pay you back, I promise."

Lièrén might not be a fixer or know how to operate aircars, but he could do something about her cashflow issues. He whipped out his prepaid percomp and, in thirty seconds, set up an anonymous account. "What's your ping ref?" he asked. She rattled it off to him, and he set it to the account. "I'm sending you an account code. It'll cover the cost of the cabs. Passphrase is the name of my cousin's restaurant."

"Incoming!" she shouted, and something slammed into the side of the ground hauler, knocking it off axis for a few seconds. The seat webbing cut into his thighs. "They sent a farking tank?!" She regained control of the ground hauler, then slammed on the brakes. The back end of the hauler started to drift alarmingly, but apparently, that's what she wanted it to do, because she steered with it, then applied forward power. "Let's see you make *that* turn, *chitsiru*!"

An awful crunching sound came from behind them, and a flash of fire licked the side window. Lièrén was very, very glad he couldn't see what was happening. Interstellar jack wars were considerably less stressful than this.

"Derrit, come here." Imara sounded cool and collected. Derrit disconnected the webbing and ran forward. "When I tell you, hit the grid switch. Lièrén!"

He fumbled with the webbing and stood. "They'll shut us down fast, so we have to rig the door first. Bring that pry bar." She pointed to the wall.

He pulled it out of the holdfast and took it to her. She pointed to the lower corner of the sliding door. "Soon as it opens, jam that in there." She pressed a plate. "Sesay Imara one four zero dot five six. Pause platform. Movement sensor override. Confirm."

A light blinked. She waved her hand over the biometric. The door slid open, and he used all his strength to slam the pry bar straight into the track. A warning alarm started wailing.

"Grab your bag," she yelled over the wind noise, as she reached for hers. He ran back and pulled it out of the holdfast and slung it over his shoulder. "Derrit, brace yourself and hit the switch!"

The ground hauler shuddered under their feet as it began a rapid but controlled deceleration. Lièrén bent his knees and leaned against the pull of the momentum, then took cautious, sliding steps toward the door.

The ground hauler hadn't finished stopping by the time she was jumping out, then turning to catch Derrit. Lièrén followed, pulling up his hood as he ran after them. Up ahead, he could see a cluster of at least twenty cabs, some secure, some commercial, some tourist. Judging from the knot of angry, shouting people, Imara's friend Rackkar had somehow hijacked cabs in mid-flight and grounded them all at the intersection.

Lièrén slowed to a fast walk, letting Imara and Derrit get ahead of him, mindful of the fact that he might be a magnet for trouble. He reached in his deep pant pocket and slid the shockstick out, then thumbed it on. The end extended downward, and a little vibration signaled its ready status. He activated his sifter senses, watching for flaring talents and the haze of violence. Derrit's shields made him a black hole. Luckily, he hadn't extended it to Imara, though he'd probably wanted to.

Suddenly, to the right, he felt violence and a flaring ramper and shielder. It was Ghisolfi, even if he couldn't see the man yet. How the hell had he gotten here so quickly? Lièrén let his talent guide his direction to intercept Ghisolfi while trying to keep an eye on Derrit and Imara at the same time.

Finally, he saw Ghisolfi, who was looking at something in his hand, then up, then back to his hand. A pedestrian jostled Ghisolfi, and Lièrén saw he was holding a tracker. It wasn't standard issue, so it was probably unauthorized mercenary tech. It was leading him straight to Imara and Derrit.

Lièrén could have kicked himself for being so stupid. They'd put a tracer in Derrit's jacket for insurance. Fortunately, Ghisolfi was so intent on his tech toy and the hunt that he forgot to shield and pay attention to what was behind him. Lièrén slid into his wake, waited for a clump of people to pass, then jabbed Ghisolfi's knee hard with the shockstick. The stunned leg collapsed and Ghisolfi tumbled forward, the tracker flying forward. Lièrén dropped the shockstick and bent over Ghisolfi.

"*Ecco, lascia che ti aiuti, testa di cazzo,*" he said quietly. *Let me help you, dickhead.* He flooded Ghisolfi's brain with happy endorphins, which made it much harder for his rage-fueled ramper talent to operate. He got a chuckling Ghisolfi to his feet, then gave him a gentle push toward a cab.

"I think he's chemmed," said Lièrén to the only woman who'd noticed anything. He shrugged one shoulder and frowned. "I told him to go home and sleep it off." She nodded and turned away.

Lièrén casually picked up the shockstick and started to turn it off, then had a better idea. He took a few steps forward and stopped, then dropped the shockstick so it landed directly on the tracker Ghisolfi had been holding. They destroyed each other with a satisfying electrical crackle.

He'd lost sight of Imara and Derrit, and he needed to tell them about the tracer. Suddenly, a huge, ugly man stepped in his way. Lièrén looked up.

"Looking for someone?" His voice sounded like a gravel pit, and his fist tightened around a spanner wrench.

Lièrén started to step back even as he flared his sifter talent again, then hesitated. "Are you Rackkar?"

"Yeah. Come with me." He spun and plunged into the crowd. People wisely stepped aside once they got a look at Rackkar's snarling face. The big man led Lièrén to a grounded secure cab. A lanky black man nodded at Rackkar. "That him?"

"Nah, Wallo, he's the farkin' Polly Lamby. Of course it's him. Strap bag, pirate jacket, Chinese, knew my name."

An older woman wearing coveralls came around the corner of the cab. "That's Dalai Lama, ziftbrain." She nodded to Lièrén. "They're back there."

Lièrén followed her direction and saw Imara and Derrit standing in front of a nondescript aircar. Derrit saw him first, and he drew a big breath to speak. Fortunately, Imara caught him in time and put a gentle hand over his mouth. "He sees you. No need to shout."

"You're okay!" he whispered loudly, then grinned.

"Yes," Lièrén said. "I stopped to help a man up who had fallen."

Imara raised an eyebrow, apparently intuiting there might have been more to it than that.

He pointed to Derrit. "Our recent playmates put a tracer on Derrit's jacket. Best to leave the whole thing here."

Derrit looked a little frightened as he rapidly unsealed the jacket and started pulling it off. He handed the jacket to his mother, then turned back to Lièrén. "Can I keep the hat? I like the colors."

Lièrén smiled. "Yes, of course. I'm pleased you like my small farewell gift." He shoved his hands in his pockets to keep himself from grabbing them both into a tight hug. They meant a great deal to him, and they weren't out of the comet trail yet. He needed to do more things to ensure their safety. "I'll be missed if I don't get back soon, and that will bring even more playmates."

Imara's smile faltered, and she put her hands on Derrit's shoulders. "We owe you everything. Thank you."

"It was an honor. And thank you. You've given me more than you know." He gave them each a short, respectful bow. "Please give my regards to Rayle, and to your admirable crew."

He kept his face serene and his body language relaxed, even though walking away from them again was ripping his heart to ice-laden shreds.

Chapter 22

* Planet: Concordance Prime * GDAT 3238.225 *

IMARA SHOOK HER head and pointed to Derrit's head. "You won't need that on the ship. It doesn't rain in space." Derrit made a face, but pulled the hat off. She'd told him several times to pack it, but somehow, it never seemed to end up in his luggage. After she'd taken the precaution of darkening and trimming his distinctive hair, he'd been wearing Lièrén's silver-blue rain hat any time he thought someone might see him. She didn't know if he was ashamed of his haircut or liked being a pirate.

The last four days had uprooted their lives dramatically, and the changes were still coming. After escaping the "Autocab Apocalypse," as the Spires newstrends called it, she and Derrit had hidden for a day in the tiny Rim apartment of a friend of Rayle's, and stayed in a new place every night.

After the Testing Center agents had loaded her into the prepaid secure cab that had taken her home, she'd packed everything she and Derrit would need to live on the road for at least a month, and spent the next twelve hours making plans, arrangements, contingencies, and converting everything she could to cashflow, because she needed every resource she could get her hands on.

After what Lièrén had told her about the Testing Center practices, she knew she'd have to prepare for war. Her only advantages were speed and unpredictability, which is why she'd been learning to use her talents in every spare moment. She had enlisted Derrit for help with that, getting him to look up the various talents and come up with techniques for her to try. She made a deal for a used aircar that she could fix when it broke down. She and Derrit would move to the other side of the continent, if necessary, and take cashflow-only day labor jobs so they wouldn't starve They'd stay in the shadows until the CPS forgot about them.

Rayle's call last night had given her an option that not even the great forecaster Ayorinn himself could have anticipated.

"I won the lottery!" Rayle was bouncing up and down with excitement, meaning his head went in and out of the holo view.

Rayle must have found a new lover. "That's wonderful. What's his name?"

"No, no, no, the *lottery* lottery. Remember those people who tipped me in lottery tickets? The Argosy Planetary Jackpot?"

"Which one was that? You get lottery tickets about once a week." She loved Rayle, but she still had a dozen details to take care of.

"The frontier planet homestead lottery. I'm giving it to you." He beamed at her in delight.

"You're… what?" She sat down quickly and stared at the holo. "You can't… You could sell it for megacreds and never have to worry about rent again. Hell, you could start your own dance company."

Rayle shook his head. "Non-transferrable for cash. I'm only allowed to use it myself, and *that* won't happen, because there's no place to dance on frontier planets, or give it away, and it has to be to a person or a family, not a business or a charity."

"What kind of screwy rules are those? It's probably a scam."

"That's what I thought, so I asked my brother to check it out." His brother, the stuffy finance king in New Geneva, who Rayle only reluctantly talked to once a year for propriety's sake. "It's granite. Some exploration scout from sixty or seventy years ago thought poor people should have a chance at homesteads, and she didn't want them tempted by the money. You'd have to follow the same rules if you accept it."

"You have other friends…"

Rayle shook his head, his expression becoming serious. "They don't need it. You do. Let me do this for you and your son."

She was silent for a long moment. "I don't know how I could ever repay you."

"You can repay me by being happy." An impish smile crossed his face. "And inviting me to your new-home blowout bash, and nursing me through the hangover, and introducing me to the best-looking men in the neighborhood, and teaching me to evade a Ground Div tank in a ground hauler."

A news organization had caught her maneuver on high-def vid. Her authorized road-crew ground hauler had cleared the turn with only a meter to spare. The "observer only" military tank had lost control and destroyed an entire sector block. Central Command said the incident was under investigation. The CPS was blustering. The city was outraged. Journos were in heaven.

It was idiotic to spit in the eye of fate, her grandmother used to say. "I accept your incredibly generous gift. Tell me what we need to do…"

Derrit's voice brought her back to the present. "Are we going to eat when we get to the space station?"

"Yes, the sandwiches are in my backpack." From what her customers said, space station food was expensive and inedible. She hoped the meals on the interstellar ship the lottery foundation arranged would be better. It was a charter, so she couldn't find any details on it.

They were waiting for Rayle, who was bringing a new percomp that her friends had all chipped in to buy. The CPS agents had stopped pinging them for her whereabouts a couple of days ago, but she had no doubt communications and movements were being monitored. Which was why she and Derrit were meeting Rayle in the maintenance loading area of a quiet transfer hub in the Rim. From there, she and Derrit would take a few hops to the flitterport where she'd booked a last-minute cheap shuttle to the space station. Thank Neptune their family name was as common as sand, and her cashflow account was flush from selling the aircar for a profit, after she'd fixed its annoying whine.

A luxury secure autocab approached from the south, right on time, and slid into the clamps. She pulled Derrit back with her into the shadows and extended her talents. She knew right away it wasn't Rayle in the cab.

Lièrén stepped out onto the dock.

Derrit looked up at her with entreaty in his eyes. She nodded, and he launched himself like a rocket toward Lièrén and wrapped himself around the man like an octopus.

"I knew you'd come!"

She snorted. It was more than she'd known. She'd resigned herself to never seeing him again. Lièrén hugged her son easily and comfortably. She stepped into view as Derrit pulled away, and Lièrén looked up to meet her gaze. The warm smile on his face made her heart skip. She'd been holding thoughts of him in so tightly, saving them for later, so she could do the thousand things that had to be done to survive. Her memories of him would be her reward.

"Rayle set this up, didn't he?" she asked as she moved closer.

"It was a collaboration. I'm very… visible at the moment. He's attending a luncheon for me so I could bring you this and say goodbye properly." He held out a sleek percomp like it was an offering.

She took it and put it in her pocket to look at later. She wanted more memories of Lièrén. "I don't think I've ever seen you dressed so..." She didn't want to be insulting, but the corporate look wasn't for him.

A corner of his mouth quirked up. "Rayle's phrase was 'dull as an accounting cube.'"

Derrit snickered.

Lièrén shrugged. "It's expected."

She suspected he was playing a deep game, and thought it was better if she didn't know. She couldn't afford to even be a flicker on the CPS's scanner right then.

"The percomp has images from your friends, and I added some entertainment and... other data that I hope may be of interest." He gestured behind him. "This cab is programmed for the south flitterport. I'm told the traffic-control system is still glitchy after the incident four days ago, which must explain why it stopped here."

She really did have the best friends in the galaxy. "Oh yes, of course." She turned to Derrit. "Go get the cart with our luggage, *binata*, while I talk to our friend."

After Derrit scampered off, she stepped closer to Lièrén and slipped a hand into his. The warmth of his skin soothed something nameless in her.

Lièrén?

Yes. He welcomed her into the walled garden of his mind. The connection with him felt right.

Is the Testing Center is still after Derrit?

Unlikely. A subtle sense of satisfaction accompanied the thought. *The newstrends reported that, owing to an unexpected systems failure in the building, the staff is temporarily being assigned elsewhere. I believe some records may have become lost.*

My luck is amazing these days. She brought his hand up to the level of his heart and squeezed his fingers. *I'm glad I met you, and glad you were there for Derrit. You're a good man.*

I'm not, but I hope to rise to your good opinion of me. You and Derrit deserve to be safe and free. Behind the garden wall, she felt vibrations of sadness and determination.

So do you. She took a deep breath, then lowered her mental defenses and showed him everything she'd bottled up, every joyously complicated feeling that centered around him. *You deserve love.*

His garden walls melted, and for a long moment, she was connected to him on a level she'd never dreamed was possible. He was deeply honorable and deeply lonely, and she and Derrit filled a void in him he hadn't even recognized. She felt his heartbeat, his aura, the music of his emotions, texture of his thoughts, the shapes of jagged memories.

His containment gently pushed her away from the details, and she let him. She didn't want to uncover his secrets or become his vulnerability.

Imara, I'm still a transient...

I know. She sent him a wave of amusement. *So am I.*

Something tugged at her. "Mom, kiss him and say goodbye, or we'll be late."

Her focus expanded to include her son, and then reality snapped into being again. Derrit pulled on her sleeve again. A transportation hub's maintenance bay wasn't the ideal place for discovering the person you were in love with returned that feeling.

She smiled at Derrit. "All right, all right. Get in the cab and give us another minute."

"A kiss takes a whole minute?" asked Derrit, a thread of disbelief in his words.

"Yes, if it's the good kind." She tilted her head toward the cab. "Now scoot."

Derrit gave an exaggerated sigh and clomped his feet as he walked, but did as she asked.

She took Lièrén's handsome, smiling face in her hands. "I believe I owe you a kiss."

CHAPTER 23

THE HIGH SPIRES CPS office was elegant and understated, and the air was decidedly cool. Lièrén was glad of the protection of his drab, conservative corporate topcoat.

"I must admit, Agent Sòng, you have an impressive educational background and record."

Lièrén kept his face serene and his body language neutral. "Thank you, Regional Supervisor."

"Please, call me Jane," she said with a smile. She said it at every meeting, and he nodded respectfully, but had no intention of doing so.

Pennington-Smythe looked older, with patrician, classical features that implied generations of carefully controlled lineage, or that she was a regular customer of an excellent body shop. She wasn't a minder, or if she was, hid it extremely well. Lièrén still hadn't figured out how Fiy... Nothenil had made his primary talents seem low, and hidden his teke talent altogether. It would be a skill worth knowing.

The other person in the room, a round-faced man with a slight wheeze, cleared his throat. Garindi didn't seem to be doing well in the perpetually damp climate of the Spires rainy season. For all that he was a senior OII investigator and a mid-level sifter, Pennington-Smythe was the more dangerous.

"Which is why I find it so hard to believe that you knew nothing of your partner's extracurricular activities." She accompanied her statement with a compassionate look that said she'd be supportive no matter what Lièrén had done.

"I wish I *had* known. I respected him, and he abused my trust." He allowed a shimmer of anger and betrayal to escape his containment, in case the telepath he'd felt earlier was still around.

"I can certainly understand that. What about your supervisor, then?" She often veered from one topic to the next, perhaps hoping to throw him off balance. It was to his advantage that they thought him young, idealistic, and naïve, but it was wearing to be treated like an idiot.

"I'm sorry, I can't speak for Agent Talavara."

They had yet to tell him that he was the only surviving member of the field unit. They were playing a lengthy strategy, which meant he wasn't going anywhere anytime soon. A short delay was fine with him, because it gave him time to make plans for his career and future. He wouldn't be content to wait for long, though.

He'd spent the majority of his life conforming to what others expected, letting them isolate him, and locking his heart in an unbreachable containment field. Falling in love with a fast-thinking, generous woman and her cheerful, talented son had made him realize what he'd done to himself. He was still a transient, and would be for some time. The CPS still owned him. Admitting his longing for her would have been unfair, so when he'd met her at the maintenance platform for what was to have been their final farewell, he'd planned to avoid letting let her get close, planned to avoid kissing her, and most of all, planned to avoid connecting with her and letting her wrap him in her mesh of talents. He was glad none of those plans had worked out.

"I'm afraid I have some bad news for you," said Pennington-Smythe. "Agent Talavara is dead."

Lièrén blinked in surprise. He didn't think they'd admit it so soon. "How did she die?"

Garindi cleared his throat and shook his head minutely. "It's still being investigated." Pennington-Smythe thinned her lips in annoyance.

Lièrén saw an opportunity to force their hand and took it. "If I may ask, who is my supervisor now?" CPS rules said they had to give him a name.

Pennington-Smythe and Garindi glared polite daggers at one another for a quick moment. Lièrén glanced at his percomp to make them believe he hadn't seen the exchange.

Pennington-Smythe drew a deep breath and let it out slowly. "About that…"

Lièrén sat comforably in his booth at the Quark and Quasar, and smiled when Rayle approached.

"Welcome back, *hansamu*. What may I bring you this rare, cloudless evening?" Rayle's hair was newly mottled brown and styled to look like wood bark, with coppery pointed ends that complemented the coppery pointed tips of his ears and the realistic-looking small horns sprouting above his temples. His eyelashes were dark and long, and his eyes a striking shade of brilliant green. The fantasy body mods took a little getting used to, though his unique synaptic signature was the same as always.

Rayle's willingness to alter his appearance had been very useful in convincing the OII watchers that Lièrén was enjoying a fine luncheon with his cousins at their exclusive restaurant, instead of giving his heart to Imara and Derrit on the maintenance dock of a city transportation hub. It had only taken Rayle about ten minutes to learn to walk, sit, and gesture like Lièrén, at least enough to fool external security eyes.

Lièrén tilted his head quizzically and glanced at the stylus and pad in Rayle's hands. "Forest fauns can't remember orders?"

Rayle's sunny expression morphed into peeved. "Forest fauns have no trouble, but their rockbrai… respected coworkers can't remember shit." He tilted his head toward the bar, where the new bartender, Gunn, was closing the door of the new dispensary. "She's not the one losing the tips when she sends a bad order out."

"My sympathies. It's unpleasant when one's coworkers can't be trusted."

Rayle smirked. "Isn't it, though, *Agent* Sòng."

"I would be grateful for a redberry fizz, and something for yourself, when you have a break." Rayle nodded and went behind the bar.

Lièrén had seen no reason to move out of the residence suites, since the CPS was still footing the bill. His favorite booth was smaller than before because when the hotel had repaired the combo gun damage, they'd squeezed in four booths where there used to be three. He didn't mind, though there were more people around to brush against his talent. He was getting better at keeping his senses always tuned to his surroundings, even when his mind was on other things.

His uncertain status had reaped an unexpected benefit of no one monitoring his usage of enhancement drugs, but he knew the CPS medics would catch up with him sooner or later. There was no arguing with a bureaucracy that believed in the efficacy of one tool for all situations, but there were workarounds. Lièrén planned to add several to his toolbox. Imara's extraction of Derrit had taught him the value of having multiple contingency plans.

Rayle came back with Lièrén's redberry fizz and a small glass of what smelled like chocolate espresso for himself and sat.

"Tomorrow's the day. You sure you don't want me to ping you?" Rayle blew across the top of his glass, then took a cautious sip.

"Thank you, but I'll likely see you sooner than I'd see the ping." Lièrén had a new prepaid percomp, but chose not to carry it with him when in the CPS offices. He'd destroyed the previous one after securing its contents elsewhere. Nothenil had thought the field unit's entire hypercube would be good insurance, and Lièrén had to agree.

Tomorrow was GDAT 3238.229, when Imara and Derrit should arrive on Abasarran, the frontier planet they'd be calling home for the foreseeable future. They'd promised to ping Rayle the moment their feet touched solid ground. Lièrén was surprised by a wave of longing so intense, it almost took his breath away. He struggled to contain it so it wouldn't impact the empath sitting across from him.

Rayle put his hand on top of Lièrén's. "I miss them, too," he said softly.

Lièrén nodded, not trusting his voice. He planned to do everything in his power to see them again, but it was going to take a longer, deeper game than anything Pennington-Smythe or the OII dreamed up. Fortunately, he was no longer stubbornly isolating himself from friends and family, meaning he had the resources of the Sòng Family Trust, and more importantly, his forecaster great-grandfather on his side. He'd pinged them as soon as he'd left Imara in the interrogation room, and been touched by their warm response. Even his great-grandfather had been welcoming, probably because Lièrén was thwarting the CPS.

He had no idea how, and would never be able to prove it, but he suspected his family was responsible for Rayle winning the frontier homestead lottery. It had been risky, because they didn't know Rayle well enough to know he'd never leave the big city, or that he'd give the prize to Imara and Derrit. The gamble had paid off, and had put them safely out of the hands of the CPS, which had no jurisdiction on planets that weren't members of the Concordance. Frontier governments could invite the CPS in to provide medical support, conduct testing, or deal with minder issues, but only as guests.

"When is your show?" Lièrén asked. "I'd like to come see it."

"Three days. I'll give you my other comp ticket, if you don't mind sitting with my plasma-hot date." Rayle fanned himself and grinned. "Detective Hǎinán. You met him the day the bar got shot up. He's teaching me Mandarin, and I'm teaching him the horizontal hula."

Lièrén laughed. "The 'horizontal hula'? What dance style is that?"

Rayle shook his head in mock disapproval. "Your cultural education is sorely lacking, Agent Sòng. You need to come to another dance class."

Lièrén smiled. "Regrettably, Server Leviso, I must decline your generous offer. I value my limbs in their current operational condition."

Rayle's eyes twinkled. "I'll take that as a maybe."

From behind the bar came an annoying whine that rapidly increased to a painfully loud squeal.

Rayle gave a long suffering sigh and slid out of the booth. "The rock… my respected coworker needs help with the blender again." He bowed. "Until tomorrow."

Tomorrow, indeed.

CHAPTER 24

* Planet: CGC Frontier / Pozivol Corp. "Abasarran" * GDAT 3239.081 *

THOUGHTS OF TOMORROW teased Imara yet again. *Focus*, she told herself.

Imara pushed in the last, hard-to-reach connection on the energy converter of the mobile glass extruder, then closed the access panel. Crossing her fingers, she keyed the start sequence. Green lights blinked.

"Hey, Chief, LeBoe needs… Hey, you got it working! That's abzee."

Elmeri, a plain young woman with angular limbs and a ready grin, was enthusiastic about everything under the sky, and was a font of slang that Imara was half convinced Elmeri made up as she went along.

Imara rubbed her grimy hands on her dusty pants. She'd been operating the grader earlier. Despite the protection of the cab, she was covered in pulverized bedrock. As far as she could tell, the only thing that being named road construction chief had gotten her was the chance to do everyone's jobs, but it was better than being stuck in an office all day.

"It'll do for now. We need to print a new converter." The road construction office got priority use of the township's high-resolution parts printer, but it'd still take a day or two to track down the right high-temperature printing substrate. If the city of Erdo Beselt didn't have any, they'd have to send to Prime Vaeros for it. "What were you saying about Manager LeBoe?"

"Oh, right. Rocksy got lost again waybo in the western preserve, and they're at least three hours out. He needs you to sub for him in that one o'clock meeting with CPS Rep Wazner about the traffic system."

Imara sighed. LeBoe was a tolerable administrator but largely a coward. He didn't like meetings with anyone who might be unpleasant, and found ways to foist them off on his staff. He'd pinged Elmeri to relay the message rather than take the chance that Imara would be irritated with him. "Where's Archer?" The nascent traffic-control system was his responsibility.

"Meeting with Pozivol." Meetings with the settlement company that still owned about half of Erdo Beselt and most of the city of Prime Vaeros were usually pointless or frustrating. Pozivol wasn't happy that the settlers were ahead of schedule in paying off the settlement debt, and was constantly finding ways to halt progress. No wonder LeBoe was hiding out "way beyond" on the other side of the forest.

"Okay, I'll have to take the Rook to make it on time. Tell Torgny to start the forms for the conduit, and make the fiber channels wide enough for an energy recapture array node. I'll be back around... oh hell, I don't know. When I can. Remember I'm off tomorrow, though." She'd lost the flip of a token with Archer to see which of them would have to attend the town council meeting that evening, because LeBoe always found a way to duck that, too.

She pinged Derrit as she strapped herself into the road crew's battered Rook aircar to tell him she was headed home for a quick shower, then into town. He pinged back that he was at the neighboring homestead, helping feed the animals. It was a large, blended family, and one of the daughters, who Imara thought Derrit might be interested in, was forever rescuing small mammals, including a few hybrids from the pet trade. She'd already given Derrit a ferwinkle, a soft-furred, omnivorous ferret-feline cross, to "foster," which likely meant Derrit had a pet for life. Imara didn't mind, as long as most of the menagerie stayed next door.

Their own small home, barn, and landing pad wasn't much to look at now, but she had plans. Tomorrow would be the start of them.

Focus, she told herself, or she'd find herself in mismatched boots or something for the rest of the day. She pulled out her second-best pair of pants and a belted blue tunic. She carried a warm copper-colored hooded vest, in case the Abasarran's weather prediction AI was wrong about the forecast for the evening. Spring weather on terraformed planets sometimes flummoxed even experienced artificial intelligence systems, and Abasarran's was young.

She landed the aircar on a wide community pad her crew had formed and textured the first month she'd arrived. It irritated her that the name of the Citizen Protection Service still had the power to make her uneasy, even though she knew they couldn't touch her or her son. In her experience, the CPS didn't always feel bound by legal proprieties.

When she'd asked around about Representative Wazner, the consensus of opinion said she was an ineffectual older woman who was looking forward to her planned retirement on a "civilized" planet. That suited the locals just fine.

Conventional wisdom in the Concordance said frontier planets were rampantly prejudiced against minders, but at least on Abasarran, no one gave a damn one way or the other. They were more concerned about making a new life in a new world, building a sustainable infrastructure, figuring out how to profitably preserve and manage the vast forest lands, and getting out from under the stifling terraforming and settlement company debts as soon as possible. If a little telekinetic push on an energy converter's connector or a plant affinity talent for finding rare, valuable fungi in the forest got the job done more quickly, all the better. No one talked about their pasts much, but she and Derrit weren't the only minders on Abasarran who'd slipped through the claws of the CPS.

She pinged her arrival for the meeting from the aircar, then spent a few seconds banking down her talents and solidifying the one-way glass shields around her mind. Imara didn't know what Wazner's talents were, but if the woman wanted to snoop, she'd have to work for it.

The wide entrance the CPS's prefab building was always open because of the minder clinic that took up the whole first floor. She rode the lift to the smaller second floor and stepped into the vestibule.

A phantom brush against the edge of her talent put her on alert as she followed the lighted display down the short wide hall to the right. The double doors at the end slid open to reveal a round-looking woman wearing sandals, a delicate, frothy sheathe, and an actual string of pink pearls. She looked like she was ready for a summer garden party instead of a business meeting. Imara sensed a hint of what she thought might be filer talent from the woman.

"Right on time. I'm Vivian Wazner." She smiled as she stood back and ushered Imara into the large, airy, but seriously under-furnished office, and gestured to the man seated behind the large, centered desk.

Tomorrow had arrived a day early.

Imara fought to keep her face calm and her body relaxed. She should be irritated, because she and Derrit had all sorts of plans, but she could adapt.

"Road Construction Chief Imara Sòng, I believe you may know Agent Lièrén Sòng, or should I say, CPS Representative Lièrén Sòng. He's my replacement, starting today."

Imara nodded politely, waiting for a cue from Lièrén. He stood and matched her polite nod.

Wazner's smile faded into puzzlement. She fluttered her hand and looked back and forth between them. "I'm, uhm… with the same family name, I'd assumed you, er, might know each other…"

Lièrén smiled sympathetically. "It's understandable. The Sòngs are spread across many worlds. It would be unlikely for us all to have met one another."

"Oh, that explains it," she said dubiously. She gave them a weak smile. "Well, I'll leave you to your first meeting, then." Brightening, she added, "I have a farewell party to attend, and since I'm the guest of honor, it wouldn't do for me to be late." She gathered her things from the only visitor chair in the room, told Lièrén she'd see him later, and was gone, leaving a cloud of floral perfume in her wake.

Imara hardly noticed, too busy drinking in the sight of Lièrén. She didn't know why she thought he might have changed, since it had only been five months since she'd left Spires. His clothes were casually conservative, and his hair was a little longer, but his handsome face and eyes dark and inviting enough to drown in were exactly as she'd remembered.

As soon as the doors closed, Imara took a step toward him, then hesitated and looked up at the corners of the room. "Are we being monitored, Representative Sòng?"

He shook his head. "Representative Wazner said no system was installed. She's a high-level filer and saw no need for it, though she did budget for it, per policy. I agreed that it was good to follow policy."

Imara relaxed and allowed a wide grin to take over her face. "I'd forgotten how good you are at that." She took a slow step toward him.

"At what, Chief Sòng?" he asked, stepping out from behind the desk and toward her.

She met him halfway and held out her hands to him. "Lying with the truth," she whispered conspiratorially.

He took her hands in his and pulled her close, lowering his face toward hers, and inviting her into his mind. Their thoughts wrapped together as he kissed her deeply and thoroughly. He tasted of black spiced tea and Lièrén.

I hadn't forgotten how good a kisser you are. She set her talents free to mesh with his. She reveled in the perfect fit.

I've missed you more than I can say. He wrapped her in his arms, and she sank into his warmth, sliding her hands up his solid, well-muscled back. It felt like coming home.

A worry surfaced in her thoughts. *Are we going to have to hide our relationship?*

Just from Wazner, until she leaves for Prime Vaeros tomorrow. It would be better if she didn't mention anything interesting about me in her transfer-of-authority report.

How long have you been here? Derrit and I made elaborate plans to welcome you tomorrow. She made an effort to hide the details behind her containment so they could still surprise him.

He sent her a wordless apology. *About two hours. You may thank Sòng Tiān Cì for my early arrival. When he said he'd provide transport from Concordance Prime, I didn't know it would be him personally piloting his racing yacht. I believe he secretly breaks the laws of physics. My own impatience to see you brought me from Prime Vaeros on the first available flitter. I didn't anticipate Wazner's eagerness to leave.*

She chuckled. *Ah, the yacht. Your great-grandfather is sun struck, like every other forecaster I've ever met. Ask Derrit to tell you about the ritual he insisted every Sòng adoptee go through. It involves singing risqué songs and wearing nothing but winter solstice tinsel.*

You didn't mind the… proposal to join the family trust, then?

She felt the trepidation behind his thoughts, and the worry that she'd resent the obligation to him and his very wealthy family. She tightened her arms around him and twined her mind deeper with his. *It seems I was fated to fall deeply in love with a man who is honorable, loving, and does the right thing even when it costs him dearly, and who also happens to be one of the crazy-like-a-fox Sòngs. It'd be stupid to spit in the eye of fate.*

"I love you," he murmured. "You and your son." The warm pressure of his breath in her ear sent a tremor through her.

"We know. It's what's kept us going." She gave him one more kiss and stepped back, though she slid her hand into his. She wasn't ready to relinquish their connection just yet. "So, what does the CPS expect you to do here?"

* * * * *

Her directness was a breath of fresh air, especially after five months of playing *n*-dimensional chess with the CPS and the media, and acting the part of martyred saint, as his advocate had described it.

"Not much, and everything." He caressed her calloused palm with his finger. He reveled in the pleasure of touching her, of being close enough to smell the soap in her damp, still crazy hair. He wanted to remove the tie and bury his face in the liberated locks, and soak in her warmth. "It seems some of my former trade office coworkers were fluxing their personal cashflow accounts by influencing the results of negotiations in favor of the highest bidder."

It was the official story he'd been directed to repeat. The CPS might have gotten away with quietly spacing their dirty laundry out the airlock, but the Mabingion Purge story, coupled with the TSAC march debacle, had resulted in increased scrutiny of CPS activities. Media companies began questioning the high number of recent CPS staffer deaths that all pointed to the same obscure trade office.

"The Office of Internal Inquiry fully exonerated me, but as long as I was in the Concordance, I was a constant, visible reminder of the scandal, and the target of near-daily interview requests from news reporters. My regional supervisor believes I am innocent, but that I am rather naïve, and not a good enough liar to fool the press. She and the OII agreed I should be reassigned, for the remainder of my CPS contract, to a less accessible, quiet post where I'll have the opportunity to broaden my experience. The upcoming vacancy on Abasarran came to their notice, and here I am."

Imara laughed out loud. "'Came to their notice'? You devious man, you played them like a teslaharp." Her laugh washed through him like healing waters.

He smiled and shrugged modestly. "I had help. My sister and great-grandfather are very crafty. I've been led to infer that if I do what the CPS wants, I'll be rewarded for my cooperation with a better post later."

"What does the CPS want?"

"Officially, I'm the CPS representative on Abasarran, available for consultation when minders or Jumpers are involved, or if the planetary government would like to engage with the CPS. I supervise the local minder clinic and the larger one in Prime Vaeros, and provide support for occasional CPS visitors. I'll have to travel some. The CPS offers free trips to a Concordance planet for people who want minder testing."

"And unofficially?"

"The CPS believes it's in the best interests of the galactic government for frontier planets to aspire to Concordance membership. I am to use my skills in keeping Abasarran on that path."

She raised an eyebrow. "Not your talents?"

He so loved a smart woman, especially the one in front of him. "Regrettably, since the nearly fatal flitter accident that killed my partner, my talents have tested sub-par. It is hoped that, with time, one of the Abasarran minder clinics can design a different enhancement drug protocol that will help." He'd tell her later about how he'd learned to mislead the talent testing instruments and how he planned to handle the required periodic drug testing. He wanted as few secrets from her as possible, though some were unavoidable.

She sighed and melted into his arms. "Do we really have to talk about the traffic system? I only know what I read in the reports."

He laughed. "No, I was going to reschedule the meeting for next week. Then I heard you were attending instead of your manager, and couldn't resist fate." He rested his cheek against the top of her head. "I know I keep saying it, but I missed you. Derrit, too."

Short coded messages through Rayle, and a few longer ones disguised as boring Sòng family business, had been better than nothing, but he'd felt like he'd never be warm again until she was in his arms.

"I missed a lot of things, at first, but you most of all." She drew back and looked up at him. "Do you have a place to stay yet? Our home has space for you. Derrit and I planned it that way." Through their deepened connection, he felt her hesitation, that she didn't want to pressure him or presume too much.

He smiled and let her feel how much her offer meant to him. "Nothing would make me happier, but you may not want me as a partner until I've learned a few things."

"Such as?"

She'd built a house from scratch, and made a home for her and her son. Her road-crew experience made her a valued member of the community. He'd lived a life of room service and restaurants, and knew how to interrogate computers and people, then twist their memories of it. Not exactly useful skills for frontier life.

"How to drive ground-based vehicles, or how often to change bed sheets, or how to operate a recycler, or…" He didn't even know what other things to mention.

She was shaking with laughter in his arms. "Or?" she prompted.

"Or… how to boil water. According to Derrit, it's an important domestic skill."

She gave him a quick kiss. "Your 'office' skills might be more useful than you think. I'm sure we can work a trade. You can teach Derrit and me to use our talents, and we'll make sure you don't crash the ground sled or starve while you're learning."

He shook his head. He was pretty sure they were getting the short end of the stick, but he wasn't going to complain. "What time were you expecting me tomorrow?"

"We didn't know, so we took the whole day off."

"If it's convenient, you could come for me at the hotel any time after eleven, when Wazner's flight leaves." There was only one hotel in town, so he didn't need to tell her the coordinates.

"We'll be there. Don't eat lunch. Derrit's cooking." She smiled. "How much luggage do you have?"

"Not much. I didn't know what I'd need, other than a corporate suit or two for…" He shrugged one shoulder.

"Meeting expectations?" Amusement laced her tone. "We'll tell you what to order from the autotailor in Prime Vaeros, though I'll always have a soft spot for the flyboy look. I liked you in the sexy, tight, black snap tunic. And out of it." It was the tunic he'd been wearing the night he'd been mugged. Or set up to be murdered, if he believed Nothenil. He shook the thought off.

"I gave it to Rayle, but I can order another." He put it at the top of his mental to-do list. "Rayle sends his regards, by the way, and several wrapped presents."

Imara smiled. "Knowing him, at least one of them is a box of sex toys."

Lièrén grinned. "That would explain the proposition I got from the spaceport entry inspector."

"What do you think of his new lover, Detective Hǎinán? The only details I ever get from Rayle are about his shows. Impossible man."

"He's good for Rayle, I think. Grounds him. Loves him even when he's being impossible. Hǎinán's boss, Commander Arfan, is still a blustering idiot. Oh, and you might get a recommendation request from Rackkar Horis. After you left, the city eliminated your shift leader position, so Rackkar didn't get promoted. Last I heard, he was mumbling about moving to a frontier planet, where there's no politics."

She snorted. "Poor Rack. I kept telling him sex isn't the oldest profession, it's politics, but I guess he'll have to find out for himself." She glanced at the clock. "Speaking of which, I need to check in with my crew. They're forming and programming the road in front of the settlement company manager's house, and I need to make sure they don't leave any, uh, personal messages for her."

She let go of him with one arm and pulled out her percomp, the one he'd brought to her on her last day in Spires. Already he was missing the feel of her warm, soft-in-the-right-places body against his, but he had tomorrow, and a lot of tomorrows after that, to make up for it.

"Give me your local ping ref, and I'll send you mine, and some others you'll need." He pulled out the ordinary-looking but very powerful percomp his great-grandfather had presented on his arrival on Abasarran, with a strict admonition not to lose it, because it would bring good fortune. He'd already synced it to the local comms and acquired a local ping ref, so he showed her the key. With her glorious filer's memory, all she needed was the once glance.

She kissed him one more time, with a hot intensity he felt down to his toes, then strode out of Wazner's office. His office now, he supposed. His mostly empty office.

Since it was unlikely that Wazner had many visitors, he imagined the official furniture and decorations had somehow found their way into her household belongings. He didn't mind. His research said Erdo Beselt featured a local cottage industry of making unique pieces out of deadfall trees, and he'd never owned anything handcrafted before.

He unfolded the old, slow office deskcomp and dutifully opened the files on the traffic system, but didn't understand what he was reading. He made a note to ask Wazner why she'd asked for the meeting in the first place.

From all he'd gathered, the CPS expected little out of him for now, other than making sure the planetary government saw the CPS as an ally. Lièrén planned to operate his little tendril of the CPS as it should be, not as he'd seen it lately. His first act would be to open the minder clinics to all settlers, whether or not they were minders, and establish a working relationship with the only body shop in Prime Vaeros. Isolation wasn't going to help minders become accepted members of the community, and healers would be a good bridge. He also planned to volunteer and send CPS staff to help with community projects and respond to emergencies. After that, minders and non-minders alike needed to see that the CPS minders could effectively deal with other minders who abused their talents.

It wouldn't be a straight and easy road, but he felt he owed a debt to the universe for the wrongs that had been done in the name of the CPS. He'd corrupted the Testing Center data hypercubes and made sure that recruiters like that farkin' lopar Ghisolfi paid the price, but making amends for what his field unit had done would be a long journey.

By the time the OII investigators had gotten around to accessing the field unit's hypercube, they'd found it to be fractured beyond recovery. Lièrén suspected it was Nothenil's last, parting gift. Both he and Lièrén had the complete records. Nothenil probably kept his for insurance, in case the CPS ever came calling. Lièrén had already begun mining his copy for the names of people who had suffered as a result of his field unit's actions, with an eye toward making anonymous reparation, in whatever form it took. A windfall inheritance here, a private scholarship there, a new job offer… He had the resources, and intended to use them, starting tomorrow. Well, the day after.

Tomorrow was for throwing himself on the tender mercies of the woman and boy he adored, and hoping they'd overlook his flaws, and be patient with him, and anchor him with their love.

"I thought toad-in-the-hole was with bread and egg in the middle," said Lièrén as he watched Derrit deftly serve browned sausages that had been baked in a savory custard. It smelled wonderful. The winsome creature named Zuzu that looked like a mink-brown cat with a pointed snout and a naked tail apparently thought so, too, because she circled around everyone's feet under the table and trilled often.

Derrit nodded. "This is the British version. I looked it up. It's so we'll remember the Quark and Quasar."

Imara gave her son an indulgent smile. She may have looked just as he remembered, but Derrit had grown several centimeters, and his face was starting to fill out. His hair was still closely cropped, as it had been for their final flight. Lièrén looked forward to seeing Derrit come into his own.

"Then I hope it's the first thing you teach me how to cook." The house's kitchen looked significantly less intimidating than the one in the residence hotel's restaurant.

Derrit grinned. "You got it." He brought a pitcher of red fizz from the cold box, then slid into his chair. He picked up his fork, then put it down again and looked to his mother. "Can I ask him now?"

Imara nodded.

Derrit turned to Lièrén. "We're going to be a family, right?"

Warmth flooded from the center of Lièrén's heart as he looked at Imara's shining face, then Derrit's. "It's what I want more than anything."

"So I can't call you Tatay, because that was my dad, but could I call you *Shúfù* Lièrén?" Doubt crossed his face. "Did I say 'Uncle' right? I'm trying to learn Mandarin, but I'm always messing up the accent."

Lièrén nodded. "You said it exactly right, and I would be deeply honored."

"Good, then let's eat before it gets cold." Derrit cut a slice of sausage and popped it into his mouth.

Imara laughed. "We'd better do as the chef says. I've heard he's very temperamental."

Lièrén smiled at Derrit. "Quite right. It always pays to be on the chef's good side."

Derrit nodded happily.

Lièrén took a deep, steadying breath. "I hope I say this often enough in the future, but in case I don't, please know that I love you both very much." He caught and held Imara's gaze. Her eyes shone brightly with unshed tears, and he felt answering tears of his own.

"Hey, no kissing until after lunch," said Derrit.

Lièrén took Imara's hand in his and stood, pulling her up and into his arms. "In this case, I must respectfully ignore the chef's wishes."

He kissed her lightly and lowered his containment to share all the promise and hope that was in his heart. She wrapped her talents around his, and he was home.

At long last, he was home.

Epilogue

JANE PENNINGTON-SMYTHE glanced at the control panel of the officer's quarters that had been loaned to her for the trip to New Kulam. The display said the next meal period would begin in twenty minutes, which would be long enough for her to finish the last of today's administrative tasks and still give her time to dress for dinner. It wasn't strictly necessary, as neither the Space Div ship's commodore nor captain would be present, but standards were important.

The latest communication packet had brought three new memos. The first was from the CPS External Relations Division, reporting the routine transfer of the CPS diplomatic legation on Abasarran from Wazner to former agent Sòng. She fired off a quick response, thanking them for the notice and reminding them that Sòng would not be eligible to return to the Covert Operations Division. It was too bad he'd been permanently disabled, because he'd had useful minder talents and an exemplary record before his accident. His diminished capacity and his involvement, however blameless, with the corrupt field unit had sealed his fate. She was *still* receiving media requests for information. Parking him off the net and isolated on an out-of-the-way frontier planet was be best for everyone.

The second memo was one she'd been expecting, since it had been her idea. She was gratified that CPS High Command was commending the employees for their hard work and dedication to the Service, considering the number of days that less-than-complimentary stories about the CPS had dominated the galactic newstrends. Morale was almost as important as procedure in effective operations.

She was equally gratified that Command had adopted her recommendation to direct all CPS field offices and units to report on the presence, activities, and membership of Minder Corps veterans and support organizations. They'd be better served by working with the organizations, not making enemies of them, if the CPS hoped to monitor what potentially powerful minders were doing after leaving the CPS. For example, the routine reports from the minder clinics on the activities of their Minder Corps patients hadn't been at all useful in predicting the unexpectedly high participation in the recent TSAC marches on Concordance Prime.

The last memo, multi-factor encrypted and with a one-view self-destruct, wasn't at all what she was expecting. The CPS Statistics Division had detected indicators of the resurgence of a dangerous urban meme after an eight-year absence. Trusted staff members, such as herself, were ordered to covertly report the appearance of the name "Ayorinn," especially if connected to the root concepts "forecast" or "legacy." The CPS hoped to intervene earlier than last time, and stop it before the contagion spread.

She entered the sequence to destroy the memo and its virtual trail, then allowed herself a minute to contemplate the bad news. She'd started out in the Statistics Division before moving into Covert Operations, and she hadn't needed a minder talent to love data and analysis. Some people were more susceptible to memes than others, of course, but the Ayorinn Legacy meme seemed to have wider demographic appeal than most. The first occurrence twenty-five years before had resulted in significant unrest and turmoil, but only on one planet, and had been easy to eradicate. Or so the CPS had thought.

Instead, it had gone underground and spread, like a hidden cancer, to hundreds of civilized planets. Twice since, the pernicious meme had resurged and had required mobilization of Jumpers and Minder Corps teke platoons to quell the resulting troubles on multiple planets. This time, it looked like the CPS was finally learning from its past mistake of dismissing the meme as inconsequential.

CPS upper echelons had a tendancy toward complacency, which she knew all too well, since her job for the last ten years had been to clean up messes that could have easily been averted had the managers been paying attention. It was frustrating to have to fix the same mistakes over and over again.

An insistent chime from the control panel reminded her of the time, and that dinner would be served soon. The military was fond of its regimented schedule, and while she understood the need for it, it was limiting. While the CPS was considered military, they weren't bound by all military rules. The CPS's mission was keeping galactic security and peace, by whatever means necessary. The Covert Operations Division preferred discretion and timing, subtleties that often escaped regular military personnel. Fortunately, she would soon be moving to a new assignment to manage special projects.

Nothing like a good challenge to keep the career interesting. If she did a good job, she'd be well positioned for a step up into CPS upper echelons herself. If so, she'd make it her personal goal to shake some of the complacency out of the CPS. If they didn't wake up, she didn't need a forecaster to tell her that they'd all soon be living in perilous times.

ABOUT THIS BOOK

Thanks for reading *Minder Rising*, and I hope you enjoyed it. This is the second in the Central Galactic Concordance space opera series. *Overload Flux*, Book 1, introduced the CGC universe. Book 2.5, *Zero Flux* features Luka and Mairwen from *Overload Flux* (Book 1) for a very cold case. *Pico's Crush*, Book 3, features new and returning characters (including Lièrén Sòng) in a fast-paced adventure on a paradise planet. Book 4, *Jumper's Hope*, has new characters on the run from whoever wants them dead, this time for real.

If you're enjoying the series, please post a review of this book and the others at your favorite ebook retailer. Even if it's short and sweet, it really helps. Reviews are what get books noticed and read by others. Think of it as paying forward for the last time someone recommended a book you really liked.

Find out about new releases before anyone else by signing up for my newsletter at http://bit.ly/CVN-news. I promise not to send photos of my cats or vacations (unless it's somewhere off-planet).

I'd love to know what you think about the story, and what you'd like to see in future books in the series. Visit my website and blog at Author.CarolVanNatta.com and comment or drop me a line, or connect with me on Facebook at CarolVanNattaAuthor.

I owe thanks to my friends and brave beta readers T3, Jill, Meredith, Ann, and Roger, who kindly pointed out ways to improve the story I wanted to tell. I am also grateful for the professional editing services provided by Shelley Holloway of Holloway House, and a fabulous cover by Gene Mollica Studio.

ABOUT THE AUTHOR

Carol Van Natta is a science fiction and fantasy author. She shares her home in Fort Collins, Colorado with a sometime-mad scientist and various cats. Any violations of the laws of physics in her books are the fault of the cats, not the mad scientist.

Sign up for her newsletter at her website, http://Author.CarolVanNatta.com.

BOOKS BY CAROL VAN NATTA

Space Opera

Overload Flux (Central Galactic Concordance, Book 1)
Minder Rising (CGC Book 2)
Zero Flux (CGC Novella 2.5)
Pico's Crush (CGC Book 3)
Jumper's Hope (CGC Book 4)

Fantasy

In Graves Below
Shift of Destiny

Retro Science Fiction Comedy

Hooray for Holopticon (with Ann Harbour)

www.ingramcontent.com/pod-product-compliance
Lightning Source LLC
Chambersburg PA
CBHW060936180626
46817CB00004B/1586